A PERIL SO DIRE

ERIC THOMSON

A Peril So Dire
Copyright 2023 Eric Thomson
First paperback printing June 2023

Published in Canada
By Sanddiver Books Inc.
ISBN: 978-1-989314-96-8

— **One** —

Commodore Howard Jacques, Commonwealth Navy, had no idea his career was about to end. Not with presentations, certificates, and champagne, but in the squalor of corruption charges.

It wasn't a particularly remarkable case. Yet it had the highest profile since Anti-Corruption Unit 12 (Military) was formed. That it was sordid certainly helped. Still, in my personal opinion, the Armed Forces' security folks would have sufficed to investigate the matter.

However, ACU 12 took over when the Navy asked us to. Or rather, they'd asked my boss, Assistant Chief Constable Taneli Sorjonen, head of the Constabulary Professional Compliance Bureau's Anti-Corruption Division.

And since it involved a flag officer, I'd taken the case personally, and brought along my wingers, Chief Inspector Arno Galdi and Warrant Officer Destine Bonta. They were officially ACU 12's adjutant and operations officer respectively, but those duties didn't take up much of their time. Besides, my four teams, each under a chief superintendent or superintendent, were pretty much autonomous, at least once I'd assigned them a case.

As a result, Arno, Destine, and I had been on Caledonia for the last few weeks seeing as how Commodore Jacques was a director in the Fleet's procurement arm with his duty station at HQ in Sanctum, Caledonia's capital.

Working and living among Armed Forces members was strange — except for the Constabulary liaison staff, we were the only ones wearing Constabulary gray in a sea of Navy blue, Army green, and Marine Corps black. Which meant we were noticeable. And the Professional Compliance Bureau badge on our right breasts above our name tapes, a stylized owl with outstretched wings over the scales of justice, made us even more so.

We had spent most of our time avoiding Commodore Jacques and investigating his division, which dealt with the procurement of Class 1 and

Class 6 routine consumables, including foodstuffs for starships, bases, and stations. It was our way of not spooking the target too soon. Yet we still quietly delved into Jacques' professional and personal lives, and it quickly became apparent that peccadilloes in the latter were driving corruption in the former. As I said, it was sordid, and in the grand scheme of things, it was small as well.

The morning of the Jacques affair's denouement, we had breakfast as usual in the HQ officer's mess, but we wore service rather than work uniforms as per Assistant Chief Constable Sorjonen's direction on dress when making arrests. I understood why. We anti-corruption investigators were often of lower rank than the people we're arresting, but we have experience and then some. The fruit salad of ribbons on our service uniform's left breast, along with qualification badges, was often more impressive than those worn by our targets.

"You know, I'm going to miss this," Arno said, pushing away his empty plate and picking up his coffee mug.

I glanced up at him. "Oh? And why is that?"

He took a sip. "The food here is much better than that served by our mess back on Wyvern. And my quarters here are much nicer, too."

"I enjoy the food at home."

"But you don't have as refined a palate as I do, Chief."

I let out a snort. "Right. Although I have to admit, working here has its compensations."

"Like?"

"We're at the heart of our customer demographic. It makes for interesting observations and conclusions."

Arno guffawed. "Customer demographic? Is that what we're calling it now? I suppose it's less aggressive than calling it a target-rich environment."

"Their feet run to evil; they are swift to shed innocent blood. Their thoughts are sinful thoughts; ruin and destruction lie in their wake," Destine Bonta intoned. "It's from scripture. Considering the size of Fleet HQ and the stats concerning corruption, our customer demographic around here is indeed a target-rich environment. I agree with the Chief. Working among the military but not part of them makes for interesting observations."

I glanced at the time. "And on that note, we have an appointment with Commodore Howard Jacques."

We finished our coffees and headed into the bowels of the base, where a network of tunnels and shuttles connected the various buildings and, if legend was to be believed, could offer HQ personnel a bomb-proof shelter if ever Sanctum was attacked. After a few minutes of waiting at the foot of the stairs leading up into the mess, one of the shuttles came to a gentle halt, and we climbed aboard. Since we took our time this morning and were heading in later than during the usual rush, we had the automated, open car to ourselves. Still, we remained silent for the five-minute drive to the underground doors giving onto the Fleet Procurement Branch's wing.

At one minute to oh-nine hundred, we walked into Jacques' outer office, and the leading spacer who jealously guarded her commodore stiffened to attention in her chair. Though she kept a bland expression, I could read worry, fear even, in her eyes. Whether it was because we were, unaccustomedly, wearing service uniforms or because she had an inkling that things would go down with Jacques shortly, I couldn't tell.

"Good morning, Assistant Commissioner."

"Good morning. We're here for our nine o'clock meeting with Commodore Jacques."

"Yes, sir. If you'll please wait." She rose and vanished through the connecting door, which closed behind her.

After a minute had passed without her reappearing, I glanced at Arno. "Shall we?"

"Let's."

I walked over to the connecting door, which opened at my touch, and saw Jacques sitting behind his desk, a worried look on his dark-complexioned face. The leading spacer was sitting casually on a corner of the desk to his right, her arms crossed. Both stared at me as I entered, followed by Arno and Destine.

I glanced at the leading spacer and said in a sharp tone that brooked no discussion, "You may leave us."

When she gave Jacques a frown, I said, "Now."

The word whipped across the room, leaving both stung by its intensity, and she scrambled to stand, then made her way around the desk, around us, and out of the room, closing the door behind her.

Beads of sweat had appeared on Jacques' hairless scalp, and his flattened nostrils flared as he took a deep breath. But his piggish eyes, small and forlorn beneath heavy lids, held mine with a steadiness that belied his growing anxiety.

I took one of the chairs in front of his desk while Arno and Destine remained standing behind me. Neither was small, so they loomed over me, an effect we'd cultivated long ago.

"Thank you for seeing us, Commodore," I said in my most reasonable tone. "I'm Assistant Commissioner Caelin Morrow of Anti-Corruption Unit 12. With me are Chief Inspector Arno Galdi and Warrant Officer Destine Bonta.

Jacques made a vague hand gesture that could have meant anything but didn't speak. His discomfort was visibly increasing, the sure sign of a guilty conscience. We'd seen it many times before, and I enjoyed drawing out the moment, one of my many failings.

"We've completed our investigation, and I'd like to share some of our findings with you." Yes, I know. I was being deliberately cruel, but Jacques was so sordid I figured he deserved a little extra. "What would you say if I told you there was deep-seated corruption in your division?"

"I find that hard to believe," he said, speaking for the first time since we entered his office. His voice was deep and surprisingly steady.

"Did I say your division? I'm sorry. I meant your office. Commodore Howard Jacques, I'm charging you with committing corrupt practices, stealing, offenses concerning documents, and conduct prejudicial to good order and discipline under the Code of Service Discipline. You do not have to say anything. But it may harm your defense if you do not mention when questioned something which you later rely on in court. Anything you do say may be given in evidence." I paused. "Do you understand?"

Jacques stared at me as if he didn't quite grasp what was happening.

"Do you understand?"

"By what right are you charging me? You're not an Armed Forces investigator, and your rank is beneath mine."

"My unit, ACU 12, has been mandated by the Grand Admiral to conduct investigations into military personnel suspected of corruption. We have the power to charge, arrest, and detain said personnel. And my rank doesn't matter. I could arrest a four-star if I find reasonable grounds to believe he or she is guilty of corruption. Now, do you understand the caution, or do I need to repeat it?"

He kept his eyes on me, but his Adam's apple was bobbing nervously.

"I demand to see my commanding officer."

"Your commanding officer is aware of my charging you this morning." I pause for a few heartbeats. "Won't you ask me about the grounds for those charges?"

"No." He spat out the word.

"A shame. By the way, your friend Melissa Dufour has been picked up by the Sanctum Police Service for her part in your theft and resale of naval supplies, and I know she'll be singing like a little bird."

That got his attention. Melissa Dufour was Jacques' secret mistress — he was married with three children — and probably the mastermind behind the entire scheme. Whether her hold over him stemmed from blackmail or simple lust remained open to question. But I had enough to see Jacques court-martialed. As I said, it was a case Fleet Security could have handled just as well.

Jacques suddenly seemed to deflate as he slumped back in his chair. I repeated the caution, and this time, he acknowledged it. I then produced a tablet and handed it to him so he could read the charges and the caution and thumbprint them, making everything nice and official. Once that was done, I pulled a memory chip from the tablet and handed it to him.

"Your copy. You are hereby suspended from duty and placed on paid leave until further notice. You will depart from these premises and not return, but you are granted freedom on your own recognizance, although you will remain in Sanctum. Further information as to the disposition of your case will come from the Judge Advocate General's office in due course. Do you understand?"

Jacques ran a thick-fingered hand over his face and scalp, then nodded.

"Yes. Can I make a confession now, to you?"

"Certainly." I placed the tablet on the desk between us, set it to record, and voiced the usual preliminaries. Then I said, "Go ahead."

His jaw muscles worked for a few seconds while his eyes focused on a spot above me and to my left. "I didn't set out to divert supplies to the civilian black market. But Melissa's tastes are so refined and expensive that I needed money. And she gave me a way of making some. At first, it was exciting. Then it became difficult, but Melissa wouldn't let me stop."

Jacques spoke for over fifteen minutes, making a rambling statement proving it had been both lust and blackmail that held him. When he fell silent, exhausted, I stood.

"Thank you. Now, if you'll grab your briefcase and beret, Warrant Officer Bonta will escort you to your car and see you off."

That evening, Jacques' wife found him in his den, dead from a self-inflicted gunshot wound to the head. When I received the news the following day, I felt sad but unsurprised. Suicide was a frequent escape for those we charged. But as Arno was fond of saying, it saved the taxpayer the expense of a trial and a lengthy prison term.

I'd reported back to ACC Sorjonen after we charged Jacques and was waiting for news of our next assignment or orders to return home. His response arrived quickly and took all three of us by surprise.

ACU 12 was transferred permanently to Caledonia at Grand Admiral Larsson's request and would co-locate with Fleet HQ. Considering the speed with which the orders were transmitted, the change of duty station had been in the works for a while.

— Two —

"Wow." Arno sat back and stroked his luxuriant beard once I told my team about our new home base. We were in the spacious office set aside for us in a corner of the Fleet Security wing, one of several vacancies in that area. "ACC Sorjonen must have heard me yesterday when I said I'd miss this place."

"I hope both of you remembered to pack your belongings before we left Wyvern, so they can ship them here without swearing and cussing."

Arno and Destine nodded. Packing our lives into containers was standard practice among PCB investigators since we never knew how long we'd be gone. Those who lived in government issue quarters often vacated them and stored the containers in the local warehouse, so we didn't have to pay rent during months of absence.

"I cleared out my apartment," Arno said. "And I believe Destine did so as well."

"As did I. So we're good on that. The message didn't say when the rest of the unit would arrive. But I suspect they'll trickle in over the coming weeks as they finish their current assignments and are diverted to Caledonia instead of returning to Wyvern. I—" A chime from my communicator interrupted me.

I pulled it out of my tunic pocket and glanced at the display.

"Well, isn't that interesting? I've been summoned to meet Grand Admiral Larsson tomorrow morning at oh-eight-thirty."

Arno grunted. "Moving up in the world, Chief. While we're on the subject, I wonder how we'll get our cases now that we're a few light-years distant from ACC Sorjonen."

"Perhaps it's one of the things the Grand Admiral wishes to discuss. I can see them coming directly to me since we're now co-located with our customer base."

"Makes sense. I hope Fleet Security received a message announcing our transfer to Sanctum because while you're schmoozing with Larsson, Destine and I will look for permanent offices able to take the entire unit."

"I'm sure they have." Climbing to my feet, I said, "And now, since it's almost seventeen-hundred hours, how about we head for the officer's mess and drink to our new duty station?"

"Right there with you, Chief. Especially if you're buying."

"I'll pay for the first round."

When we entered the three-quarters full bar, I felt many surreptitious eyes on us, a sensation I hadn't noticed since our early days here once the novelty of PCB officers working with the Fleet wore off.

"We're generating a bit of interest," Arno said in a soft voice as we took an isolated table.

"Probably because of Jacques," Destine replied in the same tone. "HQs being the gossip pits that they are, word of our charging him and his subsequent suicide must have made the rounds by now. Though I don't sense hostility."

We ordered our drinks — beer for Arno, wine for Destine, and a gin and tonic for me — from the table's built-in menu, and a few minutes later, a serving droid trundled up with them. We took our glasses from it, and I held mine up.

"To our new home. May it be just as interesting as our old one."

"I'm sure it'll be even more so," Arno replied.

We took a sip, then placed the glasses in front of us.

"What do you think precipitated our unit's transfer here?" Destine asked.

I shrugged. "Search me. It makes sense to have ACU 12 closer to Fleet HQ, though. Or right in the middle of it."

"I think it's testimony to ACC Sorjonen trusting you implicitly," Arno said before taking another sip of his beer.

"It's no different from when I headed the Rim Sector PCB Detachment on Cimmeria, reporting to DCC Hammett on Wyvern. In fact, we're much closer to Wyvern here, meaning faster communications for one."

"Except our cases are a lot higher profile and more complex now than they were back then."

I grimaced. "Not based on the Jacques case. The only high profile it had was the star on his collar."

"Ah well, perhaps we'll get better ones by living in a target-rich environment. Who knows? Maybe stuff Fleet Security would have handled before will now come to us since we're immediately available."

I raised my glass again. "Here's to hoping."

After supper, we headed back to our apartments in the various residential buildings clustered around the mess — Destine was in the warrant officers' block, Arno in the junior officers', and I in the senior officers' — and once in mine, I looked around, picturing it as my newest home. Two bedrooms, a living room, a kitchen, and a dining area, along with a balcony, made it spacious for a single person with few possessions. The furniture was standard issue but still reasonably stylish and comfortable. In other words, it was nice.

Going to bed that night, knowing this was my home for the foreseeable future, made a difference. I wasn't sure what sort, but still.

The following morning, I showed up in the anteroom of Grand Admiral Larsson's office five minutes before the appointed time of oh-eight-thirty wearing working uniform, with rank insignia on my collar and my sole qualification badge — jump wings — on my left breast. Of course, I also wore the PCB owl over the scales of justice on my right breast.

I still wasn't sure whether the latter insignia was inspired or a drag on those of us working for the PCB. Others viewed us with suspicion and often disliked or hated us. Perhaps being evident about who we were was better, more upfront.

A Navy captain, who was the Grand Admiral's senior aide, rose from his desk in front of the inner door and smiled.

"I'm Alan Bittner. Welcome, Assistant Commissioner. The Grand Admiral will receive you shortly. If you'd like to take a seat." He indicated a settee group around a low table to his right. I sat, crossed my legs, and composed myself to wait.

The Grand Admiral's outer office was enormous, richly paneled in oak, and had a golden-brown hardwood floor. A sideboard held a coffee urn with cups, while several mahogany bookcases and shelves displayed various volumes, statues, and other assorted military knickknacks. Paintings of long-ago naval and land battles covered three walls, while the fourth was all windows overlooking the parade square.

A few minutes later, a tall, lean, older woman with shoulder-length black hair entered the antechamber. She had a sharp face that seemed permanently set in a frown and wore a Marine Corps uniform with the three stars of a lieutenant general at the collar. I recognized her as Tania Terak, the Commonwealth Armed Forces Provost Marshal and Head of Fleet Security. She ignored me as she sailed by the settee group, and Captain Bittner waved her into the Grand Admiral's office after a few seconds spent on the intercom.

More minutes passed, then Bittner stood again.

"The Grand Admiral will see you now, Assistant Commissioner."

He ushered me into an office big enough for a gravball tournament, with the same golden paneling as the antechamber. A huge desk sat at the far end, backed by a stand of flags, while a conference table occupied the left side, and a group of easy chairs around a low coffee table occupied the right. One wall had windows overlooking the parade square, while the others were covered in paintings, prints, images, and plaques.

Larsson, tall, thin, ascetic-looking, with blond hair mostly gone gray, sat behind the desk, and Terak had taken a chair in front of it. Both watched me approach with intelligent eyes that gave nothing away.

I stopped three paces from the desk, came to attention, and saluted. Larsson returned the compliment with a grave nod.

"Thank you for accepting my invitation, Assistant Commissioner. Please sit." He gestured at the vacant chair beside Terak. "I believe you haven't met the Provost Marshal?"

"No, sir." I turned to Terak and bowed my head. "A pleasure, General."

She studied me for a few seconds, then inclined her head silently as I sat.

"How do you feel about your unit being transferred to Caledonia and assigned a duty station co-located with my headquarters?"

Of all the possible questions Larsson could have asked, that was one I hadn't expected.

"I suppose it makes sense to have ACU 12 closer to its—" I hesitated, not knowing how to phrase customer demographic politely.

Larsson gave me a wintry smile. "Potential targets?"

I smiled back at him. "Yes, sir."

"It certainly means you'll be able to respond more quickly whenever a suspected case of corruption or malfeasance arises, which is why I asked for your unit to be transferred here. And based on your results to date, I'm confident that cases will be swiftly and efficiently dealt with. The one thing the Fleet cannot afford, especially these days, is senior personnel who veer off into darkness."

Intriguing turn of phrase. But why, especially these days? I asked him, and he grimaced.

"I fear the Commonwealth is about to go through interesting times, the sort that'll need a steady, reliable Fleet so those times don't get too interesting."

"Understood." I knew what he was referring to. Or at least I thought I did.

"I invited General Terak to this little meet and greet," Larsson said, changing the subject, "because you two will work closely together from now on. Tania will give you targets to investigate, and you'll turn them over to her if you find them guilty."

"Yes, sir." I wasn't surprised. I'd expected something like that when I saw Terak enter Larsson's office. "Just as long as you and the general understand I am outside the Fleet's chain of command and independent of it and both of you. I will pursue cases as I deem fit under the Code of Service Discipline and Commonwealth law and charge individuals likewise. We may not always agree on my actions."

A sideways glance at Terak showed her expression hardening at my words. She didn't like my upfront statement of complete and utter independence. Tough.

Larsson gave me a brief stare, which I couldn't interpret, then nodded.

"I understand, Assistant Commissioner. And so does Tania. But I hope you'll develop the sort of working relationship that sees you always acting in harmony."

"Of course, sir."

"Then that's all I had. Tania, is there something else you wanted to discuss?"

"No, sir. I will review my working relationship with Assistant Commissioner Morrow later."

Terak's voice was a deep alto but scratchy as if she'd suffered vocal cord damage in the distant past.

Larsson's faint smile returned.

"In that case, thank you for coming, Assistant Commissioner. I hope your tour of duty here on the Fleet's own world will be pleasant and fruitful."

I stood.

"Thank you, sir." Then, I saluted, did a precise one-hundred-and-eighty-degree pivot, and marched out of Larsson's office, feeling both his and Terak's eyes on my receding back.

I returned to our temporary billet only to find it had become permanent, along with the other offices lining that previously disused corridor on the fifth and top floor of Fleet Security's wing. A sign now hung beside the corridor entrance announcing it as the home to the Constabulary's Anti-Corruption Unit 12, complete with the owl and scales of justice insignia. And the office at the end of the corridor now bore a sign above its door showing it belonged to AC Caelin Morrow, Commanding Officer, ACU 12.

— Three —

I found Arno and Destine in the office next to mine, getting comfortable behind a pair of desks, one labeled Adjutant and the other Operations Officer.

"That was quick," I commented upon entering.

Arno grinned at me and tapped the side of his nose with an extended index finger. "It pays to cultivate friends in all the important places, such as Fleet Security's HQ adjutant. How did your meeting with the Grand Admiral go?"

I grabbed a chair and gave them a verbatim run down of my brief meeting. When I was done, Arno made a face.

"I get the feeling General Terak will want more than just a harmonious relationship."

"Which is why we were given this entire corridor so quickly and easily. But be that as it may, I'm used to dealing with three stars and keeping them at arm's length. Though I think Terak might not be quite as easy to deal with as DCC Maras was."

"Maras knew intimately what the PCB was and understood the lines of delineation between her command and yours."

"Yes, and I'll simply need to make sure General Terak comes to the same understanding. That said, did anyone bother to sweep this office and mine?"

"Finished it five minutes before you showed up, Chief," Destine said. "We're clean. But I figure we'll need to sweep every office daily until further notice."

I gave her a wry smile. "Isn't it nice to be paranoid at the heart of Fleet HQ?"

"They're not PCB," she replied as if that statement said everything it had to about the Professional Compliance Bureau's position within the Constabulary and with the Armed Forces.

"Indeed, not." I climbed to my feet. "I'll get settled in."

My office, wonder of wonders, had windows overlooking the spaceport portion of the HQ complex. It wasn't small, with room for a desk, several chairs, and a conference table for twelve. But it was bare. No stand of flags, no pictures on the walls or books on the shelves, let alone the usual sort of decorations one would find in the office of an assistant commissioner who was also a unit commander. Yet it didn't bother me a bit. I'd never been keen on knickknacks, paintings, or other adornments. Not when I spend most of my time working elsewhere. Although now that my unit was up to four full teams, I doubted I'd be gallivanting across the Commonwealth anytime soon. If I took any high-profile cases myself, they'd most likely be from right here, in Sanctum.

I turned on my workstation and called up the Jacques case for one last look before I closed it and noticed a data dump from Wyvern had arrived — all of ACU 12's files and relevant documents from elsewhere in the PCB and the Constabulary. In effect, we had a ready-made database which cheered me up to no end.

I was reviewing documents flagged by ACC Sorjonen, or more likely his adjutant, when an amused voice at my office door brought me back to the here and now.

"An office with windows. My, how generous of Fleet Security."

"Hera! Welcome. You're my first visitor." I smiled at her.

Rear Admiral Hera Talyn, who headed Naval Intelligence's Special Operations Division, entered my office and dropped into one of the chairs facing my desk. We'd been friends for years, having first met on Aquilonia Station when she was a commander and I a chief superintendent, and we'd socialized frequently over the last few weeks. She, her husband, Colonel Zack Decker, who commanded the 1st Special Forces Regiment, and the latter's daughter, Saga Decker, a scarily smart intelligence officer, had made Arno, Destine, and me most welcome.

Hera had changed little over the years since we first met — shoulder-length brown hair, an unremarkable, narrow face, and a gaze so deep it seemed endless. She still exuded that predatory aura, though she had a few more lines around her mouth and eyes.

"I hope you swept this office before settling in. Fleet Security has a thing for bugs."

"No worries. Destine took care of it earlier this morning and detected nothing."

"Good." She crossed her legs and folded her hands in her lap. "Because you and I need to discuss a few things now that the Constabulary officially transferred ACU 12 to Sanctum."

I cocked an eyebrow at her. "Oh?"

"You're here largely at my behest, though Grand Admiral Larsson will tell you it was his idea."

"That's what he said when we met earlier today."

Hera nodded. "One of the things I like about the Big Boss is his willingness to cover for his subordinates."

She pulled out a small, flat object and said, "I appreciate Destine's ability to sniff out listening devices, but for this conversation, I'll add my jammer to the mix."

I chuckled and pulled out my own multi-spectrum jamming device. "Want to make it three for three?"

"Sure." Hera smiled.

"You were saying something about my being here at your behest?"

"Yes. I arranged for the Grand Admiral to ask your Chief Constable that ACU 12 be stationed at Fleet HQ. But not for the more obvious reasons you might have discussed with Admiral Larsson."

"Really?"

"You see, we have a problem in this HQ. Several years ago, Zack and I stumbled onto a conspiracy to undo Grand Admiral Kowalski's reforms, sponsored by what we now know was the Sécurité Spéciale. They called themselves Black Sword. And try as we might, we never unmasked every last one of them. We suspect their numbers are growing again and that they've infiltrated Fleet Security as well as counterintelligence, the two organizations which should be hunting them down. Things will get critical over the coming months, and we can't afford to have traitors stabbing us in the back."

Funny that — Hera paraphrased Larsson's comment that the Commonwealth was about to go through interesting times. But I didn't ask. If Larsson declined to answer, so would she.

"And you'd like me — us — to be your Black Sword hunters."

"In essence, yes. Oh, you'll have plenty of work with run-of-the-mill corruption around here as well. As much as we might wish it wasn't so, the thirty thousand uniformed and civilian members working at Fleet HQ do make for a good number of potential targets. That's without considering the various HQs and units scattered across the Commonwealth. Unfortunately, the Fleet is a reflection of our society, and that society has its fair share of the venal, the corrupt, and the criminal."

She gave me a sad smile that didn't quite reach her eyes. But then, her smiles never did. It was one of the unnerving things about Hera Talyn, though I knew our friendship was as genuine as she could make it.

"Still, having you around gives me an unimpeachable asset as far removed from the chain of command as possible. Someone fearless I can count on to ferret out malfeasance wherever you find it."

"I'll do my best, as usual. May I share this with my wingers?"

"Of course. And with your team leads. Although you should impress on them that your covert mission is top-secret and not recorded anywhere."

I nodded. "Understood."

"We, meaning my division, will give you targets to investigate, people we think may be traitors. What happens afterward is up to you. And if, in the course of an investigation, you come across someone who you think might be one, then by all means, scrutinize them. That's the beauty of having you here. You don't need anyone's permission to probe a military or civilian member's affairs, whether openly or covertly. You're literally a law unto yourself, and I intend to use that to the utmost." Her smile returned. "And since it's Friday and Zack will be back in town for the weekend, how about you join us for supper at eighteen hundred? We can hold a private celebration of your unit being stationed here."

"Certainly!"

At eighteen hundred, I walked up the driveway to Hera and Zack's residence, and the door opened as I climbed the short flight of steps. It revealed a grinning Zack Decker dressed in khaki slacks, a loud, short-sleeved shirt, and sandals. He was a large, muscular slab of a man with short, sandy hair, a square, honest face, and eyes of the deepest blue I'd ever seen.

"There she is."

He gave me a quick hug before leading me through the house to the patio, where I found a barefoot Hera wearing shorts and a subdued shirt sitting in one of the lounge chairs, a gin and tonic in hand. Zack vanished to reappear moments later with a glass of gin and tonic for me and a Shrehari ale for himself.

When we were seated, Hera raised her glass. "To ACU 12's new duty station."

After taking a sip, I settled back and relaxed, comfortable in the company of two steadfast friends.

"So," Zack said, still smiling — he smiled a lot, as a matter of fact, "I understand Hera roped you into being one of her covert allies in our ongoing war against traitors."

"She actually engineered my unit's transfer to Caledonia for those purposes, believe it or not."

"Oh, I believe it. That's her style. Welcome to the party. Hera is a master manipulator who enjoys lining up the pieces just the way she wants." He gave her a fond look. "I do so love her for it."

She raised her glass while wearing a smug air. "And it's for the betterment of the Fleet and the pursuance of its mission."

Watching the easy banter between Hera and Zack, their obvious attachment to each other, made me a little wistful. I'd never been one for relationships. In fact, I'm probably more celibate than a Sister of the Void, and while that rarely crossed my mind, seeing them interact just now brought it back to the fore. But I raised my glass as well.

"Here's to Team Hera."

"Team Hera." Zack took a big gulp of his ale and sighed with satisfaction.

It was well past twenty-three hundred hours when I finally left after a long, pleasant meal accompanied by intelligent conversation. The streets of the base's residential sector were empty at that hour, and I was back at my apartment block in just under half an hour, having walked there and back. The night was sultry, as most were in Caledonia's northern subtropical zone, and I lingered for a while on my apartment balcony with a glass of Glen Arcturus. As I looked out at the city lights beyond the base's confines, I wondered about this latest twist of fate that saw me drafted into a secret war at the heart of the human Fleet.

— Four —

The following Monday, after a quiet weekend spent mostly at home because of torrential rains that began in the early hours of Saturday, I was back in my office perusing the overnighters from Wyvern as well as a whole host of advisories from Fleet Security. I'd evidently been placed on the latter's distribution list. Nothing important jumped out at me, and I forwarded the lot of them to Arno and Destine for their information.

One of the few outings I'd made on Saturday had been to the base commissary to stock up on food since I'd be preparing breakfast and supper in my quarters from now on, seeing as how we weren't on temporary duty anymore and no longer entitled to free meals in the officer's mess. Arno and Destine had probably done the same, though I didn't ask when I poked my head into their office to say good morning.

Shortly after ten, I received a message from General Terak's aide, summoning me for a meeting with her at eleven o'clock sharp. I felt like declining simply because of how the missive was worded, but I figured I might as well get what I suspected would be an awkward encounter over with. So, I accepted.

A few minutes before the appointed time, I made my way to Terak's office, two floors down from mine. I was deliberately not wearing my beret to indicate my independence because usually, when reporting to a senior general, especially the commander of a command, officers were expected to wear their headdress. As a bonus, I didn't have to salute her.

I entered the outer office at eleven hundred precisely, and the aide behind the desk barring the way to the inner office, a major, stood.

"Good morning, Assistant Commissioner. The general is running a bit late. If you'd like to take a seat." He gestured at the settee group near a sideboard with the usual coffee and tea urns.

"Thank you, Major," I answered primly, wondering whether Terak was indeed behind schedule or making me wait in the oldest display of bureaucratic power still used. I sat, pulled out my tablet, and called up the novel I was currently reading.

Ultimately, I waited fifteen minutes before the aide ushered me into Terak's office. During that time, no one entered or exited it. If Terak was running late, it had to be because of a conversation via comlink. But I had my doubts.

Her office, not as large as the Grand Admiral's but twice the size of mine, had the usual desk backed by a stand of flags, a conference table to one side, easy chairs around a low coffee table to the other, and a sideboard. The walls were covered in paintings, prints, and photographs showing military police at work throughout the ages, all the way back to the Napoleonic Wars of the early nineteenth century.

Terak sat behind her desk with an expressionless face, eyes watching me approach.

"Good morning, General," I said in a cheery tone. If my not stopping the regulation three paces from the desk and coming to attention disturbed her, she didn't show it. But when I took a chair without so much as a by your leave, I could see her eyes narrow. "And what can ACU 12 do for you on this fine day?"

"Good morning, Assistant Commissioner. I thought we'd discuss our working relationship."

"Certainly."

"Let me make a few things clear upfront so you understand where I'm coming from. Primarily, I don't think having your unit co-located with Fleet

HQ is a good idea, the Grand Admiral notwithstanding. Let me explain. ACU 12's job is to investigate the most egregious corruption in the Fleet. Those we can't or shouldn't investigate ourselves because of the optics, the reality, or any other reason. You are supposed to be the instance of last resort for the Armed Forces while we, Fleet Security, investigate ninety-nine-point nine percent of cases. With you being here, I fear the standard of what we investigate will drop in your favor. For instance, my people could have easily resolved the Howard Jacques affair."

"Then we'll just have to work together so we can keep my investigations to those instances where an outside agency is called for, General."

"No, I think we'll take a step beyond that, Assistant Commissioner." She held my gaze with her hard eyes. "I will control who you investigate. That way, there will be no doubt whether a case is appropriate for ACU 12."

And there we had it — Terak's attempt at supervising me and my unit.

"I'm sorry, General, but that's not how it works."

"Oh?" She arched a thin eyebrow.

"Professional Compliance Bureau units are completely independent. I take my orders solely from my superior, Assistant Chief Constable Sorjonen, who is the only one with the power to control who I investigate."

"Sorjonen isn't here. I am, and I outrank him in any case." Her flat tone held an edge of finality.

"Still, General. You cannot exercise any sort of oversight on ACU 12. It would be contrary to the Constabulary Regulations Governing the Professional Compliance Bureau, which state that no one outside the PCB can control the activities of its units and its investigators. And that includes determining who I investigate. I will, of course, take on cases you refer to me, but I will also take on cases referred by other senior officers or those I determine are of interest to ACU 12."

"You determine are of interest?" Her voice suddenly took on a tinge of acid. "No. That's not acceptable. In the Fleet, it is my branch's prerogative to decide whether someone or something gets investigated.

"And I am not part of the Fleet, General. My actions come under the Constabulary Code of Discipline, not the Code of Service Discipline. As such, I am not beholden to you, or even the Grand Admiral, for that matter. The most either of you could do is complain to my superiors and ask for my removal."

This time, her nostrils flared as she took a deep breath.

"I don't appreciate your obstinacy on this matter, Assistant Commissioner."

"I'm sorry you feel that way, but my independence and freedom of action are enshrined in law. Were I to subject myself to even the slightest bit of oversight on your part, I would be removed from command by ACC Sorjonen the moment he found out." I tried to sound as apologetic as I could under the circumstances. "The best I can do is discuss cases with you to determine whether ACU 12 is the right organization to take them on."

Her fingers danced to a staccato beat on her desktop as she considered my words.

"I suppose we'll see about that. The one thing I will tell you, however, is that you will not communicate with anyone in Fleet Security concerning potential and actual cases without my permission. Or rather," she caught herself before I could object to her giving me orders, "no one in Fleet Security will talk with you about cases without my say-so."

I inclined my head. "Understood, General."

"When it comes to asserting your independence, just keep in mind that I can and will ask for you to be replaced should your behavior become egregious."

"As is your privilege."

"Yes, it is. That was it. You're dismissed."

As I rose, her gaze slipped to the virtual display hovering above one side of her desk, so I simply turned on my heels and left the office.

Once I'd returned to mine, Arno stuck his head through the door. "And?"

I waved him in and gestured at the chair in front of my desk.

"She's no Deputy Chief Constable Maras, that's for sure." I gave him a brief rundown of our conversation. When I was done, he let out a low whistle.

"Not overly aware of the PCB and its quirks, is she?"

"Oh, I'm sure she is. But she dislikes having the Constabulary equivalent of a full colonel swanning around her private hunting grounds where she can see me. It would be better for her if we were still based on Wyvern and came out on a case-by-case basis. That, she could ignore."

"Or is the delightful General Terak afraid you'll stumble across something you shouldn't?" Arno asked in a sly tone.

"The idea had occurred to me. But one doesn't become Provost Marshal of the Armed Forces with skeletons hiding in the closet. Or at least one shouldn't."

Arno held up an index finger. "Precisely. One shouldn't, but occasionally, an individual with something to hide reaches high rank."

I grinned at him. "We're a bunch of suspicious characters, aren't we?"

"We're characters who have suspicions, Chief."

— Five —

Over the following two weeks, my teams began landing in Sanctum, starting with that of Chief Superintendent Gil Hasreen, who led Team One and was by dint of his rank my deputy. Gil, a heavy-set man with a permanent hangdog look, was a cross between everyone's favorite grandfather and the proverbial bad cop of legend. He had more PCB experience than just about anyone else in ACU 12 but was still amazed he'd made chief superintendent.

Gil showed up in my office Friday morning shortly after oh-eight hundred, while I could hear the voices of his team members out in the corridor.

"Good morning, sir." He snapped off a smart salute. "Chief Superintendent Hasreen reporting with fifteen members of Team One."

"Hey, Gil. Good to see you." I pointed at the chair across from my desk. "Take a pew."

"Don't mind if I do." He sat, took off his beret, and sighed. "Another day, another duty station. Good thing we travel light."

"When did you get in?"

"Yesterday, just after twenty-hundred hours. I must remember to thank Arno for setting up our quarters and getting us in them lickety-split. We brought the containers with your household goods, by the way. They should be waiting for you at the base CMTT, along with ours."

The Central Material Traffic Terminal was the hub of physical goods transfers, and I nodded. "Thanks. I'll get them to deliver them to my apartment later today."

"Did you drum up any business for us?"

"As a matter of fact, yes." Surprising me, General Terak had referred a case to us just yesterday. When I looked into it, I understood why. It had the potential to get messy. "A defense civilian at the director level in procurement suspected of passing contracts to favored firms in return for kickbacks."

Gil let out a soft grunt. "It's always procurement that generates most of our work, isn't it?"

"That's where there's the biggest opportunity for graft. I've forwarded the case details to your team node."

"Then let me get my folks settled in, and we'll start on this civilian director with sticky fingers." Gil slowly climbed to his feet. "With your permission?"

"Go ahead and enjoy."

That was one of the many things I liked about my people. They were infinitely adaptable and ready to work anywhere and under any conditions. The fact most of them were without serious attachments, let alone families, helped a lot. We PCB officers had much in common with monastics, I figured. A life devoted to service and damn little else. For example, Gil had two grown children he saw maybe every eighteen to twenty-four months, his wife was long gone, and he had nothing beyond his work.

I didn't even have that much, what with my entire family vanishing into the dungeons of the Pacifican State Security decades ago, leaving me to run into the arms of the Constabulary recruiter and a way off Pacifica before I joined them.

I quit a little early after arranging with the CMTT to have my containers delivered to my apartment that afternoon. A droid with an antigrav sled showed up at my door at fifteen hundred, unloaded the containers into my living room, and trundled off, leaving me to unpack.

My winter uniforms went straight into the back closet. I'd not need them on Caledonia. The rest of my clothes filled less than half the available space, and the various pieces of my life seemed forlorn spread around the spacious rooms. But that was life in the PCB. As Gil said, we travel light because we travel far, although I could hope to spend a few years on Caledonia. Provided I didn't annoy General Terak to the point of her demanding I be replaced.

On Saturday, I received another invitation to supper with Hera and Zack, who had come down to Sanctum for the weekend again and at eighteen hundred, I walked up the driveway of Hera and Zack's residence as the rain started to come down, a harbinger of the monsoon season only a week or two away. This time, Hera opened the door, smiling.

"Welcome, welcome. And just in time, too. If this continues throughout the night, I'll have Zack drive you back."

Within minutes, we were on the covered patio, watching the downpour while enjoying our drinks — gin and tonic for Hera and me, Shrehari ale for Zack.

"I confess I have an ulterior motive for inviting you tonight," Hera said after we toasted another week gone by.

"Do tell."

"You remember eme mentioning that I need you to hunt traitors? Well, I have your first case. A Navy captain by the name of Gunter Wils. He's a senior watchkeeping officer in the Fleet HQ Operations Center. We suspect him of passing classified information to a hostile organization, perhaps the Sécurité Spéciale or one of the interstellar zaibatsu intelligence units." She pulled a data wafer from her shirt pocket and handed it to me. "It's encrypted, of course. Use the key I gave you. If you can handle this one yourself, so much the better."

"I'll take it on with my two wingers. So far, only Team One has arrived, and I've already given them a corrupt civilian director in procurement."

"Excellent."

We spent the rest of the evening discussing the constitutional convention the OutWorlds were organizing on Mykonos and the implications of it being held without the Home Worlds, let alone Earth's permission.

The rain had let up by the time I headed to my apartment, but it was like walking in a sauna, and I was overjoyed at being back in a climate-controlled environment a little before twenty-three hundred. After pouring myself a glass of Glen Arcturus, I put the data wafer Hera had given me in a reader and entered my key. Almost at once, the image of a handsome man in his early fifties wearing a Navy captain's stripes on his collar appeared — Gunter Wils.

I studied his face and quickly revised my assessment of his handsomeness. A weakness around his eyes and mouth overshadowed his firm chin and regular, almost sculpted features. Then it struck me. His lips were too sensual, while his eyes seemed too small, giving him a slightly untrustworthy look, or at least so it appeared to me. But I could merely be attributing those characteristics because Hera suspected him of passing classified information.

I read through the dossier once, then put it aside to sit on my balcony while I finished my glass of whiskey and let my thoughts roam. Caledonia was my third duty station in as many years, and in a way, it was the most congenial of the three. I just couldn't quite explain why. Sure, the weather so far had been better than any place else I'd lived, but with the monsoon coming, that would change.

And while Caledonia boasted an entire Constabulary Group — the 17th — my team and I were a tiny island of gray in a sea of blue, black, and green. Not that we weren't an island among several others on Wyvern as well. The PCB had always been apart from the rest of the Constabulary. Still, I felt more at home here in Sanctum than in Draconis, on Wyvern. Perhaps it was because of friends.

After a final sip of the Glen Arcturus, I headed back inside to prepare for bed. And a few minutes after lights out, I fell into a deep sleep. For once, it was dreamless.

I spent most of Sunday indoors, thanks to the pouring rain, and by Monday morning, I was once again raring to go. Coffee in hand, I wandered through Team One's office, wishing them a good day, then collected Arno and Destine in my office for our first case briefing about Captain Gunter Wils, Commonwealth Navy.

We went through the information on the data wafer, and when we were done, Arno let out a grunt. "Admiral Talyn didn't give us much to go on, did she?"

"Suspected of living beyond his means is a good sign," Destine pointed out. That information he can access landed in places it shouldn't is another."

"He and how many others in the operations center?"

"True."

"But," I said, "Admiral Talyn believes he's guilty, and she doesn't make mistakes often. It's up to us to figure Wils out. Let's start by digging into his lifestyle and confirm if he is indeed living beyond his means."

"On it, Chief."

***

Team Three, under Superintendent Losira Khan, showed up the following day after coming to Caledonia directly from their previous assignment on Cascadia. Losira, with long gray hair framing a narrow face creased by laugh lines, was the oldest member of ACU 12 and also had grown children whom she saw every few years.

She and her team had landed early that morning and, after finding their accommodations and dropping off their luggage, had shown up for work.

"A new place to hang our hats, but the same old crap, eh, boss?" She commented in her dry, sing-song voice when I bade her to take the chair across from my desk.

"How did Cascadia go?"

Losira shrugged.

"It was a success. Bugger was guilty as sin, and we broke him, but not after much work. How did we end up being transferred here?"

"At Grand Admiral Larsson's request. Fleet HQ is a target-rich environment, apparently, both in terms of corrupt personnel and traitors. And we've taken on the latter as well as our usual sort of case. That doesn't mean teams won't travel, but the Grand Admiral has decided a cleanup here is necessary."

"I see. Traitors. Got any for me?"

"I'm handling the first one myself. For you, I have a commodore who appears to suffer from a gambling problem. You need to find out whether that's true and, if so, whether he's compromised himself. He could be selling secrets. The details are in your team node."

"All right. No point in hanging around, swapping lies." Losira climbed to her feet. "With your permission, we'll get started on the gambling commodore."

I watched her leave my office, smiling. Losira came across as a crusty old cop, but there was nothing wrong with her instincts and her intellect. She had the enviable record of a hundred percent clear-up rate since joining the PCB almost two decades ago.

It still felt strange to have over sixty people in ACU 12 after the mere dozen or so I had in the Rim Sector PCB Detachment. And yet, we didn't lack for work because the Armed Forces, being a reflection of Commonwealth society, had its fair share of miscreants, including those whose crimes were sufficient to attract our attention.

Like Captain Gunter Wils, Commonwealth Navy.

That Friday evening, I was back at Zack and Hera's place for supper and a momentous announcement. Zack was taking a brigade to Mykonos ostensibly to train with the local army regiment. But in reality, he'd monitor the convention to ensure it wasn't disrupted by hostile elements. And he was taking his daughter, who'd just been promoted to captain, as Naval Intelligence liaison officer.

— Six —

"Wils is definitely living beyond his means," Arno reported when we met to discuss him the following Monday. "And not doing a particularly good job of hiding it, although he's trying."

"Any chances of his having private income or an inheritance?"

"No," Destine said, shaking her head. "We checked his finances, and nothing more than his pay is coming in. He's not taken out any loans either. Whatever else he's earning isn't part of his legitimate portfolio, but he clearly has another source of revenue that he's using to fund his extravagances. Like a yacht down on the Middle

Sea, a stable of flashy ground cars, a luxury house in Sanctum, and a cottage in the mountains, to name but a few. He's single but doesn't lack female companionship, all of it extravagant. And most of those expenses aren't showing up in his regular account, meaning he must have another secret account."

"Okay. So, he's definitely earning off the grid, likely by doing something illegal or, if not illegal, then questionable. Otherwise, why hide it?" I tapped my desktop with my fingertips. "We have what we need to formalize this investigation. The next step will be interviewing Wils."

"Where do you want to do it, Chief? His office or here?"

I smiled at them. "Neither. I was thinking of visiting him at his home. In civvies."

"Then early this afternoon would be a good time. He's on the sixteen hundred to midnight shift this week."

At thirteen hundred, the three of us aboard an unmarked staff car from the base motor pool pulled up outside a lovely two-story house set back from a quiet, leafy street in a posh neighborhood. We wore sober business suits, but to the practiced eye, there was no mistaking we were cops.

Captain Wils' eye must not have been practiced because he opened his front door to us after we rang and waited for less than thirty seconds. He wore slacks, a short-sleeved shirt, and sandals and frowned at us.

"Yes?"

I held up my credentials. "Assistant Commissioner Caelin Morrow, Commonwealth Constabulary, Captain. With me are Chief Inspector Arno Galdi and Warrant Officer Destine Bonta. We'd like about half an hour of your time to aid us in our inquiries."

Wils studied my credentials as his frown deepened. "What is this about?"

"If you invite us in, I can explain." When he hesitated, I said, "You're not due at the Fleet Operations center until sixteen hundred. We'll be done long before you need to head out."

He still seemed hesitant but stepped back to admit us, then led us into a spacious living room giving out on a terrace via floor-to-ceiling transparent aluminum doors. It flowed naturally into a formal dining area on one side. The furnishings were stylishly black with chrome accents, the walls white, and the floor granite and abstract art hung on the walls. It was very much a place to receive and impress visitors, not a cozy space to curl up in with a good book.

Wils gestured at a sofa as he took an easy chair across a low marble table from it. "Please."

I sat while Arno and Destine moved out of Wils' immediate field of vision. When he noticed them examining some of the art pieces rather than focusing on him, his look became quizzical, but he didn't comment. Mainly because I took the initiative.

"This is a rather nice place you have, Captain. And in an exclusive neighborhood. It must have set you back a few creds."

He shrugged, though suspicion began to show in his eyes.

"You know how it is when you're married to your work — the money accumulates faster than you can spend it, and eventually, you have enough to buy yourself a place like this. Now, what inquiries can I help you with?"

I could tell he wanted to know what Arno and Destine were doing behind his back, but both had taken seats at the long dining table to my left and were watching Wils, tablets in hand, ready to record the interview.

"Well, we were wondering how a Navy captain with no other visible source of income than his pay and no debts can afford your lifestyle," I said in a conversational tone. "By the way, I forgot to mention that we're from Anti-Corruption Unit 12, which investigates corrupt military members."

His eyes widened slightly in shock, and I saw fear creep into his gaze.

"I'm sure I have no idea what you're talking about. My lifestyle is commensurate with my finances."

"Let me see — a yacht, a cottage in the mountains, a collection of fast cars, presumably in the garage beneath our feet. The yacht alone is well beyond a vice admiral living on his pay, let alone a captain with expensive habits. How much do you spend on your dates, by the way? The fashionable downtown clubs and restaurants charge a lot, and you're squiring young ladies around every weekend."

Wils leaned forward in his chair, eyes now blazing with self-righteous anger.

"Get out of my house."

"Throwing us out won't help, Captain. Answers will. We did you the courtesy of coming to your place, in civilian, to have a conversation that we could just as well have had in my office or yours, where everyone could have seen us. I will repeat my question. How does a Navy captain with no other visible source of income than his pay afford your lifestyle?"

He glared at me for a few seconds. "I play the stock market, okay? And I make a lot of money from it."

"Then you won't mind giving us access to your brokerage account."

"I do mind. It's private, and my stock picks are even more so."

"And yet, I need to see your other accounts so I can match your lifestyle to your income. Otherwise, I'll have to assume you're taking corrupt payments from illegal sources." I gave him a sad smile as if to say I'd rather not.

"How dare you? How dare you accuse me of corruption?" Was there another flutter of fear in his eyes? "I'll have you stripped of your rank for this."

He definitely had something to hide. Innocent people didn't react this way.

"Come now, Captain. You and I know you won't have me stripped of anything, let alone my rank. Your brokerage account, please?"

"What if I refuse to give it?"

"Then I'll have no choice but to charge you with perverting the course of justice under Section 130 of the Code of Service Discipline."

I could see a hint of uncertainty competing with his contrived anger, and held his gaze until he looked away.

"It's a numbered account with LetDaan Brokerage," Wils finally said through clenched teeth.

I glanced at Destine to make sure she was ready to copy the account details.

"The number, please."

Wils rattled off a series of digits, which Destine entered into her tablet. After a few seconds, she nodded. The account existed, although we would need another warrant to access it. The one we obtained for his bank accounts wasn't broad enough to cover the brokerage. Destine nodded again, confirming she'd requested the warrant. And she nodded a third time, probably to indicate she'd requested the brokerage freeze the account.

"Thank you, Captain. Your cooperation has been noted." I stood. "Don't leave Sanctum until we clear you."

Then, with Arno and Destine following me, I made my way to the front door and out onto the path leading to the street, leaving Wils to stare at nothing in particular.

"I'll bet the brokerage account is being used to funnel funds into Wils' pockets," Arno said once we were in our car and headed back to the base. "And it's clear he's not declaring the so-called profits. Otherwise, we'd have seen them on his tax statement."

"We'll know once we get the warrant. Am I right you asked LetDaan to freeze the account, Destine?"

"Yes, sir."

"Let's hope they do so before Wils moves his funds out and closes it."

***

"Chief." Arno, with Destine on his tail, entered my office later that afternoon. "We've accessed the brokerage account."

"And?" I gestured at them to take a seat. We were back in uniform, having changed the moment we returned.

"It's a perfect example of what not to do when you're receiving money under the table. By the way, the brokerage froze it as we asked and just before

Wils attempted to close it. Anyway, the account has regular inflows of untraceable funds coming from various anonymous sources, all off-world. Those funds are then invested, and Wils draws on the proceeds of the investments in cash. The LetDaan Brokerage does not know who he is other than the owner of a numbered account."

"It was opened five years ago when he started working in Fleet Operations," Destine said. "And the inflows are substantial, averaging fifty thousand a month. He has about five hundred thousand in it as of today. The cash outflows over those five years have totaled approximately two million."

I let out a low whistle. "What the hell is he doing to earn over half a million a year?"

"That's what we need to find out next, Chief."

I glanced at the time.

"He started his shift in the ops center. How about you two arrest him and bring him here?"

"What are the charges?"

"Perverting the course of justice, for one. Money laundering, for another." I tapped my desktop with my fingertips. "Tell you what. I'll take care of it. You two can stand in the background, as usual."

"Roger that, Chief. I figured you'd change your mind."

The three of us had clearances to go just about anywhere in Fleet HQ, save for the most restricted areas, and got into the underground operations center without problems. We found Captain Wils in the senior watchkeeper's office on the mezzanine above the ops center's floor, where a three-dimensional holographic representation of human space held pride of place.

Wils looked up from his tablet as I entered, seeming momentarily nonplussed at my appearance. Then he recognized me, noted I was in uniform, and blanched. Arno and Destine stepped in behind me and closed the office door.

I dropped into the chair across from his desk.

"Captain Wils, we've examined your brokerage account. Can you explain the fifty thousand creds a month you've been getting for the last five years?"

He leaned forward, forearms on the desktop, and speared me with contemptuous eyes.

"I don't have to explain anything to you, Assistant Commissioner. I've consulted my lawyer, who says you have no jurisdiction over my personal finances."

"Your lawyer is wrong. In a corruption investigation, the personal finances of the targeted officer are fully within my remit. Now, please answer me. What are the fifty thousand creds per month you're receiving and not declaring as income? And by the way, you're violating Caledonia and federal tax laws by not declaring the profits from your investment activities, but that's beyond my current remit."

"Bull."

"I have no choice but to assume the fifty thousand you're getting every month result from corrupt activities. As a result, I'm charging you with committing corrupt practices, perverting the course of justice, and money laundering under Section 130 of the Code of Service Discipline and conduct prejudicial to good order and discipline under Section 129 of the Code of Service Discipline. You do not have to say anything. But it may harm your defense if you do not mention when questioned something which you later rely on in court. Anything you do say may be given in evidence." I paused. "Do you understand?"

— Seven —

Wils stared at me, incredulous. "You're doing what?"

"I'm charging you unless you'd like to explain the funds deposited in your anonymous, numbered brokerage account every month since you started to work in Fleet Operations."

He let out a burst of laughter that sounded hollow to my ears. "You can't do that."

"I can, and I just have." I pulled a data wafer from my tunic pocket and placed it on his desk. "The charges are on this. Please familiarize yourself with the details. As a next step, I will refer your case to the JAG's Director of Prosecutions. Unless, as I said, you're willing to cooperate with us. Although either way, your career is over."

Wils let his gaze slip to one side, visibly thinking about his predicament. I hoped I'd convinced him he had no choice but to open up because if he wanted to, he could stall me forever. We had no way of finding the source of the payments without his help, and, barring that, the Director of Prosecutions might decline to take it any further. Yet I was pretty sure that his career had come to a screeching halt no matter what because he couldn't or wouldn't explain the anonymous funds. Plus, there was the matter of not paying taxes on his gains, which would result in criminal charges on the civilian side.

"You Constabulary people have a reputation for keeping your word," Wils finally said. "If you give me immunity from prosecution, I'll tell you about the origin of the money and much more. And I'll put in for my retirement effective immediately. Oh, and you unfreeze the account too."

"A lot more? Like what?"

A sick smile appeared. "Like I'm not the only one receiving untraceable funds at Fleet HQ."

Now that was interesting. Did Hera know about others such as Wils, or suspect, and hoped I would find them, or was this something new?

"Okay. Tell me everything, and I'll withdraw the charges provided you retire from the Fleet effective immediately. But I mean everything. If I figure you're holding out on me, the deal is off." I switched on my recording device.

Wils nodded once, his features sagging as if all tension had left him. "In a sense, it's a relief to finally get out of this situation. It's not like I was going to become a commodore anyway."

He glanced away again.

"I've always had a weakness for the finer things in life. Things a Navy captain can't afford. And I've never had much by way of scruples, I'm afraid. I've been passing secret and top-secret deployment and other operational information to a so-called friend — allegiance, origin, and nature unknown — in exchange for a generous monthly stipend which ended up in my numbered brokerage account. How did it start? Like most of these things, quite innocently. I met this friend at a party for high rollers at the casino shortly after arriving in Sanctum. One thing led to another, and I found myself short of funds during a high-stakes poker game. He lent me the money, which I then lost. And so, he convinced me to pass along information from Fleet Ops as a way to repay him. Like I just said, I'm pretty much devoid of scruples. He gave as reason that knowing where the Fleet wasn't provided his people with an advantage. And then he told me the more information I could give him, the more he'd pay, allowing me to afford those finer things in life."

"And who is this friend?"

"A man by the name of Findlay Rogers. Oh, don't bother looking for him. He vanished without a trace four years ago, his job of roping me in as his employer's spy done. I've been sending the data to an anonymous and untraceable node. As long as the flow continues, I get my monthly stipend. Which ends now, I suppose." He ran his hand over his face, sighing. "It was a good run while it lasted."

"And the other or others receiving untraceable funds?"

Wils glanced at me before returning his stare to an undefined spot on the wall. "Brigadier General Aldous Greer, in J5 Plans, Navy Captain Victoria Montoni, in Naval Intelligence, and Colonel Leo Young in J3 Ops."

"How do you know?"

"I spotted the three of them laughing it up with Findlay Rogers in various high-end venues before he disappeared. Separately, of course. Not together."

"That's it?"

"Why else would they be having fun with Rogers? The man was a snake on a mission — corrupt senior Fleet officers. The more, the merrier. You can figure out if they have anonymous accounts somewhere." Wils turned his eyes back on me. "So, do we have a deal? I'll go on sick leave right now and stay on it until they finalize my retirement."

"You don't know to who you've been passing information?"

He shook his head. "No. I'd tell you if I knew."

I believed him because the data recipients would do anything to stay anonymous, effectively cutting off any possibility of investigators, such as us, uncovering them. Oh, it probably was the Sécurité Spéciale or perhaps one of the interstellar zaibatsus' intelligence services. They'd have both the need and the resources.

"Can I leave now?"

"How about you write your resignation before leaving?"

"Sure." He called up a virtual keyboard and typed for a few minutes while I watched the words form on the virtual display. Then, he hit send. "There. No going back now."

"We'll ensure your brokerage account is unfrozen, but I suggest you contact the tax office first thing tomorrow and square things with them before it becomes a criminal matter."

We stood, he put on his beret, grabbed his briefcase, and said, "Shall we? I'll let my deputy know I'm going on sick leave. He can take over the shift."

Did he look relieved as he spoke? I supposed he did. And he seemed exhausted. We saw him out of the building and left him to head for one of his fancy cars in the central parkade.

"Well, Chief," Arno said as we returned to our offices, "another one bites the dust. Though not arresting him leaves me a tad unsatisfied."

"I think Captain Wils' troubles are far from over, Arno. Once I report back to Admiral Talyn, I figure she'll send a pair of agents to his house, probably tonight, to find out what information he's been passing along. And since she's not bound by my deal, who knows what'll happen to Wils once they've squeezed him dry?"

Arno gave me a curious look. "You seem remarkably sanguine about that, Chief."

"Do I? Maybe cynicism is finally catching up with me after all these years."

"You? Never."

"Two sordid cases involving senior officers since we arrived in Sanctum might have changed my perceptions slightly. Besides, we have three more to investigate."

When I called Hera, she wasn't available, but I left a detailed message and waited for her to return my call. She did within twenty minutes, and I gave her the gist of Wils' confession.

"Nicely done, Caelin. I'll have someone interrogate him concerning what he stole and the node he used. Not that it'll do much good, but we must make the effort. You mentioned he gave up others?"

I related the names and assignments of the three mentioned by Wils.

"We weren't aware of them," she said, "but it stands to reason the opposition would have senior people in those organizations, even after the purges we conducted several years ago. I assume they're next on your list?"

"Yes, unless you tell me differently."

"Oh, no. Please go ahead and keep me informed of your progress."

"Will do. That was it."

"In that case, Talyn, out."

I sat back and stared out the window at the rapidly fading remains of the day. Superintendent Frederick Vasiliev and Team Four would report tomorrow morning and could take on Captain Victoria Montoni and Colonel Leo Young while I took Brigadier General Aldous Greer. Funny how I went from no business to full employment for three of my four teams in the space of two weeks. Team Two, under Superintendent Maria Lovan, wouldn't show up for at least another three weeks since they were still busy on Cimmeria.

And with that, I called it a day.

***

Superintendent Frederick Vasiliev was a tall, intense-looking man in his mid-fifties with thick black hair and a black beard framing a narrow, olive-skinned face. He, too, wore jump wings, having been a Constabulary liaison with B Squadron as a sergeant well before my time with the 1st Special Forces Regiment.

"A pair of potentially corrupt senior officers? Sure," he said in his deep voice when I gave him the assignment the next day. "And you found out about them from this Wils character. How reliable is that fellow?"

"Not particularly," I admitted. "Which is why we'll have to proceed with extreme caution in case they're innocent of anything other than having had fun with a questionable man four years ago, one who subsequently vanished."

Vasiliev stroked his beard. "Roger that, sir. Not that we don't proceed with caution in every one of our investigations."

"True. Destine is getting the sealed warrants to access their financial accounts, and this time, they'll include any and all secret, anonymous, or numbered ones. When we have those, you can dig in."

"While you're digging into this General Greer."

I grinned at him. "Someone needs to deal with the high-ranking perps."

"Indeed. If that was everything, sir, I'd like to get started on Montoni and Young."

"Off you go."

Vasiliev, for all his solemnity, truly enjoyed his job. He was probably the keenest of my four team leaders, and I knew he'd soon discover whether or not his targets were guilty.

A few days later, Arno strolled into my office wearing a grim expression. We'd begun digging through Greer's finances, and they were a lot more complex than we expected, but that wasn't the reason for his mien.

"Did you hear about Wils, Chief?"

"No. Did something happen?"

Arno took a chair across from me with a sigh. "I set up an alert on his name with the newsnets and just found out that he's disappeared and is presumed dead. He was aboard his yacht when it got caught in a freak offshore storm and foundered. The wreckage was discovered earlier today, but no sign of Wils' body. Convenient, if you ask me."

"What? That he got caught in a freak storm? An assassin could hardly whistle one up at his or her convenience."

"I know. But still. An embarrassment to the Navy conveniently gone shortly after being secretly interrogated by Naval Intelligence, presumed dead by misadventure, although we'll likely never know."

"No, we won't. And our involvement with Wils was over once he confessed and put in his retirement papers. Anything after that is none of our business."

"Aye." He climbed to his feet. "I just hope the traitors we uncover don't all end up dying in mysterious circumstances. It would be enough to make me doubt my vocation as a grand inquisitor."

"And if they do, will you quit on me?"

Arno gave me a wistful smile. "No. I'll stick with you to the bitter end, Chief."

— Eight —

Investigating General Greer was fast becoming a painful experience in bogging down. For one thing, he and his partner didn't live beyond their means. And we'd found no indication so far that he was receiving funds from untraceable sources. On the surface, Greer was as pure as the proverbial driven snow. But something bothered us about him and his financial arrangements. We simply couldn't figure it out. And getting warrants to look into his civilian partner's affairs had proved impossible.

"It's her. It has to be," Arno said with a faint air of disgust on Friday when we regrouped to discuss the week's business. "I'll bet anything that if Greer is being paid to pass on information, she's getting the money in a numbered account somewhere so he can look squeaky clean."

"That does appear to be the only reasonable explanation other than he's not being paid, meaning he's ideological rather than mercenary, or he's wholly innocent of any wrongdoing."

Arno shook his head. "No, Chief. He's not innocent. I can feel it in my bones. That man is up to no good."

I accepted Arno's judgment of Greer because he'd never been wrong before. At least not since we started working together when I took over the Rim Sector's PCB Detachment.

"Should we try again to get a warrant for his partner's financial accounts?" Destine asked.

I shook my head. "We have no further evidence to convince the judge just yet."

Arno snorted. "Civilian judges on Caledonia are a lot harder to convince than elsewhere, I guess. I'm thankful that we mostly deal with the military version. They're not hard to convince at all."

"At least not when the Constabulary's Anti-Corruption Unit asks. Was there any other business we need to discuss before the weekend?"

When both Arno and Destine shook their heads, I nodded. "In that case, we can—"

Just then, my communicator chimed, and I glanced at its display. General Terak.

"If you'll excuse me, the Provost Marshal of the Armed Forces is calling." They immediately stood and left my office while I accepted the call. "General Terak, what can I do for you?"

"Were you investigating a Captain Gunter Wils who vanished when his yacht was wrecked in a storm and is presumed dead?"

How did she find out? It certainly wasn't one of my people talking out of turn. They were too experienced as PCB investigators to even so much as hint at any case we might be working on.

"I'm sorry, but I cannot comment on any past or current ACU 12 investigation."

"Don't give me that bull, Assistant Commissioner. You were seen in his office three days before he disappeared, the same day he resigned from the Navy."

Ah. That explained it. She heard through the grapevine I'd had a heart-to-heart discussion with Wils.

"Under whose authority were you investigating him? And if you didn't press charges, why did he resign?"

"Again, I'm sorry, but I cannot comment, even if I wanted to."

"Are you investigating any other senior officers?" She paused for a second or two, then said in a sarcastic tone, "Let me guess — you can't comment."

"Precisely, General."

"I'd like to know who is assigning you these cases. Surely you can answer that."

I gave it some thought. Perhaps knowing it was the redoubtable Hera Talyn would get Terak off my back.

"Rear Admiral Talyn of Naval Intelligence."

"I know Talyn. I suppose I'll have to ask her."

Good luck with that, I figured. Hera was as likely to discuss Wils with Terak as I was. As for the other three cases — Greer, Montoni, and Young — they didn't even exist beyond the confines of my offices, which were still swept for listening devices every morning.

"Please do so, General. Was there anything else?"

"No." Terak abruptly cut the link.

I let out a sigh of irritation before climbing to my feet, putting my beret on, and heading out the door for the weekend. There wouldn't be a supper at Hera's tonight because she was in Fort Arnhem, saying goodbye to Zack Decker, who was leaving for Mykonos in the morning at the head of the 1st Special Forces Brigade.

***

By the end of the week, I was ready to give up on Greer. Frederick Vasiliev's crew hadn't found a trace of corruption wafting around Captain Montoni and Colonel Young, either, making it three for three. Yet I still believed there was something about them, not least because Wils didn't have to point them out to us. He just did. And having spotted them with the man who recruited him into a life of corruption made a pretty compelling case. Unfortunately, we couldn't come up with any evidence.

But then, Hera called.

"I had my people examine the financials of Greer's spouse, Raylee Redvers, although the way they did so means the results aren't admissible in court. And my, what a treat. But Wils was right. Greer is corrupt. His spouse has set up several numbered corporations which receive a regular inflow of money. She's being smart about it — those corporations pay taxes and occasional dividends to her. But the origin of the funds is completely obscure, like those the late Captain Wils received. The corporations do nothing. In other words, they're shells, yet legal and above board as far as Caledonian and federal laws are concerned. The only mystery is the source of the money. So, there you have it."

"And there's no chance she could receive the funds on her own behalf, meaning Greer is in the clear?"

"She's a mid-level functionary in the Caledonian government's Health and Human Services Department. There's no way she has access to the sort of information that can generate the sums the shell corporations receive, let alone the authority to issue contracts sizeable enough to attract that level of corruption."

I thought about it for a few seconds. "In effect, she's money laundering for Greer."

"That seems to be the case. The sums held in the various corporate bank accounts are increasing with every monthly deposit. As I said, the only outflows are taxes and periodic dividends, the latter not significant enough to make a dent in the totals. They're probably using the corporations as retirement accounts, which is the way to go about it — wait to draw them down once he's hung up his uniform and is beyond our reach. I'll send you copies of the documents my people collected describing this. What you do with them is up to you."

"Thanks, Hera. It gives us something we can use to dig for admissible evidence, but I don't quite know where to start yet."

"You'll figure it out. Cheers."

And with that, her image vanished. Moments later, I received an encrypted message from her and decoded it before saving its contents on ACU 12's private node — the documentation recovered by Hera's agents. Then, I called Arno and Destine and got them up to speed on Greer's spouse and her shell corporations.

"I knew it," Arno said with an air of satisfaction when we finished looking at the documents. "The guy is dirty as hell, just smarter than Wils."

"The question is, how do we get this information legally? Because without that, all we can do is watch Greer. And no, I don't propose confronting him with this evidence, knowing it's not admissible. Greer strikes me as the sort who'd explain it away convincingly enough to leave us with nothing or simply deny everything."

Arno made a face. "I wouldn't reject the idea out of hand, Chief. We've broken a few criminals with inadmissible evidence."

"Sure. But I'd like to explore other means of getting at him before we try that."

"Well, I can't see any, Chief, but the more I think about it, the less I figure it'd do us much good anyhow. He'll simply point at his spouse and profess ignorance, and that'll be it. And once he knows we're onto him, he'll shut everything down. Those shell corporations have enough money in them to fund a nice retirement."

"That's if he can," Destine said. "He may be under pressure to perform, which means no quitting. But how about we go after Raylee Redvers and see if we can't get her to roll over? Or at least get Greer alarmed enough that he makes a mistake or two."

"That's not a bad idea, Chief." Arno scratched his beard. "We come at it like we're after money laundering rather than corruption. Use a bit of obfuscation by not mentioning we're ACU 12 and let her think we're from the Caledonia Constabulary Group. Of course, you'd have to stay in the background. Can't have an assistant commissioner running this sort of investigation."

I considered the idea for a few moments, then nodded.

"Okay. It's worth a try. You'll take the lead on this, and I'll be one of your colleagues, rank not mentioned, along with Destine. We'll wear civvies, of course."

"Right." Arno and Destine stood. "Let us plan something for next week."

After they left my office, I returned to the account statements for the shell corporations, convinced more than ever they were used to launder the proceeds of Greer's treasonous behavior.

That evening, I had supper with Hera at her place and told her about our proposed approach. She approved and offered the use of covert recording equipment, which I accepted. She also offered to have her agents watch the shell companies' accounts to see if anything had changed following our meeting.

I spent the weekend in my apartment, except for lengthy, vigorous exercise periods at the base gym on both days and read. By the time Monday morning rolled around, I was ready to dig into Raylee Redvers.

— Nine —

Arno and Destine spent a few days observing Raylee Redvers to determine the appropriate moment for an approach. It wasn't until Wednesday afternoon that we finalized a plan to speak with her while she had her lunch in a park near her workplace, which she apparently did every day. And so, the next morning, we strolled into the park a few minutes before noon, Destine and I wearing sunglasses that doubled as video recorders. We saw Redvers appear on the path to the heart of the green expanse, where she usually took a bench to eat over the noon hour.

She was in her early fifties, of middling height, with shoulder-length brown hair parted in the middle, framing an unremarkable, narrow face dominated by an aquiline nose, and wore an expensive-looking charcoal business suit. Redvers carried a small bag — her lunch, no doubt — and seemed preoccupied enough that she didn't scan her surroundings as she headed for an empty bench near the pond that formed the park's center.

We ambled along behind Redvers, and when she sat, Destine and I stopped behind the bench while Arno sat beside her.

"Raylee Redvers?" He asked.

She gave him a startled look. "Yes."

"I'm Chief Inspector Arno Galdi of the Commonwealth Constabulary." He held up his credentials long enough for her to scan them. He gestured behind them. "My colleagues, Destine Bonta and Caelin Morrow."

When she glanced over her shoulder, Destine and I flashed our credentials at her, in my case, with a finger obscuring my rank.

"What is this about?" Her voice was high, though melodious. She sounded more curious than alarmed and shifted her position so she could look at Arno without craning her neck.

"We're investigating money laundering, and your shell companies have come to our attention."

I moved to my left so I could see Redvers' face while remaining out of her immediate field of vision, sunglasses recording the encounter.

"Money laundering? Good heavens. Why should my little corporations interest the Constabulary?"

"Because there's no visible source of the income you're receiving. Would you care to explain that?"

"Not particularly. I receive revenues from off-world. I pay the requisite corporate taxes on them and take dividends from time to time. The end. I don't launder money."

"Those revenues are from what and where?" Arno asked, hardening his voice ever so slightly.

"That's really none of your business, Chief Inspector."

"Well, if you won't provide the origin of the funds you receive, I will have to assume money laundering and freeze your accounts while we conduct a forensic audit."

Of course, we couldn't do that, but I hoped she didn't realize it and would either cooperate or get perturbed.

"You'd need a special warrant to freeze my accounts, Chief Inspector, and I don't think you have sufficient evidence of wrongdoing to get one. My simply refusing to discuss the origin of the money won't do."

She sounded confident, more so than I'd expected. This was no pushover who'd collapse at the first sign of police interest.

"Why not tell us and be done? We'll turn our attention elsewhere once we're assured the funds are of legitimate origin."

"Come back with a warrant, Chief Inspector. Now if you'll excuse me, I'm here to eat my lunch, and you're preventing me from doing so."

Arno knew we were beaten and stood. "Enjoy the rest of your day."

Redvers opened her lunch bag, ignoring us, and pulled out a sandwich. Arno and I exchanged a quick glance, then we walked away, headed back to our vehicle, an unmarked staff car from the base motor pool.

"That was a bit of a bust," he said once we were out of earshot. "She's a remarkably confident individual."

"She would be if she's facilitating her husband's corruption via her shell companies. Or even if she's just receiving iffy revenues from undisclosed sources. But we'll know soon enough whether our little intervention stirred something up. If she's honest, she won't do anything to the shell company accounts. If she's not, we might see funds disappear over the coming days. We might even witness General Greer get alarmed at the idea the Constabulary is looking into his spouse's financial affairs."

"Or not, if he keeps his cool knowing we have no warrants, something Raylee Redvers already sussed out." Arno sounded pessimistic. "We're obviously dealing with people who know what they're doing."

"That's what it seemed like to me. In fact, if you ask me, Redvers was a little too calm and collected," I said.

"Perhaps. Oh well, let's see what, if anything, happens now."

We returned to the office none the wiser, and I busied myself with administrative matters for the rest of the day. When I arrived at work the following morning, I found a message from Hera. It simply said Redvers had closed the shell corporation bank accounts after withdrawing the funds in untraceable cred chips the previous day and that her people were looking for the money.

When I told Arno and Destine, the former grunted softly.

"I guess we spooked her after all. She wouldn't have closed the accounts if she had nothing to hide. And I'd say good luck to Admiral Talyn's folks finding the new accounts. She'll be more careful now."

"Without a doubt." My communicator chimed for attention, and I glanced at its display. "I've been summoned to General Terak's office in thirty minutes."

"Summoned? As in, she's ordering you to show up?"

"It appears so. I'm half tempted to beg off by claiming a prior engagement, but I'm curious."

"You know what they say about curiosity, right, Chief?"

"Sure." I smiled at him. "But I'm not a cat."

At the appointed time, I showed up in Terak's office antechamber and was bidden to wait by the same aide as before. Fifteen minutes passed before he admitted me into the holy of holies, as I'd decided to call it since she was clearly trying to put me in the role of supplicant.

"Good morning, General," I said in my perkiest voice as I entered and took a chair across from her desk without waiting for an invitation. "And what can ACU 12 do for you?"

"You can explain why I've received a formal complaint from Brigadier General Aldous Greer of J5 Plans that you were harassing his spouse yesterday, accusing her of money laundering. Oh, I understand it was a Chief Inspector Galdi attempting to question her, but you were present."

I cocked an amused eyebrow at Terak, though I was feeling a surge of irritation with Greer taking a pre-emptive step against us, further proof he and his spouse had something to hide. And since Terak was now involved, I had to tell her something.

"It was hardly harassment, General, and we didn't accuse Redvers of anything. We merely inquired about the source of funds she's receiving in her shell company accounts as part of a greater inquiry into money laundering. She declined to answer, and we left her in peace. That's all."

Terak scowled at me. "Why is ACU 12 investigating money laundering in the first place?

Isn't that a job for the Constabulary's Caledonia Group?"

"Raylee Redvers came up in an investigation we're carrying out."

"And that investigation is into who? General Greer?"

"I cannot discuss active investigations with anyone outside the Professional Compliance Bureau, General," I replied in a reasonable tone. "Sorry."

She pressed her lips together in frustration, and her eyes narrowed. Then she said, "Since General Greer put in a formal complaint, it must be investigated and its merits evaluated."

"Not by ACU 12."

"Of course not. That would be like asking a poacher to act as gamekeeper."

"Then by who, General?"

"By Fleet Security."

"That's not how it works. Another branch of the Bureau investigates PCB officers, not outsiders. You can request my behavior regarding Raylee Redvers be probed by the sector PCB Detachment or by one of the Bureau's central teams on Wyvern. I would suggest the latter since the sector detachment is probably overworked. I certainly was when I handled the Rim Sector."

"And it will take what? Weeks to get another PCB team here? No, this complaint needs to be sorted out as soon as possible. My people will investigate it."

"You're free to do so, but neither my officers nor I can cooperate in this matter, especially since it touches upon an active PCB investigation. And please note, General, that I said can, not will. We're constrained by our regulations, so even if I wanted to help you, I couldn't."

She glared at me. "You PCB people think you're above everyone and everything, don't you?"

"No, General. We don't. We're merely humans tasked with one of the toughest jobs in policing, and we do it well because we follow the rules and regulations to the letter."

But not always the spirit, I silently added, if it's in the cause of uncovering the truth.

"And approaching a civilian like Redvers to ask about the source of her corporate revenues was in accordance with the rules?"

"Certainly. ACU 12 might be focused on the military, but we can still make inquiries wherever we see fit."

"Even if you don't properly identify yourselves?"

"We identified ourselves as Constabulary members and by name, which is all we're required to do when engaging a potential witness in conversation. And before you ask, there is nothing wrong with my letting a more junior officer take charge. Of course, that changes if we make things formal and caution people. But we didn't caution Redvers because we had no reason to do so."

Terak remained silent for a few moments. Finally, she said, "You will not communicate with Brigadier General Aldous Greer or Raylee Redvers until I've cleared his complaint to my satisfaction."

I stared back at her, unwavering. "I'm sorry, General, but you don't have the authority to issue such an order to me. Only Assistant Chief Constable Sorjonen or Deputy Chief Constable Hammett do. You may contact either of them and request they order me to stay away from Greer or Redvers, and if they do so, I will obey."

"You are a most frustrating individual, Morrow. Do you know that? Especially for someone who's only the equivalent of a full colonel, none of whom would dare gainsay me."

"So I've been told many times. However, I'm good at my job and enjoy my superiors' confidence. Otherwise, I wouldn't be here on Caledonia, operating independently."

And suddenly wondering whether putting up a commissioner's star would help the military take me more seriously. Or at least Terak.

"Be that as it may. I will appoint a team to investigate General Greer's complaint, whether or not you like it, Assistant Commissioner. That was all. You're dismissed."

"Aye, aye, General."

I jumped to my feet, gave her a sweet smile, and turned on my heels to leave her office, feeling her eyes boring into my back.

No sooner was I sitting behind my desk than Arno and Destine showed up.

"So?" Arno asked. "What did General Terak want?"

I gestured at them to sit, then ran through our conversation. Once I was done, Arno let out a low whistle.

"Greer's feeling the pinch, is he? Putting in a formal complaint because we spoke with his spouse is a bit over the top."

"Sure, but it's one way of deflecting attention. Or so he hopes," Destine said. "Obviously, he doesn't know us PCB types, nor does General Terak. Both of them are about to be surprised."

"Since he's fired the first shots, I think it's time we sat down with Greer and opened a dialog. But on Monday. Let's give him the weekend to stew."

— Ten —

"No, Assistant Commissioner, I will not be coming to your office so you can interrogate me on my wife's corporate holdings, something that doesn't concern you in the slightest." It had taken five tries before Greer answered my call the following Monday, and his tone had been dismissive from the very start. "Besides, I don't respond well to individuals who are inferior to me in rank and presume to order me around."

I'd been exquisitely polite with him, but his taking the offensive wasn't exactly unexpected.

"I did nothing of the sort, General. But you and I will have a long chat, either in my office or in yours. It's your choice."

"You're not listening to me, Morrow. I won't discuss anything with you because there is nothing to talk about. End of story. I'm not required to speak with you in any case unless you charge me with corruption. And if you planned on doing so, you'd have said something, meaning this conversation is utterly futile. Goodbye, and don't bother me again."

He cut the link, leaving me to stare at my communicator's blank display. Then, I chuckled — the poor deluded fool thought he could keep me from interviewing him? Oh, dear. The more they struggled, the more I dug in.

I glanced up at Arno, who'd witnessed the exchange from beyond video pickup range. "Shall we pay General Greer a visit?"

"Now? Sure. There's no time like the present. How are you going to play this, Chief?"

"Straight up, I think."

We both stood, and I put on my beret while Arno fetched his from the neighboring office. Then, we headed for the J5 Plans division in another distant part of the sprawling HQ complex via the underground passageways. I would gladly have walked the tree-lined aboveground paths, but it was pouring rain, a true Caledonia monsoon day.

Our credentials got us through the added security — the J5 shop dealt with a lot of top-secret stuff — and we quickly found Greer's corner office. We could see him having a pleasant conversation with a colonel through the open door, and, based on the laughs, they probably weren't discussing business.

I exchanged a glance with Arno, then we entered Greer's office without so much as an invitation.

"General Greer, I'm Assistant Commissioner Caelin Morrow of Anti-Corruption Unit 12, and I'd like about half an hour of your time."

He and the colonel stared at me as if I were a two-headed Caledonian Archaeopteryx. I turned to the latter and pointed at the door.

"You'll have to leave. Now."

I put enough command in my voice that he was halfway out of his seat by the time Greer recovered from his surprise at our unannounced interruption.

"No, stay, Ely. Morrow and her minion will be leaving."

"I told you we'd have our conversation either in my office or yours. You rejected my offer, so here I am. Leave Ely." The last two words came out like the crack of a whip, and the colonel scurried out after one last apologetic glance at Greer.

Arno closed the door behind him but remained standing while I took the chair vacated by the hapless Ely.

"How dare you enter my office uninvited, Morrow? Who do you think you are? You're nothing but the equivalent of a colonel and therefore have no right to impose yourself on me." Anger flared in his eyes, though his tone remained low and measured.

I held his gaze but didn't reply for several heartbeats.

"General Greer, it has come to our attention that your spouse is receiving so-called dark money into the bank accounts of the shell corporations she controls. She withdrew the funds in those accounts right after we spoke with her last Thursday and closed them."

Alarm replaced the anger in his eyes.

"Since she won't disclose the source of the funds, I can only assume they're the result of corrupt activities, either by her or you. And since you're in a vastly more important official position than she is, I'm guessing it's you."

"I'm not having this conversation, Morrow. Now get out of my office."

"Not until I have some answers."

"You're not getting any. Not from me, not from Raylee." He crossed his arms and leaned forward. "Leave. My. Office."

But despite his words and harsh tone, I saw uncertainty reflected in his eyes for the first time.

"Do you know a man by the name Findlay Rogers?"

He did. I was sure of that simply by the minute change in his expression.

"No."

"You met him about four years ago when you started your current job. He's a recruiter."

"So?" A scowling Greer leaned forward until his arms rested on his desk. "Who or what is he supposed to have recruited me for?"

"We don't know just yet, but we have a few candidates in mind. Do you admit to meeting him?"

"No." He glanced away, a sure sign he was lying. "Are you going to charge me based on my supposedly meeting this Rogers, a recruiter for a mysterious employer, four years ago?"

"The funds regularly deposited in the corporate bank accounts, do they come from Rogers' employer?"

"No." Greer looked at me momentarily before glancing away again.

"Then where do they come from?"

"None of your business."

"Oh, but it is my business, General. Dark money usually stems from corruption, and I run one of the Constabulary's anti-corruption units. If you don't tell me about the origin of those funds, I'll have to recommend you be relieved of duty pending investigation on suspicion of corrupt activities. You realize that even if we find nothing admissible in a court of law, your career will be effectively over."

Greer glared at me. "Try. Just go ahead and try. I've lodged a formal complaint against you, and I'll add to it by describing your current behavior toward me. We'll see who gets relieved of duty."

I gave him a sad smile. "I'm sorry you feel that way. But if you refuse to talk, I'll have to take this matter up with the J5 himself."

The J5, a vice admiral, wouldn't be overly impressed with me accusing Greer of corruption, but he didn't know that. Fear took over from the anger in his eyes, and he looked away again. I'd ratcheted the pressure about as high as I should have for the first interview and stood.

"I'll leave you to think this over, General. We'll talk again soon."

Arno and I left his office without another word, Arno closing the door behind him. The colonel — Ely — watched us leave, a perplexed expression on his face.

Once back in our unit lines, Arno asked, "Do you think that'll do him? He seemed pretty shaken by the end."

I shrugged. "It may take a second interview to make him crack, but if there was any doubt that he's guilty of something, it's gone."

Arno nodded. "Big time. The man is carrying a burden. Are you really going to see the J5?"

"Not if I can avoid it. I get the feeling Admiral Talyn would like traitors to vanish rather than face a messy court martial, meaning the fewer people who are aware of them, the better. Besides, the evidence we have in Greer's case isn't admissible in court."

"Vanish?" Arno took a chair across from my desk as I sat behind it. "Sounds ominous."

I gave him a mock frown. "Resign, retire, go AWOL, that sort of thing, Arno. Though with Admiral Talyn…"

Arno put on an expression of exaggerated innocence. "Like Captain Wils, who conveniently disappeared at sea?"

"Considering the state of his yacht after the storm, chances are good he drowned accidentally."

"But we'll never know, will we?"

"Probably not."

***

The next day, when Arno and I returned to General Greer's office, he wasn't there and hadn't been seen nor heard from. Colonel White — Ely — was somewhat worried since Greer never missed a day and would have called if something had occurred to keep him away from work.

"When did you last see him?"

"At around sixteen-thirty yesterday. He waved at me as he left for home," Colonel White replied.

"How did he seem?"

"Preoccupied. More so than usual. I suppose it has something to do with you."

"Probably. Thanks, Colonel." I turned to Arno and gestured at the door.

"Another vanishing act, do you think?" Arno asked in a low voice once we'd left the J5 offices.

"I hope not." Yet somehow, I knew Greer had either done a runner, was incapacitated, or was dead. "Let's call Raylee Redvers and see what she says about her husband."

But when I contacted her office, identifying myself as a Constabulary officer, I was told she hadn't shown up for work either, nor had she called.

"Should we visit their place?" Arno asked. "In case something untoward happened?"

"Yes, and we'll take Destine and her surveillance kit with us."

And so, the three of us signed out an unmarked staff car, changed into civvies, and headed for the suburbs, where Greer and Redvers owned a comfortable but not too flashy home. Certainly not as opulent as that of the late Captain Wils.

We arrived shortly before noon and found the neighborhood deserted, its inhabitants at work. After parking in front of Greer's house, Destine pulled out her handheld sensor and scanned it from inside the car. After a minute or so, she shook her head.

"No human life signs and no active security system. You'd think they would have security engaged if they're absent."

"Criminality is low on Caledonia, to begin with," Arno said, "and in a nice quiet suburban environment like this one, it's probably non-existent. Check the neighboring houses."

Destine did so and glanced up at him. "No active security systems, either. You win, Chief Inspector."

"Do you have your entry tools?" I asked her.

"Yes, sir."

"Then let's see if we can get in."

Arno gave me a curious look. "You suspect something untoward happened, Chief? We rarely break into people's homes."

"Let's just call it a gut feeling."

I climbed out of the car, followed by my companions, who looked around as they adjusted their jackets to make sure they could reach their weapons quickly. We pulled on gloves, then walked up the path to the front door, where Destine scanned the locking mechanism up close. I tried to peer through the windows, but they were polarized, and all I saw was my reflection.

Destine produced a small, cylindrical object and pressed one end against the door's control panel. It was a not-quite-legal electronic lock override, the sort many police officers quietly carried in case they needed to enter a building surreptitiously or in case of an emergency. Moments later, we heard a faint click, and the door swung open.

But before we entered, Destine scanned the foyer for any hidden dangers. Finding none, she went in, followed by Arno, with me closing the order of march and the door behind us.

The interior was bright, cheerful, and airy, uncluttered, with cream walls, gray marble floor, and tasteful paintings hanging on the foyer walls and the hallway beyond. A short, rectangular cleaning droid was puttering around, arms extruded, but it ignored us as we checked out each room on the ground floor — living room, dining room, and kitchen. They were spacious, with minimalist wood, leather, and metal furniture, and exuded a clean but lived-in aura. The living room gave onto a covered terrace at the back of the house while the kitchen windows looked out on the front. A garage sat to one side, with two cars in it, yet no one was home.

We took the stairs to the second floor and found four bedrooms, each with an ensuite bathroom. Two showed signs of routine occupancy though the beds were made. One was obviously a guest room, and they had transformed the fourth into an office.

"Separate beds," Arno said in a thoughtful tone of voice. "Either one of them — or both — snores uncontrollably, or they're not that into each other."

"It could be a lot of things," Destine replied. "Not that it matters."

We peeked into the closets, but they seemed to hold a normal amount of clothes, along with boxes of various knickknacks.

"Okay. Let's do the basement." I gestured at the stairs.

We made our way down and found a fully finished games room, a home theater, and a walk-in stasis cabinet, probably used for food storage. I opened the cabinet and immediately wished I hadn't. Greer, naked as the day he was born, lay on the floor, open eyes staring into the Great Void. I entered, knelt beside him, removed my right glove, and reached out to find a pulse on his neck. The moment I touched him, I knew he was dead.

— Eleven —

"In here."

Arno and Destine crowded at the door and took in the sight.

"Dead?" Arno asked.

"As a doornail."

"Any sign of the cause of death?"

I shook my head. "Not immediately, no. I don't want to move his body to check all sides."

"What do we do now? This is local police jurisdiction. And we're technically not supposed to be in here."

I stood, looked at the body again, studying it for a bit, then exited the stasis chamber and closed the door, restoring the stasis field that kept everything fresh, including dead bodies.

"We'll call the locals and let them know about Greer. I'll deal with questions related to our entering this place unbidden."

Once back upstairs, I fished my communicator from my jacket pocket and called the Sanctum Police's Crimes Against Sentients Division directly rather than go through the main desk or their operations center.

"This is Staff Sergeant Mattias. To whom am I speaking?"

"I'm Assistant Commissioner Caelin Morrow, Commonwealth Constabulary. I head Anti-Corruption Unit 12."

"And what can Crimes Against Sentients do for you, Assistant Commissioner?"

"I'm calling to report the suspicious death of a military member in his off-base home, a Brigadier General Aldous Greer. The address is Twelve-Sixty Mudlark Drive. We found him naked in a basement stasis room used to store food. His body temperature is low, so he was likely placed in stasis several hours after death. I didn't touch him other than to ensure he had no pulse and vacated the stasis room immediately."

"What were you doing in this General Greer's house, if I may ask, Assistant Commissioner?"

"We've been investigating him as per my unit's remit, and when he failed to appear at work today or call in, I feared something untoward might have happened. We entered the house, searched it, and eventually found him. There's no sign of his spouse, Raylee Redvers, who also failed to appear at her place of work this morning, and both of their cars are in the garage. We didn't find any indications of a struggle."

"Okay. I'll have a team there within the next thirty minutes. If you can exit the house to avoid further contaminating the scene and wait for them outside, that would be appreciated."

"Will do."

"Mattias, out."

I glanced at my team, who'd overheard the conversation and nodded at the front door. "Let's go sit in our car while we wait."

"First impressions?" I asked once we left the house.

"Since there's no trace of Redvers, perhaps she had something to do with Greer's death," Arno replied. "If a third party was responsible, we should have found her body along with his. There's enough room in the stasis chamber."

"Agreed," Destine said.

Arno leaned against our vehicle instead of climbing in. "Both cars are in the garage, which means she either left on foot, hired ground transport, or left with a third party."

I nodded. "Or her body is somewhere on the property, but we haven't found it. We didn't actually look inside the cars, did we?"

"No. I guess we'll have to leave that to the locals." Arno glanced at the garage. "Or should we take a quick peek?"

"Let's."

We returned to the house and entered the garage from the inside door. A quick search proved neither car contained a body.

"Okay. That answers that. Time to return outside."

Eventually, a pair of unmarked police cars and a coroner's van pulled up to the house and disgorged eight cops, six of them wearing crime scene jumpsuits, the other two street civvies. I pushed myself off our car and held up my credentials.

"I'm Assistant Commissioner Caelin Morrow."

"Detective Inspector Ahmed Greval," the older of the two in civvies replied, holding up his credentials. He was of average height and slender, black-haired, swarthy, with intelligent brown eyes.

We put our credentials away and shook hands. Then I pointed behind me. "Chief Inspector Arno Galdi and Warrant Officer Destine Bonta."

Greval nodded at them. "Pleasure." He pointed at the other detective, a lean, tall, narrow-faced woman with short gray hair, watchful blue eyes, and a sallow complexion, and said, "Detective Staff Sergeant Ericka Leung. So, what do you have?"

I explained we were investigating Greer, showing up at the house because he'd fallen off the face of the planet and eventually found him in the basement stasis room.

Greval consulted a small pad in his hand, proof he had what I told Mattias. "How about the wife — a Raylee Redvers?"

"No signs of her. Both cars are in the garage. No signs of a struggle, either. As for the cause of death, I couldn't tell from my cursory inspection of the body."

"Did you touch anything?"

"We wore gloves throughout, though I briefly removed my right one to check Greer for a pulse."

"Good. It's always a pleasure to work with pros." He gave me a curious glance. "How did you get into the house, by the way?"

I nodded at Destine, who briefly produced the lock override. Greval gave me a knowing look.

"We'll leave it at that, then. How'd you like to show me around, Assistant Commissioner?"

"Sure." I led Greval and Leung up the path to the front door and into the house. We walked through each room on the main and upper floors, popped our heads into the garage, then went into the basement, where I opened the stasis room door and stepped back to let them by.

Both detectives studied the body without touching it. Then Greval raised his communicator to his lips and said, "Come on to the basement."

He glanced at Leung. "Check the security system for any recordings."

She vanished. Moments later, I heard footsteps on the stairs, and the six in crime scene suits appeared, carrying cases. Greval turned to me.

"You're cleared to leave now, but I'll need statements from you and your people."

"I'd like to stick around and see what the probable cause of death is if your folks can determine it here. As I said, we're investigating Greer for corruption, and I have no doubt his death is directly related."

"Was he aware of your investigation?"

"Yes. We interviewed him yesterday morning. His wife — a civilian government employee — is also involved in it, which makes her disappearance part of my case."

Greval stared at me for a few heartbeats, digesting my words. Then he nodded once.

"Right. So we have overlapping cases and overlapping jurisdictions here. You'll excuse me if I'm not dancing with joy, Assistant Commissioner."

I gave him a small smile.

"Getting the feds involved is always a joy for planetary police forces. I suggest that we compare notes going forward and help each other out. I'll send you what we have on Greer's corruption case. In the meantime, I suggest you issue a BOLO for Raylee Redvers. She might try to leave Caledonia with all the funds she withdrew from her corporate bank accounts late last week. Several million creds which we think are the proceeds of Greer's corrupt activities."

Greval let out a low whistle. "What sort of corruption was he involved in making that much money?"

"Selling military secrets. He worked in the Fleet's plans division where he had access to plenty of highly classified material, the sort wanted by many shadowy organizations."

Greval scratched his chin. "I see. You get a lot of customers doing that sort of thing?"

"A few. But my unit is still fairly new, and we just transferred from Wyvern to Caledonia a few weeks ago, so I expect to get more in due course."

One of the crime scene suits came out of the stasis room, a medical sensor in his hand.

"I can't give you a cause of death without an autopsy, Ahmed. But I can tell you he died approximately eight hours before someone put his body in stasis."

Greval turned to me. "When was he last seen?"

"At sixteen-thirty, leaving the office. Figure about half an hour to get here from the base, so he could have died anytime after seventeen-hundred yesterday."

"And we'll never know the correct time of death, thanks to the stasis chamber," the man with the medical sensor said. "I'll have his body removed and brought to the morgue now. The scene is yours."

Sergeant Leung came down the stairs again. "The security system has been disconnected from the central, and its records have been wiped."

"Redvers?"

"Possibly," I said. "She seemed quite self-possessed when we attempted to interview her. I could see her deleting the system's records before vanishing, especially if she was involved in Greer's death."

"I suppose I should issue that BOLO. Where did she work?"

"Caledonia Health and Human Services."

He moved away and murmured into his communicator while Leung and I watched as the crime scene people placed Greer's body in a bag and carried him out to the waiting coroner's van.

Greval rejoined us. "Done. I had them pull images from her work credentials. Time to search the house in detail, room by room. Assistant Commissioner, could you record your statements and send them to me?"

"Sure. No problems. I'll send them at the same time as our case notes on Greer."

"And I'll let you know about any developments."

With that, we were dismissed, but I couldn't see much point in staying. We had to tell the J5, Vice Admiral Egon Yuell, that he needed a replacement for Greer, warn the Joint Base Sanctum Provost Marshal that he'd be getting a call from the Sanctum Police, and figure out the next steps.

***

"Dead?" Vice Admiral Yuell seemed puzzled by my statement. "How can he be dead? He was fit, young, and healthy."

Perhaps not young, but compared to Yuell, who was in his seventies?

"His death is suspicious, sir."

"Meaning he was murdered? Poor Raylee. How is she taking it?"

"We don't know. She vanished without a trace."

"Oh." A pause. "Are you saying Raylee is involved?"

"We don't know that either, sir."

Yuell's lips compressed together, and his fingers momentarily danced on his desktop as if he were holding an internal debate.

"Well, I'm not sure if I should say so, but there was always something hard and unfeeling about her. The few times we met socially, I mean. And she gave me the impression of dominating Aldous if you get my meaning. It was as if she were in charge of their marriage."

Interesting. I noted his words and knew Arno, sitting behind me and to one side, was recording them for the case file.

"I see. Is there anything else about Raylee Redvers you remember, sir?"

His fingers tapped the desk again, then he shook his head. "No. I'm afraid not."

"In that case, thank you for your time." I stood. "I'll notify the base provost marshal of General Greer's death, so you may expect a call from him or one of his people."

"Thank you, Assistant Commissioner."

Arno and I left the J5 wing and, since the weather was holding, crossed the base to the base security offices above ground to better digest a lunch that had been wolfed down rather than enjoyed.

The Joint Base Sanctum's Provost Marshal was a Navy commodore named Stepan Gordiev. We'd met before when I first arrived at Fleet HQ and made my manners with him. He didn't give me the impression of being overly pleased with an independent police agency operating on his territory without oversight, but then it could just have been his way. Gordiev struck me as a taciturn man who never smiled and always kept his own counsel. Stocky, broad-shouldered, he had hooded eyes set in a square face dominated by a sharp nose and wore his mop of dark hair swept back from his forehead.

"What can I do for you, Assistant Commissioner?" he asked in his low, gravelly voice when I stuck my head through his open office door.

"You have a few minutes, Commodore?" When he nodded warily, I entered, trailed by Arno, and took a chair across from him. "We found Brigadier General Aldous Greer, of the J5 division, dead under suspicious circumstances in his home this morning. I was investigating Greer, and we went to his place when he failed to appear at work. Since it occurred off-base, the Sanctum Police are handling the case, but I thought you should be aware before they contact you."

"Greer, eh?" I could almost see Gordiev parsing his memory for a face and a few facts. "And you were investigating him, you said?"

"Yes. And I already spoke with Vice Admiral Yuell, Greer's superior."

I figured he was debating whether to ask me about it, but discretion won out.

"Okay, thanks for letting me know. I suggest you also tell General Terak about this." He gave me a veiled look I couldn't interpret. That he'd be in tight with her was no surprise. Terak probably handpicked Gordiev for the job.

"I will." And with that, I climbed to my feet, and we left.

— Twelve —

"So you're now what? Three for three, Morrow? I'm beginning to think you're a jinx for anyone suspected of corruption." How Terak managed to stare down her nose at me while we both sat at the same height was interesting. "It's most careless of you."

Disturbingly, she was right, at least in part, to attribute the three deaths to me. Jacques committed suicide because of the disgrace of being found out. Wils had perished in an accident at sea that could well have been deliberate — no sailor goes out into a storm unless he has to, even a relatively inexperienced one. And now Greer, dead within twenty-four hours of my interviewing him about the proceeds of corrupt activities.

"Perhaps, General. But I can do nothing to control the reactions of those I investigate. They'll do as they will. Besides, Greer almost certainly died at the hand of someone else. His spouse, maybe? The Sanctum Police have issued a BOLO for her."

"What? You suspect Raylee Redvers?"

This time, it was my turn to be surprised. "You know her?"

Terak's face took on an air of inscrutability as if she figured she might have betrayed herself somehow.

"There aren't that many Marine flag officers in this town, so I knew Greer in passing and met Raylee a few times during Marine Corps mess functions."

I didn't know how she interpreted not all that many because there were over a hundred Marine generals in Sanctum, from the Commandant, who doubled as deputy commander-in-chief of the Armed Forces, down to the most junior brigadier general. And to remember the name of a spouse she'd met a few times over the years seemed a bit out of the ordinary. But perhaps Terak had a better-than-average memory for names and faces, just like I did.

"I see. Well, that's what I had for you, General." I waited a few seconds to allow her to broach other subjects or continue this one, then stood. "Enjoy the rest of your day."

She kept staring at me as I politely nodded and turned to leave her office.

"Take care you don't lose any more suspects, Morrow. Your fitness to command ACU 12 might be questioned."

"Yes, General," I said over my shoulder.

***

The following day, I received a message from Inspector Greval asking me to call him at my convenience. He had the preliminary autopsy results on Greer.

"Our man suffered cardiac arrest," Greval said once we connected. "And yes, I know that it's the cause of most deaths. But his heart was in perfect condition for a man his age, and he suffered from no obvious ailments."

"In other words, his heart shouldn't simply have stopped."

"Right. Our current theory is a dissipating poison that stops the heart and breaks down immediately afterward, leaving no trace."

"Which explains why the body wasn't placed in the stasis room until several hours after death, to ensure the poison was completely gone from his system."

Greval pointed at her with his index finger. "Just so. It means we're dealing with a well-organized killer who left nothing to chance. Would Raylee Redvers be such a person, Assistant Commissioner?"

I thought about it briefly before giving him a half-shrug. "Perhaps. Did your BOLO bring any results so far?"

He shrugged. "No. But I'm not surprised. If Redvers is our well-organized killer, she'd surely have changed her appearance and identity by now."

"How long had she been working for the Caledonian government?"

"Four years. Almost exactly as long as she and Greer have been married. We're still trying to figure out who she is by interviewing her work colleagues and neighbors. So far, we have found no relatives or friends, though both are off-worlders, he from Scandia, she from Celeste. They arrived on Caledonia at roughly the same time and met shortly after that."

"And then, Greer met a recruiter, and Redvers set up shell corporations to receive dark money."

"What are you thinking, Assistant Commissioner?"

"That Redvers is more than she seems. Perhaps she's actually an agent of the organization Greer sold secrets to."

"And married to keep an eye on him? That sounds a bit farfetched."

"Trust me on this. There are organizations out there who'd do it without a moment's hesitation if the prize is big enough, and being a senior planning officer, Greer had access to secrets they'd pay a lot for and did, as you might have seen from the documents I sent."

"Yeah. That's quite an impressive amount of money. Anyway, that sort of stuff is in your remit, not mine, but if she's a secret operative, everything makes sense. Not that it gets us any further. In fact, if she's an agent, she'll have plenty of resources to disappear for good. Still, I'll continue investigating her possible involvement in Greer's death."

"Thanks for the update."

"De nada. Cheers, Assistant Commissioner."

As his image vanished, I sat back and crossed my legs, eyes staring out the window. My gut instinct told me I was on the right track to consider Redvers as a hostile agent who married Greer because he was a big prize in the world of betrayal and the theft of secrets. And I had to decide whether to brief Vice Admiral Yuell on our suspicions about Greer so he and his people could make a damage assessment.

Where Wils had dealt with the ephemeral, passing along current deployments, something that stopped the moment we strong-armed him into retiring, Greer handled a sizeable chunk of long-range planning which had more intrinsic value to any hostile elements. The damage his betrayal could do might resonate for years.

I called Yuell's office and asked for an appointment to discuss Greer; as luck had it, he was available right then.

***

"So, you see, sir, I have grounds to believe General Greer was selling secrets and died because he learned I was on to him and told his spouse, who could well have been a hostile operative controlling him."

Yuell, who'd listened to me speak without interrupting, rubbed his chin with his left hand when I sat back.

"That's very troubling, Assistant Commissioner. Very troubling indeed. I understand sniffing out corruption is your stock in trade, and from what I've heard, you're rather good at it, so I'll take what you told me at face value. Of course, this means the damage assessment will be a humongous task, considering the top-secret and above material Greer had access to over the last four years and some." He let out a soft sigh. "But I suppose it must be done. A shame he's no longer alive to tell us what he sold, but I suppose that's why he was killed in the first place."

"More than likely, sir. You'll receive my written report by tomorrow. Did you have any questions?"

He sighed. "No. You were succinct, and I thank you."

I stood. "In that case, I'll be off."

Once back in my office, I put in a call with Hera while I briefed my team on Inspector Greval's findings and my discussion with Vice Admiral Yuell.

"You decided to call it, then, Chief?" Arno asked once I fell silent. "Even though our evidence is circumstantial and inadmissible in court?"

"Yes, if only so the J5 can carry out damage assessment. We won't get any more certainty than we have now. I'm afraid Raylee Redvers no longer exists, and whoever she transformed into is probably booked on the next liner headed away from Caledonia."

"You're most likely right on that count." Arno scratched his beard. "I guess the Greer investigation is over for all intents and purposes."

"It is. I'll file it as incomplete, unlikely to resolve."

I hated unresolved cases, but they happened. At least Greer was no longer able to betray the Fleet, which was the most important thing. Of course, the damage he might have done was incalculable, but that wasn't my problem. As a PCB officer, I learned to not take our targets' misdeeds personally. We simply put them out of action and moved on to the next. Whether the system prosecuted them rather than let them disappear quietly wasn't really my decision.

Except being the Fleet's conscience made it mine, if only because I was dozens of light-years removed from my superior and entrusted with his confidence that I'd make the right call every time. I'd done so with Wils, allowing him to retire rather than face a messy prosecution, knowing Naval Intelligence agents would debrief him informally.

Would I have done the same with Greer? I doubted it but couldn't know for sure. I operated on instinct based on decades of experience part of the time and decided on the fly. Those decisions proved to mostly be correct. Of course, whenever I pushed my instinct aside and decided based on pure evidence, my choices were even more on the money. Where Greer was concerned, it was a bit of both. The evidence pointed at him being corrupt, and my instincts confirmed it.

My communicator sounded — Hera. I activated it and said, "A good morning to you, Admiral."

"Good morning, Caelin. What's up?"

"Brigadier General Aldous Greer is dead." I gave her a detailed account of the situation.

When I finished, Hera nodded. "I figure you're right in pointing the finger at Raylee Redvers, or whatever her real name is, for Greer's murder. A shame we couldn't debrief him before he died. Still, you ended his double-crossing career, so it's a win for the good guys."

She laughed when I told her what Terak said about my being three for three. "Don't worry about it. Back during the Black Sword business, we literally made several dozen treasonous officers vanish into the Infinite Void. None of them saw a charge sheet, let alone the inside of a courtroom. Just keep on sniffing out traitors, Caelin. It's what you do best. And if they die before you bring them to justice, then so be it."

I made a face. "Thanks. I think."

"What'll you do now?"

"File the case as unresolved and find a new one. I'll take either Montoni or Young from Frederick Vasiliev's team."

"How about you concentrate on Montoni?"

"Any particular reason?"

A faint smile appeared on Hera's lips. "Montoni's Naval Intelligence, which complicates things just a bit if she strayed from the path of righteousness. I'd feel better if you handled her personally."

"Will do."

"Talyn, out."

I liked Hera. I really did, even though sometimes I thought her soulless eyes were eerie. But there were occasions when her callous attitude toward the lives of those who betrayed the Fleet struck a sour chord, and this was one of them. I wondered about Wils again. Did he really perish in a storm by accident, or was his death engineered by Hera's people?

— Thirteen —

"You can certainly have Captain Montoni," Frederick Vasiliev said when I told him I'd take one of the two cases I assigned him. "We didn't get far with her. Either she's clean, or she covers it up really well. Or she was selling out the Fleet once and is no longer doing so."

"All right, Montoni is mine, then. How are you doing on Young?"

Frederick made a face. "Not that well either, though there are indications of money coming in from one or more unknown sources. We'll eventually crack it."

I gave him a smile. "Of that, I have no doubt."

"Was there anything else?"

"No." I watched Frederick leave my office, then I called up the Montoni file and studied her image.

She was a raven-haired fifty-something with tresses down to her shoulders, olive skin, and almond eyes above high cheekbones. Unmarried, with no known attachments, and a modest lifestyle, although she took the leave she was entitled to and spent it south, by the sea, where she rented a small bungalow. Montoni lived in the same senior officers' apartment building as I did, two floors down from me, though I didn't recall ever coming across her.

She worked in Naval Intelligence as one of the section heads in the Political Analysis Division. Zack's daughter, Saga Decker, also worked in Political Analysis, and she might have been helpful in getting to know Montoni better. But Saga was off on Mykonos with her father for the constitutional convention.

So far, the investigation hadn't come up with anything unusual about her — no extra income, no questionable associates, and no behavior that could lead to being blackmailed. Montoni was the epitome of the warrior nun, including a dedication to physical fitness that saw her in the base gym for over an hour and a half every day of the week.

And yet, the late Captain Wils identified her as having spent time with Findlay Rogers, the recruiter, four years ago. Wils had been right about

Greer, and it seemed likely he'd also been right about Young. Was this a three for three situation, or was Victoria Montoni wholly innocent of corruption?

How would I tackle her? The moment that thought entered my mind, I saw the glimmer of a plan forming, one which would involve me more closely with the target than usual. Yet if it worked…

That afternoon, I went to the gym at the same time as Montoni and finally saw her in person, though I took care to avoid staring. Montoni was in the bodybuilding center, working on one of the multifunction machines, a thin sheen of sweat on her skin, eyes narrowed as she strained. She wore tight black shorts and a tight red t-shirt, molding her slender body.

I was no slouch myself in the fitness department, but her physique was finely developed compared to mine, with well-defined muscles evident on her bare arms and legs as she strained against the apparatus' resistance.

I took a nearby machine and began my routine, and I quickly zoned out, as usual, when working muscles tight from spending too much time behind a desk. Soon, I sported a sheen of sweat as well, yet the sensation of endorphins flowing through my bloodstream was glorious.

Eventually, I reached my daily quota and glanced at Montoni, who was cooling down with stretching exercises. I stepped out of my machine and imitated her, feeling at peace with myself and the universe. Around us, hundreds of men and women were exercising before heading home, and Montoni eventually made her way to the locker room. I followed moments later.

There, she retrieved her uniform, now on a hanger, and a gym bag and left. I did the same, also preferring to shower at home, and emerged into the late afternoon sunshine thirty paces behind Montoni, who was headed toward the residential section with an energetic pace, uniform hanger tossed over her left shoulder. We weren't the only ones walking home on the surface, taking advantage of the nice weather rather than using the subterranean passage system. I caught up with her by the time we reached the senior officers' apartment block and entered right on her heels.

When she turned her head, having finally sensed me behind her, I smiled. "Another great day to be alive, isn't it?"

Montoni smiled back. "It is."

She gave me a curious look as she called the lift. "Are you new around here? I can't recall seeing you before."

"I moved in a few weeks ago. Caelin Morrow." I offered her my hand. "I'm on the sixth floor."

"Victoria Montoni." We shook. "I'm on the fourth."

As we entered the lift, she asked, "What do you do around here, Caelin?"

"I head the Constabulary's Anti-Corruption Unit 12. And you?"

Surprising me not at all, I saw no reaction to Montoni hearing the name of my organization. Her expression and her eyes remained impassive as if ACU 12 were just another outfit.

"I'm in Naval Intelligence." The lift stopped on the fourth floor, and she stepped out. "Enjoy the rest of your day."

"You too."

Once the lift doors were closed, I muttered to myself, "Contact — wait, out."

The following day, I didn't go to the gym at the same time as Montoni, and the day after, I showed up when her routine was halfway done. We acknowledged each other with a nod, then I took a machine and ignored her finishing and leaving. That evening, I had supper with Hera at her place and told her about my plan of getting close to Montoni.

"It sounds like a good idea. But Montoni is notoriously private and self-contained. She has no known friends, though she gets along quite well with her colleagues, subordinates, and superiors."

"I privately dubbed her the warrior nun."

Hera chuckled. "That's as good a name for her as any. She certainly practices a simple lifestyle from what I've heard."

The following Monday, I got to the gym a few minutes ahead of her and was already deep into my routine when she showed up. As luck would have it, Montoni took the machine next to mine — it was one of the few still available — and when I glanced at her, she smiled.

"Hello again, Caelin."

I smiled back. "Hi, Victoria."

"Call me Vic, please." She began her exercises, and her eyes lost focus.

I judged when she'd finished and stepped out of the machine just ahead of her to begin my cool down. She joined me a few minutes later.

"I gather you don't exercise at the same time every day."

"No. Some days, I come early to clear my mind and return to work afterward. It's only on days when things have gone reasonably well that I'm here after work. You come at the same time every day?"

"Yes. Except for weekends."

"Do you do anything special on weekends?"

"I enjoy hiking the foothills. Sometimes, I'll overnight along the trail on Saturdays."

Flashing a quick smile at her, I said, "I'm also into hiking, but I prefer to come home for the night."

We finished stretching and headed for the locker room together. She noticed the rank insignia on my tunic collar as I pulled out my uniform on its hanger.

"Assistant Commissioner?" Montoni gave me a raised eyebrows look. "Your unit must be rather large and important."

"It's neither." I swung the hanger over my shoulder and grabbed my bag. "But the nature of my business is such that my people tend to be more senior than in other units."

"And what is an anti-corruption unit doing at the heart of Fleet HQ?" She picked up her uniform and bags, and we fell into step beside each other, headed for the door.

I flashed her a smile. "Investigating military members and Fleet civilians suspected of corruption."

"Isn't that a job for the Armed Forces Security Branch?"

"Small-time corruption is. We're here to go after the complex cases involving senior personnel."

We reached the front door only to realize it was pouring rain, so we backtracked and took the stairs to the underground complex, where we waited for one of the automated shuttles headed in the right direction, along with a dozen others.

"You get a lot of business?"

"Enough to keep us busy. How about you? Which part of Naval Intelligence do you work for?"

"Political Analysis. I'm a section head. My primary responsibility centers on the OutWorlds."

"Just like me then?"

"What do you mean?"

I smiled at her again. "You run a small team of higher-ranking individuals."

She smiled back for the first time, transforming her severe features into something more human and approachable. "Yes, I suppose so."

A shuttle stopped in front of us, and we hopped aboard the open, roofless platform, taking side-by-side seats. It chimed twice and moved off smoothly and noiselessly. We didn't speak during the short ride to our building, but the silence didn't seem uncomfortable.

Once there, we got off and entered the apartment block's basement lobby. Montoni called a lift, which appeared almost instantly. We entered the car, and the door opened onto the fourth floor moments later.

"That's me. See you tomorrow. Or not — depending on how you feel." Another faint smile briefly flashed across her face.

"See you tomorrow." The doors closed, and I was wafted up two floors, pleased with myself. Perhaps I could get close after all and find some sign of whether Victoria Montoni — Vic — was bent or not.

The things we did in the name of the Professional Compliance Bureau's Anti-Corruption Branch.

— Fourteen —

The following morning, Gil Hasreen came to see me so he could report that his investigation on the civilian director in procurement, Hal Jeehan, was complete. His team had found enough evidence to bring the target in for a formal interview, and Gil was running it by me before pulling the trigger.

"I think you've got Jeehan, which is just as well because we received a fresh case."

"No rest for the wicked," he replied in his deep voice. "What's the new one about?"

"A Navy commander at 3rd Fleet HQ suspected of passing secrets to an unnamed zaibatsu. I figure you can assign it to your deputy and send her off to

Dordogne with part of your team while you finish the case of the civilian. I've posted the orders just now. Destine will organize the trip."

Gil let out a soft grunt. "April does like traveling."

I chuckled. "April especially enjoys the downtime aboard starships when she can read to her heart's content."

Chief Inspector April Hong was well known in the PCB for her voracious reading habits, second only to her sharp investigator's instincts.

"True." Gil stood. "I'll give April her assignment, then reel in Mister Jeehan. If you want to watch the interview, we'll use room 2. Say in half an hour. He's currently at his desk, practicing the fine art of peculation." When I cocked an eyebrow at him, Gil let out a bark of laughter. "Oh, yes. We obtained a warrant to place surveillance on all his computers and connections, and Hal Jeehan is indeed wheeling and dealing as we speak. Of course, he's doing it in code, but we cracked that too."

Half an hour later, I switched my office primary display to the feed from Interrogation Room 2 just in time to see Hal Jeehan enter along with Gil and one of his warrant officers. The room was small yet comfortable enough to put targets at ease, with padded chairs around a table, two to each side, a large display on one wall, and posters on the others.

Jeehan was a good-looking man in his early sixties, lean, with silver-shot dark hair brushed back from a high forehead, intelligent brown eyes framing a patrician nose, and a square jaw. He wore a dark gray, high-collared business suit, the sort that was a quasi-uniform for Fleet civilian employees. His gaze took in the windowless room, and he licked his lips nervously a few times as he sat. It was the only hint that Jeehan wasn't entirely as composed as he appeared.

Gil and his warrant officer took chairs across from Jeehan, their eyes on him.

"We will make an audiovisual record of this interview," Gil said. "For the purposes of the recording, I am Chief Superintendent Gil Hasreen of Anti-Corruption Unit 12." He nodded at his colleague.

"I am Warrant Officer Francis Belleck of Anti-Corruption Unit 12."

Gil turned to Jeehan.

"Please identify yourself for the record, sir."

"I'm Hal Jeehan of the Naval Procurement Branch, and I'd like to know why I'm here."

"Mister Jeehan, I put it to you that you pass contracts to favored firms in return for kickbacks."

"I beg your pardon." Jeehan reared up, frowning, though I could spot fear in his eyes, and so could Gil and his warrant officer. "I'll have you know that I never, ever favored a firm, let alone took corrupt payments."

"Let's begin with Temujin Antimatter Controllers," Gil said, ignoring Jeehan's outburst as he glanced at the tablet in his right hand. "They came second in the bidding contest but miraculously won the contract, anyway. Shortly afterward, you received one hundred thousand creds from a numbered account, which we traced back to Temujin via layers of shell corporations. And as a good citizen, you declared the monies and paid taxes on them. Do you have any comments?"

Jeehan crossed his arms and sat back in his chair. "None whatsoever."

"Next, we have Gennadium Hyperdrives, part of the same zaibatsu as Temujin, by the way — Lakatic Corporation — though they keep the relationship nice and quiet. Gennadium came in third but got the contract. Meanwhile, you got another hundred thousand from a different numbered account that we traced back to Lakatic itself. Care to comment?"

"No."

Gil looked at his tablet again. "Then, we have Halogen Industries, Redfern Starship Parts, and Venkatri Incorporated, who won smaller no-bid contracts. You've been busy, Mister Jeehan. Fortunately for you, payments of thirty thousand, fifty-five thousand, and seventy thousand followed the attribution of each contract, all of them traceable back to the companies in question." He looked up at Jeehan. "Any comments about those?"

Jeehan shook his head, though he was licking his lips nervously again. "No."

"As you can see, sir, we have five obvious examples of corrupt practices committed in recent times. I have no doubt that if we went back further, we would find more. Now, we have evidence of the payments and their origins, which is enough to end your career. We also have testimony from certain members of your staff of irregularities committed on your orders regarding the aforementioned contracts."

"My staff would never toss me out of the airlock like that."

A faint smile appeared on Gil's lips. "Who do you think alerted us to your misdeeds and triggered our investigation, sir?"

Jeehan looked away, eyes narrowing in thought. "I'm not admitting anything."

"You're not poor or indebted. You don't have any expensive habits, apart from the odd escort once or twice a month. Why did you take the kickbacks?"

"No comment."

"Are they supposed to provide an additional nest egg for when you retire?"

A flash in his eyes told me Gil had hit on the right reason. "No comment."

He must have also seen it because his next question tried to explore the subject.

"Funny, considering the pension of a director-level civilian employee is more than generous, and you have legitimate retirement savings on top of that."

"No comment." Jeehan leaned forward. "In fact, we're done here. You'll need to speak with my lawyer from now on."

"In that case, Hal Jeehan, I am arresting you for corrupt practices and perverting the course of justice. You do not have to say anything, but it may harm your defense if you do not mention, when questioned, something which you later rely on in court. Anything you do say may be given in evidence. You have the right to retain counsel. If you cannot afford a lawyer, one will be assigned to you at no cost. Do you understand?"

When he didn't immediately reply, Gil asked again, "Do you understand what I just said?"

"Yes, and I have nothing else to say," Jeehan replied irritably. "I'll call my lawyer now if you don't mind."

"You will do so from the Joint Base Sanctum brig, where you will be escorted once we're done here."

Jeehan gave Gil a look of pure astonishment. "You're jailing me on accusations of petty crime?"

"The crimes you're accused of aren't petty, sir. And a judge will decide whether you'll be released on bail pending trial. Since you're being arrested for crimes committed against the Armed Forces while employed by them, that judge will be military unless he or she transfers jurisdiction to the civilian court."

At a signal from Gil, he and the warrant officer climbed to their feet. "Please stand, Mister Jeehan. We can do this in one of two ways. Either you promise to come quietly with us, and we won't cuff you, or you don't, and we will."

Jeehan seemed to deflate all of a sudden and slowly stood. "I'll come quietly."

I watched them leave the room, then switched off my primary display. Moments later, Gil was at my office door.

"You watched?"

"Yes. Nicely done. He strikes me as the sort who won't admit guilt until the bitter end and then perhaps even keep proclaiming his innocence in the face of overwhelming evidence."

"That was my thought as well, which is why I cut the interview short and arrested him. Maybe after a night in the cells, he'll come to his senses and call us to discuss an arrangement, but I doubt it. And then, the judge will grant him bail since he's a non-violent, first-time offender, and that will be that until the trial."

"You have a rock-solid case, so I'm not worried about a court acquitting him, though he might escape jail time and instead be fined all the corrupt payments he's received along with a suspended sentence. In any case, he won't be working for a government agency ever again."

Gil let out a disconsolate grunt. "We bring them in. The justice system disposes of them. It has always been thus and shall always be thus until the heat death of the universe."

"Amen."

With that, Gil vanished to write the first of many reports. Arresting a suspect was the simple part. Preparing the documentation for the judge, the prosecution, and the defending lawyer — three unique sets — was tedious, but it had to be done.

I prepared a brief note for General Terak since she referred the Jeehan case to us, giving her an update about its status, and sent it off via routine channels. Considering her workload as Provost Marshal of the Armed Forces, I didn't expect her to read it, let alone acknowledge my sending it, but I had to make an effort, slight as it was.

Arno wandered into my office, coffee mug in hand, shortly afterward and sat across from me. "I understand Gil arrested Jeehan."

I nodded. "He did."

"Good. That bastard was too slippery by half. How's your campaign to get into Montoni's good graces going?"

"It feels like I'm engaged in a game of slow seduction, but I've got her to crack a smile at me, so I count that as progress. We'll see when I head for the gym this afternoon."

"A smile, eh? Well done, Chief."

Unsure whether or not he was being sarcastic, I gave him a mock scowl. "You try to get the warrior nun to crack one. It isn't that easy."

"Warrior Nun?"

"It's my private nickname for Montoni."

Arno thought for a moment, then nodded sagely. "A most apt one, considering she doesn't appear to have much of a life beyond work and physical exercise. And if she has sources of extracurricular income, we haven't found the slightest trace of them."

"She could be ideological rather than mercenary."

"And those who betray because of ideals are extremely difficult to pin down."

I shrugged. "True, but we must try."

— Fifteen —

And try I did. I showed up at the gym that afternoon shortly after Montoni and took the machine next to hers. We smiled at each other and nodded but concentrated on our exercises. But afterward, during our cool-down stretches, Montoni said, "I gather you had a good day, Caelin."

"Yes. We arrested a corrupt civilian official this morning."

"Can I ask what he or she's done? Or is that confidential?"

"He took kickbacks from Fleet suppliers for improperly awarding them contracts and earned himself over a quarter million creds in the last eighteen months. That's not something you do."

"Oh, my. Was he senior?"

"Fairly. Senior enough to have known better, that's for sure."

"Interesting. You get a lot of cases like that?"

"Mainly. Corruption is most frequently related to money — those engaging in it need or want additional funds for various reasons, indebtedness being the top one."

"And your corrupt civilian?" She asked with an air of interest clear in her usually impassive eyes. "What was his reason?"

"Building himself an additional retirement fund." We finished stretching and headed for the locker room. "It was greed, pure and simple. He thought he could get away with it but hadn't counted on one of his subordinates going to Fleet Security with concerns. And since we're based here now, Security tossed it over to us. All in all, it was a classic case, the sort we see more often than any other."

I knew I'd probably told her more than I should have about an active case, but I figured it might help strengthen our tenuous relationship. We grabbed our things and, because the weather was good, took the surface paths.

"Your job seems fascinating. Investigating those who fall prey to their baser desires must give you quite an insight into the human psyche."

"It does. But in the end, they're all pretty much the same — weak psyches in thrall to their appetites, fears, and desires." It wasn't entirely accurate, but I figured I'd use a bit of misdirection. She probably considered herself to be strong and, therefore, beyond suspicion.

"And yet those weak men and women attain high-ranking positions," Montoni said with a faint air of wonder.

"Middling high. I've yet to find one at the three- or four-star level. Of course," I said, giving her a wry smile, "they could simply be better at hiding their corrupt natures. We're hardly infallible in the PCB."

"Do you get a lot of cases where you can't prove anything?"

"Some. Not many. Mostly when we're called in, it's more a matter of gathering evidence proving corruption rather than establishing the possibility in the first place. We don't investigate on spec but follow up possibilities identified by an individual's chain of command, colleagues, subordinates, or third parties. That said, we do get the odd innocent whose behavior merely appeared suspicious."

"It must be difficult to make friends with your sort of job."

"Within the Constabulary and the Fleet, sure. We're always looked at with suspicion. That's why when a member is assigned to the PCB, he or she stays with it for the rest of their career. Still, the work is interesting, the people are more experienced than any other group, and we tend to be closer to each other. Me, I'm solitary by nature and don't have many friends, period."

Montoni chuckled, a throaty sound that matched her severe looks.

"As am I, and I don't have many friends either. We seem to have that in common, at least."

Did I detect a hint of interest beyond that of a vague acquaintance making pleasant conversation?

"Oh, I'm sure we have more than a lack of friends in common."

"Such as?"

"There's our mutual enjoyment of hiking, for one thing."

"True."

"And I'm sure we can find more rather quickly. Tell me, what sort of food do you like? Caledonian, Dordognais, Wyvernian?"

"Oh, definitely Dordognais. There's a little restaurant in town called L'Habitation which serves the best Dordognais food on the planet." She glanced at me with a mysterious smile. "And I have an in with the maître d'hotel, which means I don't need reservations a week in advance. You?"

"Dordognais as well. I've never heard of L'Habitation, but now I must try it."

"How would you like to go Friday for supper? I haven't been in a few weeks and am due a dose of their heavenly prix fixe."

I gave her a big grin. "Sure. I'd love to. And if you want to show me some of your favorite hiking trails, I wouldn't say no either."

"You're in luck. I was thinking of heading upcountry on Sunday. A nice little six-to-seven-hour hike across the Thurso Valley in the shadow of Mount Caravel. I plan on leaving at oh-seven hundred."

"You're on." We reached the senior officers' apartment block and stepped aboard the lift. "If you're into gin and tonic after work, I have a nice bottle of Caledonian Blue in the freezer."

"And another thing we have in common."

"Apartment six-oh-four, say, in half an hour?"

"I'll be there." She stepped out on the fourth and smiled at me again as the door closed.

Thirty minutes later — I'd showered, cleaned up, and put out the drinks fixings by then — a soft chime wafted through my apartment. I opened the door to a smiling Victoria Montoni wearing a green short-sleeved blouse, fawn slacks, and white flat shoes.

"Come in, come in." I waved her through and into my living room. She looked around, but if the lack of personal touches in the apartment surprised her, she kept it well hidden. "Shall we sit on the balcony and admire the view?"

"Sure."

"How do you take your gin and tonic?"

"Half and half."

"A woman after my own heart." I quickly poured the drinks, then joined her on my balcony, where we sat on either side of a small, low table, facing northwest, with the mountains purplish on the horizon under the late afternoon sun.

"Nice," she said. "I'm on the other side of the building, which means I get a view of Joint Base Sanctum's full expanse."

"Along with sunshine all day. They gave me this apartment as lodgings when I was here on temporary duty investigating a commodore engaged in peculation. But that turned into a permanent change of duty station a few weeks ago when my entire unit was moved here from Wyvern under the logic that we should be closer to our customer base."

Montoni let out another of her throaty chuckles. "Is that what you call it? Your customer base?"

"It's one of the more polite terms we use."

"Should I ask about the less polite appellations?"

"No."

"Okay, I won't. So, tell me about your background. Where were you born?"

"Pacifica. But I left there under duress when I was seventeen and haven't returned since, mainly because the Secret State Police still have a warrant for my arrest."

She turned her whole body toward me, placing both elbows on the chair's right arm. "Now, that's a story I'd like to hear."

And hear it, she did. We'd downed our drinks by the time I finished speaking, and I made fresh ones.

"How about you?" I asked.

"I'm from Arcadia and entered the Armed Forces Academy after a childhood without adventures, certainly nothing like you experienced. Let me see — I'm not used to talking about myself. My parents were solidly middle class. I have two brothers, one two years older than me, the other three years younger."

"Were?"

"They passed away about ten years ago in an accident."

"I'm sorry."

"We hadn't been close for over twenty years by then. When I went to the Academy at eighteen, I pretty much cut most links with family. It's not that they were against me going, but I've always been solitary and self-contained, and once embarked on a career in the Fleet, which took me everywhere but Arcadia, I lost touch more by neglect than anything else." She gave me a sad smile. "And you lost your family in the worst way possible."

"I got over that long ago. Those days seem more like a distant dream, or rather nightmare, than something that actually happened to me. So, you're an Academy product."

"The best thing I ever did. I thrived in the highly regimented atmosphere and did well enough that I got my first choice of occupational specialty, intelligence. After graduation, I attended the Intelligence School, and when I finished that, I was posted to 3rd Fleet on Dordogne as a junior analyst." A glint of amusement crossed her eyes. "It's where I developed a lifelong love for Dordognais food."

"I only spent a few weeks there when I was a chief inspector in the Flying Squad, but it was enough to get me hooked as well."

"Flying Squad? What's that?"

"It's the nickname of a specialized group — the Sector Major Crimes Division. They sent us wherever the locals grappled with events that stretched their resources. Mass murders, serial killers, that sort of thing."

It was also my last assignment before going to the PCB when I fell out with the best friend I'd had, Gerri Kazan, because she became prone to cutting corners. But I kept that to myself. The wound had scabbed over long ago, yet I'd still rather not probe it. Seeing Gerri again on Aquilonia Station several years ago had cost me enough.

"Sounds cheerful."

"It had its moments. I'm not unhappy to have left the Flying Squad for the Firing Squad, even though joining the latter essentially means you work nowhere else ever again."

Montoni chuckled once more. "Is that what you call yourselves? The Firing Squad? Seems rather apt."

I gave her a wry smile. "Isn't it, though? We also call ourselves the Last of the Incorruptibles."

She thought for a moment, then said, "Because you're the answer to *quis custodiet ipsos custodes*, who will guard the guards themselves."

"Just so."

She finished her drink and stood. "With that, I'm off. Thank you for the excellent Caledonian Blue."

I escorted her to my apartment door and watched her leave. Only later did I realize she'd learned much more about me than I about her, proving that although she probably hadn't been a field officer for years, Montoni evidently still possessed decent interrogation skills.

That Friday, Hera called to invite me over for supper, but I told her I was going out to L'Habitation with Montoni, which elicited a soft whistle.

"The finest Dordognais restaurant on the planet. And you got reservations just like that?"

"Montoni apparently has an in with the maître d'hotel."

"Does she now? Well, enjoy. It's Zack's and my favorite. We go there regularly. Does that mean your campaign to worm your way into Montoni's confidence is working?"

"It appears to be." I told her about Montoni's interrogation skills, and she laughed.

"Typical career intelligence officer. They develop those abilities early on, especially if they do a tour as a field operative, and never forget them."

"They? Does that mean you're not a career intelligence officer?"

"No. I was a command path lieutenant, a gunnery officer when I was recruited into Special Operations because of certain traits I exhibited."

The way Hera said traits, I knew better than to ask further questions on that subject.

— Sixteen —

We met in our building's lobby at eighteen-thirty and then went down two levels to the underground garage — we'd be taking Montoni's car, an older model, trim, yet elegant, a teardrop shape in silvery gray. It made mine look positively dowdy. And her driving habits were equally elegant yet zippy, weaving in and out of traffic rather than connecting to the centralized traffic control hub and letting it get us there. I reached for the grab bar on my side a few times, something she noticed because a wicked smile appeared on her face.

We got to L'Habitation shortly before nineteen hundred and parked across the street from its unprepossessing facade, modeled after an early seventeenth-century structure of the same name that once stood on Earth's North American continent. Its windows were gaily lit, hinting at a warm atmosphere inside.

The main door gave onto a spacious, wood-paneled lobby with a chandelier, an imitation wooden wheel holding fake candles hanging from the high ceiling. Wooden benches lined both side walls, while a small podium stood beside the glass inner door. Within moments, a compact, black-suited, middle-aged man with a small mustache came through the door, smiling.

"Madame Montoni. How nice to have you back in the house."

"It's always a pleasure to be here, Etienne. This is Caelin Morrow of the Commonwealth Constabulary, newly arrived on Caledonia and eager for her first visit to L'Habitation."

He bowed his head. "Madame Morrow, welcome. I'm sure you'll enjoy yourself. If you'll follow me, your table is waiting."

Etienne led us into the restaurant proper, a cozy place with cream-colored walls above pale wood wainscoting, a wood ceiling with exposed beams, glow globes discretely hovering above tables, and a wooden floor the color of old honey. He ushered us to a corner table set for two, produced printed menus with a flourish, and wished us a good meal.

Montoni took one look at the menu and said, "Can't go wrong with the three-course prix fixe, Caelin. It's trout arancini, duck magret with asparagus, and an orange brandy tart tonight. And let me tell you, they make the duck like no one else in this star system."

"All right, then. The prix fixe it is." I put the menu to one side. Montoni dropped hers on top of it.

"I think the house red wine is more than adequate. Shall we split a bottle?"

"Sure."

The house red turned out to be a Chateau Caledon from the Pictou Vineyards, which were a mere hour east of Sanctum, and it was delightful from the first sip.

"Your health." Montoni raised her glass.

"And yours."

I placed my glass back on the table and played with its stem while looking at Montoni.

"So, what does a Political Analysis team do?"

She gave me a quick smile. "We analyze the political aspect of things. What are star system governments doing? What are they planning? Do they have any secrets? Are they up to no good? Do they have sovereignist aspirations? That sort of thing. And with the amount of shenanigans they get up to, there's always something brewing. We have five teams, each with its own set of star systems, each under an O-6, and we report to a commodore."

"A friend's daughter is on one of the teams — Captain Saga Decker. Do you know her?"

Montoni's eyebrows shot up. "You're friends with Colonel Zack Decker and, I presume, with Rear Admiral Hera Talyn as well?"

"Yes. We've known each other for years. I first ran across Hera Talyn when she was just a commander and I was a chief superintendent."

I figured I might as well get it out in the open in case she already knew of or suspected my links with Hera. We hadn't been particularly secretive about them.

"I see. Good friends to have. Saga is on Colonel Derwent's team, one of the three concerned with the OutWorlds. She's about the smartest, most perceptive intelligence officer anyone has ever seen." Montoni's mischievous smile returned. "We call her the Intelligence Witch behind her back. It's eerie sometimes how she can connect events and details, almost as if she had a Sister of the Void's abilities to perceive things normal mortals can't. For instance, she came up with the idea that the OutWorlds would hold a constitutional convention in defiance of Earth before they even announced it."

"That's what I gathered from Admiral Talyn."

We both took a sip of our wine, Montoni eying me speculatively.

"Tell me, Caelin, you're a Home Worlder by birth, like me, but you're hanging out with a pair of OutWorlders who make no secret about their distaste for proponents of greater centralization by Earth. Does that mean you've taken on an OutWorlder's viewpoint?"

The question was so unexpected that I didn't immediately answer.

"I can't say I've taken on any viewpoint on the matter, if truth be told, and we don't discuss it much, if at all." That wasn't strictly true, but I didn't want to wade into those murky waters with Montoni. "I suppose I'm too focused on my job to care overly about the subject of centralization versus sovereign star systems. How about you? Considering you didn't leave Arcadia as a refugee like I left Pacifica and soured on the world of my birth."

"Well," she said, swirling her wine glass absently, "I suppose I'm a bit like you — too involved with my work. But I can see the merits of the arguments for both sides of the debate."

"So can I." That wasn't strictly true, either. However, I needed to keep building my rapport with her. "I'm not an absolutist by any means. Relationships between human-settled worlds and Earth or each other have always been fraught. Although it seems they're in direr straights nowadays than at any other time I can remember. I couldn't tell you the answer, but I doubt it's increased star system sovereignty."

"We're in agreement on that point."

Just then, the trout arancini arrived, and we paused our conversation to take a first bite. It was terrific, and I said so. Once we were done, I picked up my wine glass again, took a sip, then toyed with it as I allowed myself an air of mischief.

"How long were you a field operative?"

Her eyebrows crept up by a few millimeters as she stared at me.

"What makes you think I was a field operative?"

My smile broadened. "Your interrogation skills, for one thing."

She chuckled. "My interrogation skills. And when would you have noticed those? Not that I'm saying I have any."

"The other day, when we were enjoying a glass of Caledonian Blue on my balcony. I didn't notice them right away, but afterward, I realized you'd learned much more about me than I about you. And I'm usually not that prone to sharing."

A coy grin briefly appeared on her lips.

"Guilty, I guess. Old habits die hard. I was a field operative for five years when I was a lieutenant. Nothing exciting, mind you. Merely the collection of raw intelligence at the source. And some of those sources — many, in fact — were human. Hence my developing those skills."

Something told me it was much more than that, even if she wasn't working for the blackest of black, Hera's Special Operations Division. Or as it would have been at the time, the Special Operations

Section. But why I got that impression, I couldn't say. Instinct, no doubt. After dealing with master dissemblers over the years since I joined the PCB, I'd developed a feel for untruths, evasions, and outright lies told in the most convincing way possible.

"Well, now that I'm aware of it, you won't get away with giving little in return," I said in a light, playful tone.

A waiter removed our appetizer plates and then returned with the main dish, succulent slices of duck breast bordered by skin so crispy, I thought I'd died and merged with the Infinite Void. We spoke little during the meal except to praise the dish.

When I finally pushed my empty plate to one side and picked up my wine glass, I asked, "What do your brothers do for a living?"

"Let me see. Last I checked — and this was shortly after my parents died — the oldest, Liam, was working for a member of the Arcadian Senate from the People's Prosperity Party as chief of staff. The youngest, Gerard, was on the verge of another business failure. He collects them like other people collect rare gemstones, poor Gerry. Never had much luck but plenty of determination. Hopefully, he finally found something that didn't go under within the space of eighteen months. But I doubt it. He's the sort who's destined for failure no matter what he tries and would be better off taking a job for someone else." She gave me a pained look. "Yet he'll never submit to a boss."

I made a mental note to check up on Liam and Gerard Montoni and see if she told me the truth. One of the other skills that a field operative must possess was the ability to twist stories so they would suit a narrative.

"Shall we have the cheese platter before dessert?" She asked.

I thought about it for a moment, but just one. Cheese was a weakness of mine, which I didn't indulge in often, so I nodded.

"Absolutely."

When the waiter came to remove our empty plates, Montoni asked for the *Plateau des maîtres fromagers* for two before the brandy tart and two glasses of the house port wine.

"You'll enjoy this. They usually have five different local cheeses, including a blue to die for."

"Then I'll have experienced many deaths tonight."

Her eyes crinkled with delight. "And aren't those the best of nights?"

"They are."

I didn't know whether there was a double entendre in her words, but she seemed more relaxed than I'd ever seen her to date.

The cheese plate showed up shortly afterward, and the blue was indeed heavenly. The port was pretty good, too, and our conversation turned to lighter matters, such as hiking trails, funny events at work, and the like. We had the dessert and lingered over our coffee cups, Montoni watching me above the rim of hers as she held it just below her eyes with both hands.

She took a last sip of her coffee, then placed the cup on the table and touched my hand briefly with her fingertips. "This was a lot of fun, Caelin."

"It was."

"And I'd like to do it again."

I smiled back at her. "So would I. And tonight is my treat since you introduced me to this splendid restaurant."

She inclined her head in gratitude. "Why thank you."

Was her face a little more flushed than usual? Or was it simply an artifact of the room's gentle lighting? We did split a bottle of wine, but that amounted to only two glasses each, plus a small glass of port.

I paid, and we walked out into the sultry night air. The area around L'Habitation was hopping — bars spilling light and sound onto streets filled with people celebrating the end of the work week. But I suddenly felt tired and was glad when I settled in Montoni's car without her proposing we continue the evening elsewhere.

She set the car on automatic, and the AI drove us back to Joint Base Sanctum at a sedate rate of speed while we chatted about our upcoming hike on Sunday.

Montoni was still smiling at me when we said goodnight as she stepped off the elevator on the fourth floor.

— Seventeen —

Sunday morning, bright and early, I met Montoni in the underground garage by her car. We were both dressed for a day on the trail — long trousers, long-sleeved, loose shirts, hiking boots, and floppy hats. I'd brought my day pack with first aid supplies, food, a water pouch, a rain poncho, and emergency items, as well as my pair of walking sticks. Montoni had a pack and sticks as well.

"Ready?" She asked with a smile as we tossed our gear on the back seat.

I grinned at her. "Totally."

The drive up to the Thurso Valley was pleasant, under a clear blue sky that heralded a glorious day.

At least until late afternoon, when the forecast called for a monsoon-like downpour. We talked about nothing in particular, mostly childhood memories of various events. Soon enough, the bulk of Mount Caravel began to stand out from the rest of the mountain chain, dark green with trees up to three-quarters of its height, then bare stone for the rest.

"I hope you're not planning on taking me up that monster," I said, gesturing at it through the windscreen.

"No fears. We won't be going up that much on the trail I've selected. But there will still be a few steep rises."

"Good. I may be fit, but not Mount Caravel fit like you."

We bypassed Thurso itself and ended up at a trailhead in a clearing just south of the town. There were no other cars, and we parked near the sign with a map and a warning. I climbed out, shrugged on my daypack, and picked up my walking sticks. Then, I went over to the sign and studied it. A single path wound its way around a spur beneath Mount Caravel for approximately twenty kilometers. It was more than I was used to, but I knew I'd make it without too many problems. At least the elevation changes seemed to be moderate, save for a bit near the beginning, where the path headed toward the mountain.

"It's a nice walk," Montoni said from behind me. "I try to do this one every few months because the view when you reach the highest point is absolutely magnificent. You can almost see Sanctum in the distance. Almost, but not quite. It's a little too far away."

"We'll certainly have the trail to ourselves, it seems."

"Probably. It's not the most popular for the city crowd. Too long and too far away." She flashed me a smile. "But I prefer it that way — all alone with nature. Come on."

Montoni led us onto the trail, which immediately went upward. It was bordered by dense native trees blocking much of the morning sun, giving it a tunnel-like appearance. Native avians flitted by, chirping and singing in utterly alien tones, and I realized that this was my first introduction to the real Caledonia beyond the terraformed parts.

Small insectoids buzzed around us, but they kept their distance since we were alien to them. Caledonia was only recently colonized, less than a hundred and fifty years ago, and much of it remained as it had always been, the vegetation a deep green, with surprising splashes of red, orange, and yellow, the tree trunks smooth and straight, and the undergrowth a riot of colorful plants. Some of the latter even exhibited behavior more like that of animals and watched us go by, their flowery heads moving in unison. It was disturbing at first.

We soon fell into a rhythm that worked for both of us, walking at a good clip, side by side, in silence, enjoying the sounds of nature on a world several dozen light-years from that with gave birth to our species. And yet, strangely enough, I felt at home in this environment, and I couldn't explain why.

After three hours of going mainly uphill, the trees gave way, and we found ourselves a fair bit up the flank of Mount Caravel, where the trail flattened, and the view became almost infinite, fading in the hazy distance beyond the horizon.

"What did I tell you?" Montoni asked once we stopped and sat on a boulder facing downslope. "Isn't this magnificent?"

"It is."

We couldn't quite see Sanctum at this distance, but we could make out just about where it was among the green of the foothills and plains, with the ribbon of river cutting through everything. From this height, the world looked undisturbed by human hands, and we might have been the only ones on the planet. Until a shuttle crossed the sky, high above us, on an approach to the Sanctum spaceport. It was silent, but there was no mistaking the small, dark dot descending purposefully to the horizon for anything else. Whether it was naval or civilian, we couldn't tell, of course.

"This is probably the best view in the settled part of Caledonia. At least it's the best I've found in my years exploring the planet. I'm sure there are better ones in the Northern Alps, but there are no roads, towns, or settlements, nothing but wind, cold, snow, and craggy stones reaching for the sky. I suppose I could hire an aircar to take me there, but then I prefer the warmer climate."

"So do I. The first settlers knew what they were doing when they established themselves on this part of the main continent, with the Middle Sea a few hundred kilometers downriver of Sanctum, just far enough to blunt any tropical storm coming ashore in a northerly direction." A pause. "I'd like to see the Middle Sea one of these days. Apparently, Admiral Talyn and Colonel Decker have a home on a small bay there, behind a curtain of Caledonian mangroves. They call it their retirement place."

"We can go next weekend if you like. A day trip or an overnighter — your choice. I haven't swum in the Middle Sea for a while. It's wonderfully warm."

I turned to smile at her. "Why not?"

She smiled back. "An overnighter?"

"Sure. I'd love that."

Montoni looked up at the sky, then glanced at her timepiece. "It's still a little too early for lunch. And it's getting uncomfortably hot. Shall we resume our trek?"

"Yes."

We both stood, stretched a little, since the time spent sitting had tightened our muscles, then headed off, downhill this time, stopping an hour later for a quick cold meal while sitting on a fallen log by the edge of the trail in the shade.

By the time the shadow of Mount Caravel encroached fully on the Thurso Valley, we had reached the parking lot, where a few cars were now sitting beside Montoni's and climbed aboard.

"That was fun. A little challenging for me, but what a beautiful forest and that view? Simply magnificent."

"I'm glad you enjoyed it, Caelin. It's one of my favorites." She switched on the power plant and sped out of the parking lot with the panache I'd gotten used to seeing from her.

When we returned to our apartment block, just after eighteen hundred, I impulsively invited her to supper at my place, but she demurred, saying she would have a light meal and then go to bed early. I didn't insist.

Instead, once showered and in light clothes, I sat on my balcony with a gin and tonic and reviewed the day. I figured we'd gotten closer, but I still didn't have a grasp of her as a person. Just when I thought I'd gained insight, she'd slipped away, turning conversations down inconsequential paths as if she was trying to avoid my prying while keeping me interested.

At this point, I didn't know whether it was the intelligence officer in her or whether she was naturally reserved. But even though I'd made another step into her confidence, if not her life, it wasn't taking me any closer to figuring out whether or not she was a traitor.

I shoved a prepared meal into the autochef and ate while reading one of the books currently on my list, a history of the Second Migration War. It was heavy going, without a doubt, but something told me it would become topical sooner rather than later, especially with the highly contested constitutional convention on Mykonos.

Later on, lying in bed, feeling my muscles and feet from the hike, I couldn't help but wonder whether Victoria Montoni wasn't innocent of treason. That Wils either tried to stitch her up, or she withstood the recruiter's blandishments. Then, I fell into a deep sleep, one disturbed by a dream of the past, of when I betrayed Gerri Kazan. Or at least that's how she saw it.

"How dare you?" Gerri, eyes blazing with fury, swirled toward me, her fists clenched at her side. "How the fuck dare you? I thought we were friends as well as partners."

"So did I. But you put me in an untenable position." My gaze slipped away from her to stare out the office window. It was raining, and long streaks ran down the panes while Squamish, Cascadia's capital, suffered under another downpour.

"Untenable position? All you had to do was look in another direction this once, and it would have been fine. No one would have complained, and the case would have been closed."

"Except it wasn't this once. It was the latest occasion you crossed the line, one of a dozen or more. The previous times I either didn't catch on until you'd presented our conclusions to the chief, or I could just stomach what you'd done, barely." I turned back toward her. "But fabricating evidence to justify arresting Corvo?"

"He's guilty. You know it, and I know it. And I didn't fabricate evidence. I merely smoothed it out to make sure it implicated him without question. Anyone in the Flying Squad would have accepted it as fair dealing. Corvo is guilty, end of story."

I let out a humorless bark of laughter. "I doubt our colleagues would think so, and I'm not the only one who's tired of you cutting corners to close cases."

"But I close them. That's what counts. If I hadn't massaged the evidence, Corvo would still be walking free, preparing to assault and murder his next victim. Who knows how many more dead bodies we'd be examining for clues waiting for you to be satisfied? One, five, ten?"

The contempt dripping from her voice was a corrosive that ate away at my self-confidence and at my heart. Part of me wished to take everything back and return to how things were. Yet it was too late. I'd gone to the chief superintendent with my concerns about the validity of Corvo's arrest under the circumstances, and the other times she'd taken shortcuts also came out.

He'd suspended Gerri with pay pending an investigation by the PCB into her conduct and to determine whether it had jeopardized our case against Corvo and rendered the judgments against the others before him unsafe.

I forced myself to hold her gaze and experience the full onslaught of her anger against me.

"We would have had him in another week or two. We were so close that jeopardizing the case by smoothing out the evidence, as you put it, was unjustified and unjustifiable. I tried to tell you, but you wouldn't listen. You wanted so desperately to bring Corvo in and reap the kudos that it blinded you to your duty."

"Oh, no, Caelin. The only one who's blind is you. And you'll pay for this betrayal. No one in the Flying Squad will want to work with you anymore. You'll be a pariah because everyone will know you can't be trusted to have your partner's back." She stared at me in silence for a few heartbeats. "In any case, you and I are finished. As partners and as friends. I never want to see you again, *Chief Inspector.*"

She spat out the last two words as if they offended her very being, then turned on her heels and left my office. It was the last time I saw her until we met again on Aquilonia Station years later.

Sadly, her prediction turned out to be correct. Even though Gerri was known to cut corners, she was seen as the victim in this whole business by most members of the Flying Squad, leaving me without a willing partner. When the PCB chief superintendent assigned to investigate her finished, he'd found enough evidence to have her dismissed for professional misconduct. But by then, she'd resigned from the Constabulary and left Cascadia for parts unknown.

He called me into the office he'd been assigned and asked me to sit.

"I realize it took a lot of courage to denounce Kazan's actions, Chief Inspector. Few members have it in them. It's easier to squint when a colleague twists the rules and tweaks the law, provided it's for a good cause. You'd be surprised how few come forward because doing so often carries a steep cost. Fortunately, your work correcting Kazan's misconduct in the Corvo case gave the Service a second chance to nab him, this time in due and proper form."

It had been difficult, especially with reluctant officers working at my side, but I'd established clean evidence unimpeachable in any court of law.

When I said nothing, the chief superintendent studied me with curiosity. "What are your plans now? You can't stay with the Sector Flying Squad, that's clear — you've been shunned by just about everyone."

I shrugged. "No idea, sir. Maybe I can change sectors."

"What you did here will follow you for the rest of your career, and I'd say your chances of making it past superintendent are pretty slim, even if you went back to uniformed duties. It has nothing to do with right or wrong. You were right, and the case against Corvo would probably have been thrown out based on Kazan's massaged evidence. Yet by shopping your partner to the PCB, you also committed a grave offense in the eyes of your colleagues."

"So, what are my options?"

"You could transfer to the PCB. I have a vacant superintendent's position in the Rim Sector PCB Detachment. You have enough time in rank as a chief inspector to qualify for a promotion, and I'd say you've displayed the right mindset to become a PCB officer. You're certainly a superb criminal investigator."

When I woke, the dream still vivid in my mind, I wondered why it had surfaced now. Perhaps I was becoming a bit too friendly with Victoria 'Vic' Montoni, even though I intended to betray her in the end, and the dream came back as a warning. The problem was, I genuinely enjoyed being with her. Just like Gerri before she took that irrevocable step over the line and our friendship turned sour when she tried to deny it.

— Eighteen —

That Monday, two things happened. First, Team Two, led by Superintendent Maria Lovan, finally arrived bright-eyed and ready to work after more than a week in space. And second, we received a veritable flood of cases from Fleet Security. I immediately got the sneaking suspicion Terak was trying to bury us because many of them, although they had an official corruption angle, concerned matters her people could investigate.

After saying hello to Maria and her team, I sat with Arno and Destine and triaged the cases.

"You know," Arno said as we went through the pile, "these investigations mean three-quarters of our people will head off to other star systems."

Destine made a face. "If we accept them all."

"I don't think we have much choice." I shrugged. "If this is a test of our willingness, then so be it. Besides, it'll give us a chance to shine some light into the Fleet's dark corners, even though a lot of them are a little beneath ACU 12's mandate. But then again, in ACC Sorjonen's absence, I set the mandate."

"A lot of the cases?" Arno cocked an eyebrow at me. "I'd say most."

"Still. We'll take care of them so long as we don't end up overstretched. And this lot doesn't quite do that. Many of the investigations are two officer problems, no more."

"Agreed." Arno let out a sigh. "I suppose they're no worse than what we handled in the Rim Sector Detachment."

I grinned at him. "That's the spirit. Let's prove to Fleet Security that we'll get our hands dirty when asked."

We finished the list, and I sat back.

"Okay. How about we apportion them to the teams? Team Two, since they just got here, get the local ones. Team One already has folks on Dordogne, so they get at least one less away case than the rest. How does that leave us?"

Destine quickly tapped her tablet, then looked up at Arno and me while gesturing at my office's primary display, which now listed the cases and the team assignments.

"What do you think?"

We scanned it and glanced at each other. "You good with that, Arno?"

"Yes."

"Alright, pass the assignments to the team leads, and thank you."

"How's your case on Montoni going, Chief?"

I briefly described the previous Friday's outing to L'Habitation and Sunday's hike. When I finished, Arno scratched his beard, nodding sagely.

"It looks as if you're getting into her good graces."

I grimaced. "Problem is, I'm beginning to like her."

Arno winced theatrically. "And it makes you think of your old partner, Gerri Kazan, who you shopped to the PCB, right?"

"Who I shopped? A little harsh, isn't it? She jeopardized a major case and not for the first time."

A slow grin appeared on his face. "You must admit that's how most of your former Flying Squad colleagues saw it."

"Yeah." I gave him a rueful shake of the head. "And you're right. I'm a tad leery about getting too close to Montoni because I remember what betraying a friendship is like, even though I did it for the best of reasons."

"And arresting Montoni if she's corrupt will also be for the best of reasons, Chief."

"I know. It's just a tad difficult for me at the moment."

"You'll get through this. You always do."

"Yep."

Arno and Destine left me to contemplate my next move with Montoni while they visited the team leads in case the work apportionment needed adjusting.

That afternoon, I went to the gym early and returned to work to avoid Montoni while I figured things out. I spent the rest of the day submerged in administrivia and didn't make it home until nearly eighteen hundred hours.

But shortly after I changed into my usual civvies — shorts, loose shirt, and sandals — I got a call on my private channel. It was Vic Montoni wondering whether I'd like to come to her apartment for drinks. I was immediately intrigued because I hadn't visited her place before and because she'd obviously monitored my arrival via the downstairs video pickup that allowed anyone in the building to watch the surface and subsurface lobbies.

"I'll be there in five minutes."

"Excellent." Montoni smiled. "See you then."

I took a deep breath once she cut the link, then glanced into the mirror. For some reason, I didn't want to look totally disheveled and adjusted my hair, though I figured my clothes were fine. And they were. Montoni was dressed similarly when she opened the door to her apartment five minutes later.

"Come in, come in, and welcome to Chez Vic." She waved me through the doorway and into a place very similar to mine, except she had more personal furnishings and items. The layout was the same but in reverse. "I had a bottle of Caledonian Blue delivered and thought we should open it together."

"An excellent idea."

"Why don't you sit on the balcony while I mix our drinks?"

Her apartment faced in the opposite direction from mine, and I could see Joint Base Sanctum in the last rays of the setting sun, with people in the distance hurrying home. It wasn't a bad-looking installation. Most of the buildings erected a little over half a century earlier had pleasing curves, reflective floor-to-ceiling windows, and pinkish granite cladding which glowed in the sunset.

Plenty of greenery separated the various structures — Earth trees mixed with Caledonian bushes and flowers — and benches everywhere, a few in arbors, others at the edge of tiny plazas. There were signs here and there, flagpoles lining the central parade square, and the odd monuments, many of which were decommissioned small aircraft or ground vehicles.

But I knew that beneath the surface, in some cases deep beneath, was a complex of tunnels, secure offices, operations rooms, data centers, and much more. At the same time, innocuous domes dotting the perimeter hid aerospace defense nodes capable of reaching into orbit. I couldn't see the spaceport from Montoni's balcony, however. It was on the far side of the installation, beyond the buildings and hidden by them. Yet, I could still get a sense of Joint Base Sanctum's sheer size. It certainly dwarfed Constabulary HQ in Draconis, on Wyvern, by several orders of magnitude.

"Here we are."

I turned from where I'd been leaning against the railing and took the proffered glass of gin and tonic from Montoni's right hand. She raised hers.

"To your health."

"And to yours."

We both took healthy sips, and I let out a soft sigh of pleasure.

Montoni smiled. "It is nice, isn't it?"

She gestured at the chairs flanking a small table, and we sat.

"I didn't see you at the gym today."

I let out a small grunt. "That's because I went earlier and then returned to work."

"One of those days?"

"Yep." I took another sip. "But then, Mondays often are. How was your day?"

"Same old. I spent most of it reviewing analyses my people filed on Friday before going home."

"Anything interesting?"

"Plenty. The constitutional convention on Mykonos is stirring up passions on every last OutWorld and colony, with many of them calling for far-reaching amendments to the Commonwealth Constitution that would rewrite most of it. Of course, since Earth isn't acknowledging the convention, to begin with, all I can say is good luck to them. Anything interesting happen in your part of HQ?"

"Fleet Security referred almost three dozen cases to us this morning."

Montoni, eyebrows raised, glanced at me. "Three dozen?"

"Yep. Fortunately, with my fourth team arriving this morning after a lengthy investigation off-world, we can handle the load without problems."

"That's a lot of corruption, though."

"For an organization the size of the Fleet? It's a mere drop of water in the ocean. I expect that now they've realized we're here and available, we'll get plenty more referrals. And that's fine. Our work is pretty much all we PCB folks live for."

Montoni guffawed. "I'd call that sad, but unfortunately, I'm the same, as are many of my intelligence colleagues. Heck, how about a lot of the Fleet in general? Moving from starship to planet to starship doesn't give most of us the chance of a life beyond the Service."

I knew she was exaggerating, but not by much. The proportion of Constabulary and Fleet members who were married was lower than the population in general, and those who married did so at a later age. We were nomads with no fixed address other than the Service we'd joined. Although I understood Caledonia was fast becoming the Fleet's home world, where members settled when they retired after putting in their twenty, thirty, or fifty years. And married each other, such as Zack and Hera, although I suspected they were still a lot of years from retirement since they both could count on a few more promotions before they reached their plateau and faced the dreaded stay stuck for ten years in the same rank and you're out.

As for us Constabulary officers, we didn't quite consider Wyvern our home world since we didn't own it outright like the Fleet owned Caledonia. Which meant I did not know where I'd settle once the Service decided it was time for me to retire. Perhaps I could start a movement that would see us former constables join our Fleet brethren right here.

"It's the same in the Constabulary in general, although the junior ranks can stay on a given world pretty much their entire careers if they choose to do so, with the caveat that their chances for advancement would be more limited. I guess only the Army has the stability to allow people families, but a lot of the senior ranks are ex-Marines who came home after a full twenty or thirty."

"And how long do you expect to be on Caledonia?"

"No idea. If I'm terminal at assistant commissioner, it could be several years, and I have few ambitions to rise any higher. Not that the promotion opportunities in the PCB are good, to begin with, since we're in it until we retire. There's no return to regular Constabulary duties. How about you?"

"I'm pretty much ending my career on Caledonia. The only positions for a post captain in intelligence outside Armed Forces HQ are as N2 for the various fleets, and there are only six of those. Well, seven once they establish the 7th Fleet later this year. And I'm not on the list of potential N2s for the new formation."

"How long will it be until the end?"

Montoni shrugged as she turned her head to glance at me. "No idea. I might still get a commodore's star, which resets the clock. Not that I'm worried about it. Intelligence officers may stick around longer than line officers because of the expertise we've accumulated, and because promotion in our branch is slower, meaning in reality, there is no ten and out for us. Does the Constabulary have an up or out policy?"

I shook my head. "No. But we have mandatory retirement ages by rank."

"And what is it for an assistant commissioner?"

"Seventy. It means I have more than two decades left before being put to pasture."

"Not quite fifty yet, are you? And an assistant commissioner? Nicely done. I understand you start in the ranks as ordinary constables."

"Yes, and you need to make at least corporal before being considered for officer training. I made staff sergeant. How about you?"

"My age, you mean? I'm fifty-six. A few years older than you, but that doesn't matter, right?"

"Of course not." Now why would she ask whether our age difference mattered? Eleven years for a long-lived species such as ours wasn't much.

"Good." She reached out and touched the back of my hand, which was resting on the small table between us, with her fingertips. They stayed there for two or three seconds while she met my eyes, and I suddenly understood the age difference question.

I smiled at her. She smiled back. Then she withdrew her fingers and finished her gin and tonic. I emptied my glass as well. In the meantime, the sun had disappeared behind the distant mountains, leaving us a last light that quickly vanished as well. Clouds were massing in the south, eclipsing the newly born starlight, and the first gusts of moist wind reached us.

I stood. "Thanks for the gin, Vic. And," I gave her a mischievous grin, "you've succeeded in getting more from me than I from you again."

She climbed to her feet.

"The former field agent in me is still constantly on the prowl. Before I forget, are we still on for an overnighter on the Middle Sea this weekend?"

"Certainly. I'm looking forward to it, never having been there."

"It's a date, then."

She accompanied me to the front door, her fingertips resting on my lower back, confirming my suspicions.

"See you tomorrow."

— Nineteen —

I'll freely admit I wasn't the most experienced with relationships — I've only had a handful throughout my life — but it seemed pretty clear Vic Montoni was harboring romantic feelings toward me. The touching gave that away, as did the eye contact, even though her gaze had remained as veiled as always. Or perhaps she was faking those sentiments for some reason. That was the problem with spending too many years in the PCB. You became suspicious of everyone and everything outside the Bureau.

The big question was what to do with that.

I was certainly not going to enter an amorous relationship with her. Not that I found Montoni displeasing. But I had to remember I'd approached her because we suspected her of being corrupt, not out of any wish to become friends, let alone lovers. And I already felt more friendship than I should under the circumstances.

Once back in my apartment, I poured myself a glass of wine to go with another autochef supper — this time chicken masala over basmati rice — and ate slowly, lost in thought, eyes staring out at the night through the closed balcony doors. It would rain soon, and there was no point in settling outside with my plate and glass.

I quickly concluded that I had to keep her from getting the impression I'd be interested in something more than friendship. If only for my self-respect. But how to do that without endangering the increasingly good rapport I'd built?

Perhaps by simply not reacting to her advances. *If* those were advances, of course. Yet considering Montoni didn't strike me as a casual toucher in the first place, she being too self-contained, I was pretty sure they meant something.

That night I dreamed of Gerri Kazan again, the same dream as before, and woke up at daybreak feeling drained and melancholy. Maybe befriending Montoni to find out whether she was corrupt hadn't been such a good idea. Perhaps I'd finally found the limits to my values and ethics, and this was beyond them.

Arno walked into my office a few hours later, coffee cup in hand, and took one glance at my face before taking a seat across from me.

"Trouble in paradise, Chief?"

"Why? Does it show?"

"Only for those who know you too well. That cloud on your face tells me something is bothering you."

I related my encounter with Montoni the previous evening and my conclusions. "So, you could say she upped the ante, which upped my discomfort with the entire operation."

"It's a little late to back out now, Chief."

"I know. Which is what's bothering me."

"If she's innocent, she never needs to know, and you'll have made a friend. The Almighty knows you don't have many."

"And if she's guilty?"

"Then you'll do your job and move on. In other news, several of our contingents are leaving this morning on the Fleet Auxiliary transport *Normandie*, which is headed in the right direction for the Fourth and Fifth Fleet investigations."

"That was quick."

"It's either take *Normandie* or wait five, maybe six days for *Carentan*." Arno shrugged. "And since they were keen on going…"

"Just as well, then."

"That's what I figured." He took a sip of his coffee.

I wasn't surprised by my people heading out on the first available ship. PCB investigators were nomads at heart. Being home-ported on Caledonia was a blessing because it gave them a touchstone rather than being wholly unmoored and living out of their luggage. But they still enjoyed traveling the star lanes to tackle cases far and wide, no matter how distant. I supposed it took a distinct personality to work for the Bureau, an uncommon one, even for a Service like the Constabulary, which saw freshly minted constables posted as far from their home world as possible after graduation.

"Look, if you're worried about my state of mind, don't be," I said, breaking the silence between us.

He waved my words away. "I'm not worried. And that being said," he stood, "I'll let you get on with it."

I didn't go to the gym that day and made sure I was home before Montoni. Thankfully, she didn't call or otherwise communicate with me. The same held true for Wednesday.

On Thursday morning, Hera called me at work to discuss Montoni.

"How are you doing with her?"

"Okay." I passed along the latest developments.

"I've had my people examine her past."

"And they obviously found something. Otherwise, you wouldn't have called."

"Right. Her last posting before coming to Caledonia was Fifth Fleet HQ on Cascadia, where she worked as N2 Operations and was a commander under the N2, a captain.”

I already knew that but didn’t mention it, preferring to let Hera tell me what she wanted in her own way.

“Now, her job isn’t important in this, but a tidbit about her private life has come to light. She was in a discreet relationship with a senior Cascadia Security Intelligence Agency official, a Magda LeTellier, who headed the Agency’s anti-terrorism branch.”

Something in her tone and use of words caught my attention. “You’re referring to LeTellier in the past tense, Hera. Does that mean she’s no longer employed?”

“She vanished shortly after Montoni was promoted to captain and left Cascadia for Fleet HQ. As in, not a trace of her has been found. Officially, she’s listed as missing. Montoni was never interviewed because by the time LeTellier became a missing person, she was already on Caledonia, and evidence indicated LeTellier was still active on Cascadia two days after her departure. LeTellier was on three weeks' leave, and concern wasn’t raised until she failed to return to work. Where it gets interesting, and the official file doesn’t mention this, they found indications in her residence that she’d been transferring top-secret anti-terrorism information to unknown recipients.”

“So, this LeTellier was a traitor?”

Hera raised a restraining hand. "Or her colleagues were meant to think so, bolstering the assumption she vanished to avoid the consequences of being detected."

"And did they?"

"The Agency appears split on that subject, with many believing she fell afoul of someone, was killed, and her body made to disappear."

"What evidence did they have LeTellier was still active two days after Montoni left?"

"Financial transactions."

I scoffed. "Someone who has access to her accounts can set those ahead of time."

"Oh, no doubt. But when the Agency found out about them, they'd already uncovered the data transfers, and it became a political hot potato, so they didn't pursue the matter beyond confirming the transactions were made by someone with all the proper credentials. If you think Montoni could be involved in LeTellier's disappearance, I'd say yes. Even though witnesses last saw her and LeTellier together eight days before her departure, two days before LeTellier went on leave."

"Interesting. Why would Montoni kill her lover?"

"That, we don't know, but there's more. Before Cascadia, Montoni was at 1st Fleet HQ on Earth. There, she was in a relationship with a Lieutenant Commander Gary Holden, who worked in operations. Holden vanished during a solo trip to

South America on holidays a week before Montoni was posted to Cascadia."

"Two in the space of a few years? That's rather careless of her."

Hera smirked. "Isn't it? Now here's where it gets really interesting. Holden was actually a counterintelligence officer working undercover, and they kept their relationship rather low-key."

"What was he doing in 1st Fleet Operations?"

"Looking for traitors. This was before the Black Sword debacle when we unraveled a conspiracy involving hundreds of officers."

"Was Montoni ever linked to this Holden's disappearance?"

"No. She was supposedly in Geneva during that time, although my agents couldn't find any corroboration."

"Sounds like my warrior nun is more of a black widow if we assume she was involved in both cases."

"They say twice is a coincidence, but I'm not convinced of that in her case. We might be looking at enemy action already."

I gave Hera's image a wry smile. "And I'm supposed to go on an overnighter with her to the Middle Sea this coming weekend."

Hera winced. "I'm not sure that's such a splendid notion at this point."

A shrug. "Considering I'm out of ideas where she's concerned, I figure why not? Even after your revelations, she may or may not have been involved in the disappearance of two former lovers. Besides, I'm nothing more than a friend and will be nothing more, and she's not due to depart Caledonia like she left Earth and Cascadia around the time her previous paramours vanished."

"All right. Just be careful, then. Talyn, out."

I briefed Arno and Destine on the latest Montoni information, and the former sat back in his chair, scratching his beard as he contemplated me.

"Two lovers vanished, eh? That doesn't bode well for you, Chief."

"I'm not her lover."

"But you're fairly close. Are you still going with her this weekend?"

"Yes. I don't really have much choice but to see this through to the end."

— Twenty —

I met Montoni at the gym on Friday, when we confirmed our plans for the weekend, with a departure the following day at oh-seven hundred. We'd be using her car again at her insistence. Although I saw Montoni differently since Hera's revelations, I hoped it didn't show. She did touch my bare arm in the lobby of our building, smiling at me, but it didn't feel as personal as the previous contacts for some reason I couldn't quite explain.

Neither of us seemed inclined to invite the other over for a drink, and so we parted ways when she got off the elevator on the fourth floor.

The next morning, I joined her in the underground parking, carrying my overnight bag and wearing light, airy clothes suitable for the tropical coast. She greeted me with a broad smile.

"Ready?"

"That I am." I tossed my bag on the back alongside hers and climbed into the passenger seat. "How long will the trip take?"

"Not that long," she replied, switching on the car's power plant and edging it out of its spot. "The highway is pretty straight and smooth, so traffic control will allow us up to two hundred and fifty kilometers per hour. We'll be there shortly after ten."

"And there is?"

"The little seaside town of Horizonte, where I've booked us a room at the Bello Inn, right on the beach."

From what I remembered Hera telling me, Horizonte was the closest agglomeration of any significance to her and Zack's place, but I kept that information to myself.

"Sounds nice."

"That it is. You'll see."

We arrived in Horizonte at ten-fifteen after a quick trip under AI control. When we got out of the car at the Bello Inn, the air was hot, humid and held a distinct salty tang. But the southern horizon was gray with dense clouds growing visibly even in the few minutes we stood to take in the sun before picking our bags from the back seat and heading for the reception area.

The hotel was a sprawling, white, two-story structure with a red metal roof built to resist the fiercest storms. Its transparent aluminum windows were polarized, as were the front doors. Native tropical trees, dark green, feathery, and supple, along with colorful bushes, surrounded it.

The reception was an airy, high-ceilinged space with tile flooring, white walls, and a granite counter. Beyond, floor-to-ceiling windows gave out on a covered terrace fronting a beach of pale sand. Turquoise waters rolled in gently, the ocean waves muted by barrier islands a few kilometers out, covered in a Caledonian analog of Earth mangroves.

An androgynous hologram appeared behind the counter and bowed its head. "Welcome back, Madame Montoni. Suite one-oh-one is ready for you and your guest." It gestured to its right.

"Thank you," Montoni replied without breaking stride as we crossed the reception area and took the indicated corridor.

Suite one-oh-one proved to be a two-story apartment, with an open area combining a kitchen, dining room, and living room on the ground floor and two bedrooms with ensuite bathrooms on the second. Broad patio doors gave out onto a private terrace, partly covered, bordering the beach itself. It was, in a word, luxurious.

"Beautiful," Montoni commented, looking around. "I've never taken one of the suites since I've always been alone. But this will do us nicely. Do you want the bedroom on the left or the right?"

"I have no preference."

"The left one it is for me then." She gave me a smile and then, overnight bag in hand, entered the bedroom in question. I went into the other one and quickly unpacked. The rooms were spacious, with wide beds, a dresser, a desk and chair, and a small sofa facing the windows.

They overlooked the beach, and as I glanced out, I saw the thick clouds had come nearer, but they still seemed to be a hundred kilometers or more out to sea.

"Do you think we'll get a storm?" I asked through the open doors.

"Maybe. It would be a perfect time to hunker down with a cup of tea and watch the angry waters play between the barrier islands and shore."

"Sounds relaxing."

"That's what this weekend is about, Caelin. Relaxation far from Sanctum and the insane demands of our jobs." She appeared in my doorway wearing nothing but a swimsuit. "Now, get changed so we can hit the water."

***

The storm struck just as we finished supper at a waterfront restaurant a hundred meters or so from the inn, and we were soaked by the time we reached our suite. Montoni gave me a wistful glance before disappearing into her room to change. I swapped my wet clothes for dry ones and headed downstairs to the sitting area by the floor-to-ceiling windows facing the raging sea, lit by lightning every few seconds. The soundproofing of the suite was impeccable because it was like watching a three-dee show on mute. Only an almost subliminal buzzing, probably from the wind, remained.

Montoni joined me moments later, holding a bottle of Glen Arcturus in one hand and two glasses in the other.

"A little postprandial libation?" She raised the bottle. "I know we had a bit to drink during supper, but I figure we're on a mini holiday."

The way she said it and her gestures seemed a little off to me, and she didn't wait for my reply but placed the glasses on the coffee table, splashed a good two fingers into each, then handed me one and took the other.

"Here's to a great day." She raised the glass in a toast.

"It was a lot of fun." I surreptitiously watched her put the glass to her lips, but although they touched the amber liquid, she didn't actually drink a drop. Senses suddenly alert, I did the same, remembering her two mysteriously vanished lovers. What with the storm outside…

We sat on either side of the coffee table, half facing the outside, half facing each other. I placed my whiskey glass on the tabletop and settled back with what I hoped sounded like a contented sigh. The atmosphere felt charged, though whether it was because of the electric storm or something closer remained debatable.

Montoni also put her glass on the table, though she eyed me and my glass sideways as if checking to see whether or not I'd taken a healthy sip. It was then that I noticed the glasses were banded horizontally with an incision, and she'd poured the whiskey right up to it, allowing her to see how much I'd consumed. Which, in this case, was not a drop.

A bolt of lightning immediately to our front reached down and touched the barrier island, illuminating the treetops with its eerie though brief glow.

"There's nothing quite like the fury of nature unleashed," Montoni said in a low, husky tone.

"Indeed. Though human fury unleashed can be even more frightening."

"True." After a while, she turned to me. "I notice you're not touching your whiskey. Would you like some tea instead? I brought a sampler."

"No, but thank you for offering. I guess I'm still full to the gills from supper."

Was she merely being solicitous, or was she intent on me consuming something she served? And if so, why? Another lightning bolt struck the barrier island, illuminating the water between it and us in electric blue. I noticed Montoni didn't touch her whiskey either, even though she was the one who'd served it.

As I reflected on our day, I realized that, in retrospect, she'd appeared too bright, too eager, trying too hard. It was out of character for the person I thought I knew.

"Tell me, what are you looking for in this relationship?" She asked out of the blue, her eyes on the spectacle outside. "I know it's not a romantic attachment."

"Friendship, I suppose. I don't have many friends and none outside the Constabulary in this star system." I allowed myself a humorless bark of laughter but sensing that she might be aiming at something in particular, I reached for my communicator in my shirt pocket and surreptitiously turned on its recording function. "Or in any other star system, for that matter. What are you looking for?"

A sad smile briefly lit up her face, though she kept staring through the window. "A friend."

"And you have one."

"Do I? Do I really? Or did you pretend to befriend me because you're investigating me?"

"Why do you ask that? Do you have a guilty conscience?" I tried a smile, but it felt so patently false that I was glad Montoni's eyes were elsewhere.

And then they weren't.

A small but deadly blaster had materialized in her hand, and it was pointing straight at me. "I wish you'd take a healthy slug of the whiskey, Caelin, darling."

Her voice was huskier than ever, but how she said that last word sent chills up my spine.

"Why?"

Her hand was steady, and I stared into the barrel of the gun for a few seconds before meeting her eyes.

"Because it contains an interrogation drug, and I'd like to know what you have on me."

"And then, am I to vanish just like Magda LeTellier and Gary Holden?"

A bark of laughter escaped her throat. "You've done your homework. Excellent. Now be a good little girl and drink up."

"It won't do you any good. I've been conditioned."

"Have you now? Interesting. I didn't know they conditioned Constabulary officers. I always thought it was reserved for field operatives like I was once upon a time. Or are you lying to me like you have all along?"

"PCB officers are routinely conditioned so that desperate suspects can't pump them full of interrogation drugs to find out what they know. I'll not be answering questions. In fact, I might die of a heart attack, depending on the type of drug and its strength."

"It's not the sort that gives conditioned people cardiac arrest, but a rather mild form of the drug. I'd prefer it if you stayed alive so you can be seen leaving this place before disappearing."

"In that case, you'll get nothing but nonsense from me, and I'll probably not be able to move coherently, if at all."

Her gaze was steady, but I saw a glint of madness behind those dark eyes, the sort that made me think my last hour could be at hand.

"Drink."

"No." I adjusted my position to face her, bemoaning the fact I'd left my weapon in my bedroom. "If you shoot me, you'll get nothing. How about we make a deal? I tell you what you want to know, and you tell me whether I'm right."

And once we were done, she'd kill me. Bleak didn't begin to describe my situation.

"Besides, shooting me will make my disappearance rather messy and more likely to be traced back to you."

"Fine. What do you have on me?"

"You were seen with a Findlay Rogers four years ago by the late Captain Gunter Wils. Rogers was a recruiter for an unknown organization who turned several senior officers into traitors, Wils included. That's it."

A faint air of astonishment briefly transformed her stony countenance. "That's it? That's what you have against me?"

"Yes."

She started to laugh. "Oh, my lord. You mean you went through the whole rigmarole of befriending me based on a single encounter four years ago? Now that's what I call dedication. It's almost a shame I have to end things."

"Your turn. Who are you working for?"

A smirk appeared. "Oh please. I won't tell you anything. Why should I? Now drink your whiskey. I'll take my chances with your incoherent movements so long as you can still move."

She jerked the gun at me to emphasize her order. When I remained motionless, she took aim at my left arm.

"The first round will hurt like crazy, but I'm close enough to ensure it's only a flesh wound. Where you're going, you don't need to leave a beautiful, unblemished corpse. Drink."

I held her gaze as I reached for my glass, lifted it, and threw its contents in her face with a flick of the wrist. The glass followed a fraction of a second later.

— Twenty-One —

Montoni yelped, and a shot went off. I felt the heat of the round as it passed my cheek when I threw myself out of the chair and her direct line of fire. She dropped her gun as her hands went to her eyes, and I lunged to one side, kicking it away from her. I knew I had a small window of opportunity to subdue Montoni while she dealt with the burning sensation of the whiskey on her eyeballs. I also knew she had to flush them out once she was subdued. And so I ran upstairs to my room to retrieve my weapon and the wrist restraints I always carried along with it.

When I returned downstairs, she'd moved to the kitchen sink and was busy splashing water into her face. Without saying a word, I grabbed her right hand and twisted the arm behind her while snapping the restraint on her wrist. The left hand followed a second later before she had time to react, and I pushed her face into the sink.

"Turn your head so the water can flush out your eyes."

"It stings like crazy, you bitch." She tried to raise her head, but I kept it down while knocking her legs apart with my feet and trying to keep her off balance.

"That was why I tossed the whiskey at you, Vic. You didn't think I'd actually drink anything laced with an interrogation drug? What was it, incidentally?"

"Gammahypnol."

"That might have caused adverse cardiac effects on me. Just as well I used it in a more productive manner. Now keep your head under the water stream and rinse out those crazy eyes of yours."

I released her and stepped back, wondering what to do next. The storm was still raging outside, and although I could conceivably get Montoni to release her car into my care and drive back to Sanctum, she was still a dangerous viper, even with the manacles.

In the end, I pulled out my communicator and asked for a link with Arno, who replied within seconds.

"What's up, Chief?"

"I have Montoni in restraints, washing gammahypnol-laced whiskey from her eyes, and need backup to bring her in."

Arno let out a soft grunt. "The story behind that simple statement must be rather entertaining. But backup, Destine and I can do. We're just down the street from the Bello Inn."

"What do you mean you're just down the street?"

"We sort of followed you here and kept an eye on you — in disguise, of course."

His less-than-contrite tone made me smile. "Figures. Okay, suite one-oh-one, if you're willing to brave the elements."

"For you, anytime, Chief. We're on our way."

Two waterlogged creatures vaguely resembling Arno Galdi and Destine Bonta showed up at the door to our suite five minutes later, and I let them in. Montoni still had her head in the sink, rinsing out her eyes and cursing beneath her breath.

"Quite the weather we're having, Chief," the bearded wet creature said in Arno's voice as he entered, his eyes immediately fixing on Montoni. "I'd say it's a good night for shenanigans if it weren't for your life having been in danger. Gammahypnol is no laughing matter for someone who's conditioned."

A barely recognizable Destine followed on Arno's heels and headed for Montoni, ready to stop her from doing anything stupid.

"So, what's the plan?" Arno asked after I finished telling them about the events of the last fifteen minutes.

"We pack up and head for Sanctum, where we'll deposit Montoni in the base brig. In the meantime, Captain Victoria Montoni, I am arresting you on suspicion of attempted murder, attempted administration of a noxious substance, perverting the course of justice, and conduct prejudicial to good order and discipline."

Montoni laughed. "Good luck making those charges stick. It's your word against mine, and you're the one who assaulted me by throwing whiskey into my eyes."

"We have your gun and the gammahypnol-laced whiskey bottle with your prints on it, for starters. And I recorded our conversation on my service-issue communicator, which means I can use it in court. Your life as a member of the Fleet is over, Captain Montoni."

"Perhaps, but I have friends in high places who can moot your so-called evidence and allow me to retire quietly and without prejudice, especially considering your attack on me."

"We'll see. Do you need more time under running water?"

"What I need is to see a medical officer."

"You can see the brig's when we get there."

"In what? Four or five hours, considering the storm? How about taking me to the local emergency now?"

"So you can attempt to escape? Not a chance."

"Then I'll add disregarding the welfare of a detainee to my list of charges against you."

Arno snorted. "You go ahead and do that. Destine, check her eyes, will you?"

Destine pulled Montoni upright by the shoulders, grabbed her chin, and forced her head to one side so she could examine her.

"They're red, inflamed, but not overly so. She'll live with her vision intact, although it'll be uncomfortable for a while. Perhaps we should put a wet compress over her eyes for the trip back."

"No thanks," Montoni said between clenched teeth.

Destine released Montoni's chin. "Do you want to flush them some more?"

"No."

"In that case," I headed for the stairs, "we pack and leave. Destine, if you could secure the whiskey bottle, both glasses and her gun. And take images of the scene."

"Will do, sir. What about her car?"

"We'll leave it for now. A flatbed from Fleet Security can pick it up tomorrow."

Arno walked over to where Montoni stood, her face like thunder. "You know, we never had enough evidence to haul you in for a talk. If you hadn't tried it out on the Chief, you'd still be walking free. Not a smart choice, was it?"

"Go fuck yourself."

Happy to have gotten a reaction, Arno simply watched her with a smile while I packed both our things, and Destine retrieved the bottle and glasses. Shortly after that, we trooped out of the suite via the patio doors to avoid the lobby, Arno holding Montoni's right arm in a grip of steel. As an added precaution, we'd muzzled her so she couldn't cause a ruckus. We got soaked within seconds, and when Montoni decided she wouldn't cooperate, Destine took her other arm, and between them, she and Arno carried her around the building to where their vehicle waited.

Once in the car — Montoni sitting between Destine and me in the back, Arno at the driver's console — I removed the muzzle.

"Four hours sitting like this will not be fun," Montoni immediately said. "Could you please move the manacles to my front?"

Destine and I exchanged an amused glance since we both had been expecting the question. I shook my head. "No. I have too much respect for your abilities to take that risk."

She gave me a dirty look but settled back, eyes to the front, face adopting her usual inscrutable expression.

"So, tell me, Vic, who are your friends in high places?" I asked once we were moving off into the dark, storm-lashed night for the long trip back to Sanctum. We wouldn't be driving at two hundred and fifty kilometers per hour, at least not until we'd outrun the bad weather.

"You'll find out soon enough."

And those were the last words she spoke for the rest of the trip, no matter what I asked or said. But I remained curious about her so-called friends. Were they also in the employ of an organization other than the Fleet? Or were they merely persons of influence Montoni thought she could call on to get her out of this mess?

It was well past midnight when we finally pulled up to the Joint Base Sanctum brig after a brief stopover at the office to change into the spare uniforms we kept there — one of us staying with Montoni in the car at all times. Arno and Destine had removed their disguises during the trip and were back to their regular selves by the time we passed through the security arches at the base's main entrance.

The desk sergeant, a Marine whose nametape said Otreya, looked up from her workstation with a faint air of bemusement as we three frogmarched Montoni into the brig's reception area.

"Yes, sir?"

"I am Assistant Commissioner Caelin Morrow of Anti-Corruption Unit 12. With me are Chief Inspector Arno Galdi and Warrant Officer Destine Bonta. We are bringing in a Service detainee,

Captain Victoria Montoni, Commonwealth Navy. I have arrested her on suspicion of attempted murder, attempted administration of a noxious substance, perverting the course of justice, and conduct prejudicial to good order and discipline."

Sergeant Otreya's eyes widened. She'd obviously never seen a four-striper brought in under arrest.

"I want Captain Montoni confined to a private cell until further notice. No one but a member of Anti-Corruption Unit 12 may see or speak with her save for a doctor to check her eyes if she so wishes.

"What about my lawyer?" Montoni asked in a sardonic tone.

"You don't get to talk with one until I charge you, and I have twenty-four hours from the moment I've taken you into custody to do so. Sergeant Otreya, please take care of Captain Montoni."

"Yes, sir." The sergeant took biometric readings of Montoni to confirm her identity, then relieved her of the items she carried in her pockets, including her credentials. Once she'd finished processing her, Otreya removed the manacles and handed them back to me. "The brig has taken charge of Captain Victoria Montoni, Assistant Commissioner."

"Excellent, thank you. Please note in the log that we'll be back to interrogate and charge the prisoner in the morning. As I said, no one outside ACU 12 is to see or speak with her."

"Understood, sir." She turned to Montoni and gestured at a door silently opening. "If you'll go through there and follow the arrows on the floor to your cell, Captain."

With a last glare at me, Montoni obeyed and was swallowed by the brig proper, the door closing behind her with a sense of finality. We watched on the desk sergeant's screen as she passed through a pair of automated security stations, then walked down a silent white corridor with doors piercing its walls at regular intervals until she reached an open one. She glanced over her shoulder, then entered the cell, whose door slid shut.

Having seen her off, I had Arno drop me at the senior officers' block after I made a mental note to get a warrant for Montoni's apartment first thing in the morning before I interviewed her. I stepped out of my spare uniform and took a long, hot shower to try to rinse off the last few hours. Then I poured myself a glass of unadulterated Glen Arcturus and sat on the balcony, staring out at the darkened landscape dotted here and there with lights. Although the storm didn't reach Sanctum, a thick cloud cover that smelled of rain occluded the stars and moons.

Try as I might, I couldn't find any sleep that night, my mind spinning in circles, trying to figure out what had betrayed me to the point where Montoni risked surreptitiously feeding me an interrogation drug. By dawn, I concluded I'd never fooled her from the get-go and that she'd merely been waiting until the right moment.

I was in the office by oh-seven-hundred and had a warrant to search Montoni's apartment shortly after seven-thirty. The moment Arno and Destine showed up, we executed it. But after an hour of carefully searching the place, including with Destine's handheld sensor, we gave up. There was nothing to find. Her apartment was, in police parlance, absolutely sterile. We couldn't even find traces of the gammahypnol she'd used in the whiskey.

"How does anyone keep their apartment so clean of anything that might indicate they're not on the level?" Arno asked as we locked the door and headed for the lift. "Usually, there's always something, the slightest bit of evidence, which betrays the owner."

"No idea. Let's head off to the brig and formally charge her so we can begin the interrogations."

Just then, our communicators pinged, and one glance told us the lab results from the whiskey were in. There was enough gammahypnol to knock out several Caledonian bathas, large hippo-like creatures which lived in the jungles south of the Middle Sea.

— Twenty-Two —

The daytime desk sergeant immediately summoned the brig commander the moment we arrived. Lieutenant Colonel Horik, muscular, bald, as broad as he was tall and utterly devoid of a neck, must have been waiting for us because he appeared moments later. I'd met him before, and he nodded politely.

"Assistant Commissioner, I understand you've detained a senior officer, a Captain Victoria Montoni of the Navy, with instructions no one was to visit her save members of your unit and the doctor until further notice, and she was not to communicate with anyone."

"Yes. I trust my instructions were obeyed."

"To the letter. The only person she spoke with was the duty medical officer, who applied ointment to her eyes but otherwise declared them out of danger."

"What I'd like to do now is charge her. Could you have her brought to an interview room?"

"Certainly." He turned to the desk sergeant. "Have Captain Montoni brought to Interview 2."

"Yes, sir."

Horik gestured toward a door behind the desk sergeant. "If you'll follow me."

He took us to the observation gallery, and we watched Montoni enter Interview 2. She looked terrible as if she hadn't slept all night. Her eyes were red, but whether it was remnants of the whiskey bath or lack of sleep was up to question. She studied the room, a white, windowless cube with a table and four chairs at its center, for a few seconds, then took a seat facing the door and composed herself to wait. I admired her calmness — no fidgeting, glancing around, or repositioning herself on the uncomfortable chair. After a minute or so, I nodded once.

"Okay, let's do this."

I led my team into the room and sat opposite Montoni, with Arno at my side. Destine took the fourth chair and placed it in the corner behind Montoni, where she sat beyond her line of sight and took out her tablet, with which she would record everything for the file.

"Captain Victoria Montoni, I am hereby formally charging you with attempted murder, attempted administration of a noxious substance, perverting the course of justice, and conduct prejudicial to good order and discipline. Further charges are possible depending on what we uncover. You do not have to say anything. But it may harm your defense if you do not mention when questioned something which you later rely on in court. Anything you do say may be given in evidence." I paused. "Do you understand?"

"I do."

"Do you wish to make a statement?"

"No, what I want is a lawyer. I'm not saying a word without one." She gave me a calm, appraising look. "Do *you* understand?"

I turned toward Destine. "Captain Montoni, having requested the presence of legal counsel, I'm suspending this interview."

"When do I get out of here?"

"Oh, you're not going anywhere now that I've charged you. Certainly not with attempted murder as one of the charges."

"I demand bail."

"And your lawyer will make the request to a military judge on your behalf. Just be aware that I will oppose any bail."

She gave me a contemptuous glare. "Big surprise there. Now, how does it work with the lawyer?"

"You'll get one assigned from the Joint Base Sanctum's Judge Advocate General's office unless you have a civilian solicitor in mind."

"And if I don't, but want a civilian lawyer anyway?"

"Then you'll start with the one from the JAG, who can recommend a civilian. But I suggest you think hard about it. Courts-martial are a different beast from civilian courts, and a civilian barrister can be at a disadvantage compared to a JAG officer."

A faint smirk appeared. "That's if it even gets to a court, which I doubt."

I stood, imitated by Arno and Destine. "We'll resume this conversation once the brig commander informs me you have legal counsel at your side."

It was Sunday, which meant some poor JAG lawyer was about to have his or her weekend ended prematurely, but that's what they were paid to do.

We returned to the office to make a dent in the piles of documentation we'd need to back up the arrest and charges, starting with my sworn statement made to Arno and Destine. Technically, I shouldn't be involved in the case since I was the victim. But because I was treating last night's incident as part of the broader investigation into allegations of treason, I could use my discretion as senior PCB officer in the Caledonia system.

It was close to sixteen hundred when Lieutenant Colonel Horik called to tell me Montoni had met with a JAG lawyer, Lieutenant Commander Amon

Galindez, and was ready to resume the interview. I told him we'd do so the following morning at oh-nine hundred. There was nothing wrong with letting Montoni stew overnight now that I'd charged her and could take my time. I sent Galindez and Montoni a copy of my statement, then went home.

Monday morning, I was at work by oh-seven-hundred again, after a better night's sleep than the previous one, and resumed work on the Montoni file. Shortly after oh-eight-hundred, General Terak called me in high dudgeon.

"I understand you've arrested Captain Victoria Montoni on charges of attempted murder and are handling the case yourself?"

"Yes, I did, and yes, I am."

"Why are you not handing it over to Fleet Security? Your brief is anti-corruption."

"Because the attempted murder happened during my investigation into Captain Montoni for corrupt practices and is thus inseparable from it.

"What? You're investigating her for corruption? How did you figure that one out? Captain Montoni is as straight an arrow as I can think of, honest as the day is long, unimpeachable."

I mentally rolled my eyes at Terak's litany of clichés. Yet, if she knew Montoni, could Terak be one of her friends in high places?

"Does that mean you're acquainted with Captain Montoni, General?"

"As a matter of fact, I am. We go back a few years, not that it's any of your business."

Oh, she was so wrong about that. But I wouldn't tell her right away.

"Was that everything, General? I have to prepare for my interview with her later this morning."

"I would like one of my officers to sit in on that."

"He can watch from the observation gallery. The only ones who will be physically present are Montoni, her lawyer, my people, and I."

"I would prefer he be in the room with you."

"No."

"What if my officer has a question?"

"He or she can ask it afterward, and I'll see if it's worth raising at the next interview."

"You really are a law unto yourself, aren't you, Morrow?"

"When it comes to ACU 12 and its cases, I'm answerable to no one in this star system, General. And Montoni is one of my cases. I'll relinquish her to Fleet Security if I find she is not corrupt. Until then, she's mine."

"I can't say I like it, but no one asked for my opinion when they posted you here. Terak, out."

I stared at my blank communicator display for a few seconds. Terak and Montoni. Strange. One was a lieutenant general of Marines who'd spent her career in security, the other a Navy captain who'd spent hers in intelligence. Not the sort you'd immediately pick as being acquaintances. Certainly not to the point where Terak herself would call me bright and early on a Monday morning demanding to know why I kept the case.

And then there was her insistence on having one of her own observe my interview. She appeared to attribute more importance to Montoni than casual association would warrant.

A few minutes before oh-nine-hundred, Arno, Destine, and I were standing in the observation gallery and watched Montoni, who now wore a dark blue brig uniform, and her lawyer, Amon Galindez, enter Interview 2. The latter was a stocky man in his fifties with short gray hair and an equally short gray beard. He wore a Navy uniform with enough ribbons on his left breast to show he'd seen a few things in his time. Both took seats side-by-side, facing the door, and Galindez retrieved a tablet from his briefcase. Then they silently waited.

At nine precisely, Terak's observer not having shown up yet, I led my team into the interview room, and we sat.

"Good morning, Captain Montoni, Commander Galindez. Commander, this is Chief Inspector Arno Galdi, who'll be assisting me, and Warrant Officer Destine Bonta, who will record the interview. Before we start, Captain Montoni, do you have any complaints about your detention?"

She gave me a sardonic look. "You mean other than being detained on spurious grounds? No."

"You've both read my statement concerning the events of last Saturday evening at the Bello Inn?"

Galindez nodded. "Yes. And I question your impartiality in running this investigation if you were the victim of the alleged attack."

"You also received copies of the evidence report on the gun Captain Montoni used to fire at me, the images of the scene, and the whiskey adulterated with gammahypnol she tried to force me to drink."

"Yes, and Captain Montoni strictly denies having fired at you or adulterated the whiskey. She maintains you fabricated the evidence when she turned down your advances."

My eyebrows shot up, and I smiled at him. "She turned down *my* advances? That's an interesting lie, especially since I'm not interested in women. But considering her gun was fired and only had her fingerprints on it, and the whiskey bottle was clearly spiked with gammahypnol, and it too had only her fingerprints on it, I'd say your client needs to rethink her statements, lest I add to the charges. Did she tell you I recorded our conversation on my service-issue communicator? No? She must have forgotten."

I pulled out the communicator and called up the recording. "Listen carefully, Commander. You'll find your client has lied to you."

"That's a fake," Montoni said. "No such conversation occurred."

"Did you know Constabulary service-issue communicators are sealed units that cannot be tampered with? Any recordings made on them will stand up in court because they are date, time, and geolocation stamped."

I replayed the conversation, leading right up to my calling Arno for help. When I put my communicator away, Galindez gave Montoni a stern look, the sort lawyers give their clients when they've been holding back on them.

"I think it's safe to say that a court martial will find Captain Montoni guilty of the charges I laid. The only matter up for debate is the penalty it will assign. I doubt she'll be sentenced to a prison colony on Parth. Perhaps five years in a penitentiary on Caledonia will be it. Less if she cooperates. But her career is over. She'll be released from the Navy under Item 1 — Misconduct as per Chapter 15 of the Code of Service Discipline. The only thing up for debate is whether it will be a 1(a) or a 1(b). Not that it matters. Whether or not she's dismissed with disgrace, she'll not be eligible for any federal or Caledonian government job, and her pension rights will be forfeit."

"Unless a court releases her under Item 2 — Unsatisfactory conduct," Galindez said. "I don't know if my client is open to cooperating if we can parlay her release into an Item 2. What, for instance, would you consider sufficient to reduce the charges so she faces an Item 2 instead of an Item 1? On top of prison time, of course, which would also be suitably reduced."

"How about I let you and your client discuss whether she's open to cooperating first?" I stood without waiting for an answer, followed by Arno and Destine, and we left.

By the time we entered the observation gallery, the sound feed from Interview 2 had been cut. Watching them silently discuss matters was a distinguished-looking Marine colonel in his late fifties. Tall, with thick silver hair swept back from a broad forehead, a black mustache beneath a patrician nose, and inquisitive brown eyes, he wore an impressive array of ribbons on his left breast beneath Pathfinder wings. He nodded politely at me.

"Assistant Commissioner Morrow, I'm Saul Butler from General Terak's staff."

I nodded back. "Colonel. Any questions or comments on what you've seen so far?"

He shook his head. "No. Although I am intrigued by your communicator's sealed, and dare I say, secret recording function. We weren't aware of such a thing."

"That's because we don't use it often and advertise its existence even less, for obvious reasons."

"Indeed." His accent was Cimmerian, and his diction was distinctly upper-class. "It must come in handy at times."

"When we need it, we really need it. Otherwise, we use conventional recording devices."

"Do you think Captain Montoni will give you something in return for reduced charges?"

I shrugged, aware Butler was carrying out Terak's agenda and possibly, if not probably, in her confidence. "Doubtful. She doesn't have much to offer."

My eyes were drawn to the display where Montoni and Galindez were having an animated conversation, much more so than I'd have expected.

"I would give a lot to hear what they're saying right now," Butler commented as his gaze followed mine. "But solicitor-client confidentiality is paramount."

"That it is." I paused for a few seconds. "Have you worked for General Terak long, Colonel?"

"More years than either of us can count, I suspect. The Fleet Security branch is in many ways a closed shop where you serve with the same people over and over." He gave me a small smile that didn't reach his eyes. "Why do you ask?"

"Out of sheer idleness while our suspect and her lawyer are debating." I had a pat answer ready to go. "What is it you do for her?"

"I'm her executive assistant. I do whatever she needs me to." He briefly glanced at the PCB's owl above the scales of justice badge on my right breast, then nodded at my left one. "I see we attended the same school, the one where you're made to jump out of perfectly good shuttles from low orbit."

"We did. I served two years as a Constabulary liaison with C Squadron, 1st Special Forces Regiment, as a sergeant. You?"

"I served with B Squadron as a private and lance corporal decades ago before moving to Fleet Security. I daresay my time predates yours by a bit."

"Probably." I saw Galindez get up and head for the door. "If you'll excuse me, Colonel."

We filed back into the interview room and took our seats. I looked at Galindez with an air of expectation. "So?"

"Captain Montoni maintains her innocence and, therefore, has nothing to offer."

It was what I'd expected. If she was a traitor, the last thing she'd want to do was expose her treason.

"In that case, let's get on with the interview. Captain Montoni, I put it to you that you were recruited by a man who called himself Findlay Rogers four years ago to pass along Fleet secrets."

Galindez gave me an astonished glance at my sudden change of tack but refrained from speaking, for which I was grateful.

"No comment," Montoni replied.

"Do you deny meeting with Findlay Rogers?"

"No comment."

"Who do you work for? The *Sécurité Spéciale*? Or one of the zaibatsu intelligence organizations?"

"No comment."

"Or do you even know to whom you're passing secrets?"

"No comment."

I tried a few more questions, but her answer remained the same, so I ended the interview.

Once Destine had ceased recording, Lieutenant Commander Galindez said, "I'll be seeking bail for Captain Montoni."

"Good luck with that. Because she's suspected of committing treason on top of everything else, we consider her a flight risk and will so advise the prosecution when we meet this afternoon to go over the details of the case."

"Nevertheless, Captain Montoni will exercise her right to request bail. I've scheduled an appearance before a military judge tomorrow morning."

My teammates and I stood. "As I said, good luck. Let me know if your client wishes to discuss anything or cooperate."

— Twenty-Three —

"I can't say I wholly approve of your methods, Assistant Commissioner." The prosecutor assigned to the Montoni case, Marine Colonel Azira Delios, sat back in her chair once I finished giving her the details. Tall, dark, and slender, with shoulder-length black hair and brown eyes framing a strong nose, she'd studied me intently throughout my monologue. "But then, I'm unfamiliar with the Professional Compliance Bureau's practices. Be that as it may, I believe we have an open and shut case against Montoni. I am concerned about the allegations of treason, however, since they potentially carry a much harsher punishment, including death. Certainly, life on Parth would be an appropriate sentence."

"Unfortunately, we have little evidence, although her attempt on my life, because I was investigating her for corruption, indicates I was on the right track. If she were innocent, she wouldn't have reacted that way. Then there are previous incidents." I related the disappearances of Magda LeTellier and Gary Holden. "Realistically, there's no way we'll ever be able to pin those on Montoni short of her confessing to their murder, and she seems prepared to go to prison for a full term rather than cooperate."

"Which isn't surprising if she's betrayed the Fleet. Cooperating with us by revealing her treason won't gain her much, but it will paint a target on her back, one her former employers will gleefully aim at. She has a greater chance of staying alive by remaining silent."

She seemed remarkably knowledgeable about the matter, and I asked her why.

"I was involved in the Black Sword traitor hunt years ago, prosecuting those who survived the purge. There weren't many, let me tell you. Most either died by their own hand or were killed by our black ops people."

Meaning Hera, Zack, and their colleagues.

"I can understand her staying silent, Colonel. Either way, she'll no longer be in a position to betray the Fleet, so in a sense, my job is done even if I didn't end up charging her for corrupt practices. This sort of ending to my cases happens more often than you might think." I shrugged. "Was there anything else you needed from me at this moment?"

"No." She closed Montoni's file. "I have all the evidence I need to prosecute the case. Like I said, it's open and shut, thanks to your recording of the events."

Moments after I returned to my office and reset my communicator to accept links from outside my team, Terak called again. I should have figured she would after Colonel Butler reported I was actually investigating Montoni for treason.

"How did you decide Vic Montoni was a traitor, Assistant Commissioner?"

"I decided no such thing, General, but as Colonel Butler surely told you, she was seen with a recruiter for an outside organization specializing in turning officers four years ago. That's the basis on which I was investigating her when she betrayed herself Saturday evening by making an attempt on my life. If she hadn't decided to interrogate and kill me, Montoni would still walk around a free woman."

"That's if she actually did what you say, which I find hard to believe."

"I've presented my evidence to the JAG prosecutor. She considers the case an easy prosecution. I'm sorry, General, but your friend is going away for a few years after an Item 1 release. There's no way for her to beat the charges."

"I'd like to see that evidence myself."

After briefly debating whether I should tell her no, which was my right, if not exactly my obligation, I figured there was no harm in sharing the evidence.

"Certainly, General. Stand by to receive." She was silent while I transmitted the evidentiary file to her message queue, perhaps slightly stunned by my agreeing to a request for once. "There. You have it. As you'll see, it's incontrovertible. Captain Montoni would do well to plead guilty and accept her punishment."

"And the evidence of treason?"

"I have none, but it doesn't matter anymore. Captain Montoni can no longer sell secrets, and I'll count that as a win."

"How many other senior officers are you investigating for possibly betraying the Fleet?"

"I can't tell you that, General."

"This is the whole sorry Black Sword business all over again, isn't it? Except this time, it's the Constabulary hunting down potential traitors instead of Naval Intelligence to keep things strictly legal."

"I was a chief superintendent in the Rim Sector in those days, so I couldn't possibly comment." Why did she call it a sorry business, I wondered? So I asked her, and she appeared flustered for a few seconds as if she hadn't been fully aware of her choice of words.

"Because it wasn't one of the Fleet's most glorious moments. It was a witch hunt, pure and simple, and I suspect several innocent officers were caught in the deadly web cast by Naval Intelligence."

"Were you involved?"

"What do you mean by that?"

"You were what? A brigadier or major general at the time, one of the top Fleet Security officers? Surely Security would have been involved."

A bitter laugh came over the link. "We were essentially sidelined by intelligence on suspicion of harboring traitors."

"And were you?"

"Yes. Sadly. Some of them were people I'd known for years. And some of them whom I was and still am convinced were innocent, but they lost their careers and, in some cases, their lives anyway. But intelligence was equally penetrated, including the Special Operations Division, which spearheaded the effort." There was bitterness in her voice as she spoke that last sentence. "Anyway, let me look at that evidence. If it's conclusive, maybe I can convince Vic to plead guilty in return for a reduced sentence and an Item 2 release."

"It's conclusive, General. But whether Captain Montoni will listen to reason is anyone's guess."

"Terak, out."

I glanced at the time and decided to hit the gym, then go home.

The next morning, Lieutenant Colonel Horik, the brig commander, called to inform me that Captain Victoria Montoni had passed away during the night of what appeared to be natural causes, perhaps cardiac arrest brought on by the stress of her situation. They had taken her body to the base hospital for an autopsy.

When I told Arno, he shook his head. "Bullcrap. She died of *un*natural causes, mark my words. A fit woman like her unable to deal with incarceration? Someone slipped her a suicide pill. Another traitor who wanted to make sure Montoni wouldn't talk."

"I'm inclined to agree. We'll see what the autopsy says."

"I can tell you what it'll say, Chief. Cardiac arrest, with no discernible reason because the suicide pill will have dissolved, and the poison dissipated by the time she's on the autopsy table. Someone in the brig is in on it. Maybe even the commander." He snapped his fingers. "Tell you what. It could be that Colonel Butler, Terak's executive assistant, visited Montoni late last night. Since they're all Fleet Security, maybe he won't have been recorded in the brig's log as a favor to a high-ranking officer. The Almighty knows we've seen the like in our own Service — senior people slipping into detention areas unrecorded and unseen to help detainees or interrogate them illegally."

Arno had a point and one I'd have come to myself seconds later. I remembered at least two cases where junior Constabulary members in the Rim Sector held on corruption charges mysteriously died in custody after unrecorded visits by superiors we eventually nabbed. In both cases, the superiors ended up in a prison colony on Parth for life.

I contacted the base hospital and asked that they send me a copy of the autopsy report since Montoni was my case. It must have been a slow day because I received it early that same afternoon.

"You nailed it, Arno. Cardiac arrest with no detectable reason. Her heart was healthy, as was the rest of her. The autopsy report is therefore inconclusive as to the reason for death."

I touched my communicator and asked it to link me with Lieutenant Colonel Horik. He answered within moments.

"What can I do for you, Assistant Commissioner?"

"I presume you've received the autopsy report for Captain Montoni."

"Yes."

"Since it's inconclusive, I intend to treat her death as suspicious and investigate it myself."

Horik didn't immediately reply, and his eyes shifted to one side.

"I'm sorry, sir," he finally said. "But you don't have jurisdiction. This is a Fleet Security matter, and I can already tell you her death will be treated as natural. It won't be investigated."

"That's where you're wrong. I do have jurisdiction, not only because Montoni is my case, and I consider her unexpected and inexplicable demise part of it. I will investigate. Tell me, do you have a lot of deaths in custody, Colonel?"

He shrugged. "Two or three per year."

"You don't have an AI keeping watch on each cell?"

"Sure, but by the time it alerts the watchkeepers and they reach the cell of a suicide, it's usually too late."

"And the AI didn't detect Montoni going into cardiac arrest?"

"It did, but she was gone by the time my people got there."

"At what time did it happen?"

"The AI alerted the desk sergeant at oh-one-thirty-seven." Then, realizing he was actually cooperating with my investigation, Horik frowned. "But be that as it may, you're overstepping your bounds, sir. As I said, this is a Fleet Security matter."

"I'd like to interview the desk sergeant who was on duty, see the brig's logs, and subject Montoni's cell to an intensive scan."

An air of exasperation appeared on his normally inexpressive features.

"For the last time, Assistant Commissioner, you don't have jurisdiction. Besides, the cell has already been sterilized for reuse by the next inmate to come along, so you won't even find any of Captain Montoni's DNA."

"Why do I think you have something to hide, Colonel Horik? Should I widen the scope of my investigation to include you and the brig? And yes, I can do that without needing General Terak's or Grand Admiral Larsson's approval. You understand I can investigate whoever or whatever I deem fit, right?"

His eyes slipped to one side again for a second or two.

"I'll need General Terak's authorization to let you interview the desk sergeant and see the logs."

"What part of I can do anything I want without her approval did you not understand, Colonel? I expect a copy of the logs within the next five minutes and an appointment to speak with the desk sergeant within ten. If I don't get those two things, I will charge you with perverting the course of justice under Section 130 of the Commonwealth Defense Act."

That got his attention. He stared at me with widening eyes, clearly indignant.

"You can't."

"You wouldn't be the first senior officer I charge for failing to cooperate with an anti-corruption investigation. Five minutes for the logs, Colonel." I cut the link and glanced at Arno. "Hopefully, he'll be smart about it rather than obstinate."

"What do they call Security folks again? Meatheads? I wouldn't be surprised if he digs in."

"Then he'll experience the brig from the other side."

My communicator chimed just then, indicating the arrival of a message. It was the overnight log.

"I guess Horik isn't as much of a meathead as you figured, Arno."

— Twenty-Four —

We reviewed the logs but found nothing related to Montoni until the AI monitoring her cell reported her heartbeat had stopped. No visitors to the brig were logged from sixteen hundred yesterday until this morning, and the last visitor had been a JAG officer visiting one of the other detainees. I wasn't sure what I was expecting or hoping for since anyone visiting Montoni after hours for nefarious purposes would have made sure they left no traces. Logs had been falsified before, in my experience, even those of detention centers or brigs.

I forwarded the file to Destine so she could analyze it for discrepancies, such as entries having been replaced or excised. It was challenging to change logs without leaving some artifacts behind.

The desk sergeant called me eleven minutes after I threatened Horik — it was Sergeant Otreya, who'd been on duty when we brought Montoni in. Otreya confirmed no one had visited Montoni during her duty shift and that she discovered her lying on the bunk with vital signs absent when she entered her cell. She'd found nothing suspicious in the cell.

"Are you surprised?" Arno asked once I cut the link with Otreya. "Colonel Butler called Fleet Security a closed shop yesterday, remember? If someone visited Montoni after hours to slip her a suicide pill, they'd never tell."

"They might not have known about the pill part, though. I'll grant them at least that much. Mind you, Otreya sounded credible."

"She could simply be a good liar. Montoni's heart didn't give out just like that while contemplating a few years in prison."

"I'm aware of that. But we have no way of proving it. That's the thing with these fast-dissolving poisons. It was long gone by the time they did the autopsy, just like Greer's case."

My communicator chimed again. General Terak. And I knew exactly why she was calling me.

"General."

"Did you really threaten to charge Anton Horik with perverting the course of justice?"

"Yes. He was refusing to provide me with evidence germane to the case of Captain Montoni."

"There is no more case against her, Assistant Commissioner. She died of natural causes."

"I have a case for as long as I determine there to be one, General. At this point, I consider her death suspicious, which ties it back into my investigation."

Terak's lips compressed together to where they almost disappeared as she glared at me.

"A death in custody is a matter for Fleet Security."

"Not this one."

"And if I decide Fleet Security will no longer cooperate with you in this matter, will you offer to charge me with perverting the course of justice?"

"If I have to, General. I carry out my work without fear or favor."

"You assume a lot."

"I only assume that which is in my power."

"And you consider investigating Montoni's death against the wishes of the Provost Marshal of the Armed Forces within your power."

"I do. That's why ACU 12 is here, General. To investigate corruption cases completely insulated from the Fleet's chain of command. And I've been given the latitude to do as I see fit within the bounds of legality and Constabulary regulations. Note that I said Constabulary regulations rather than Armed Forces regulations. I am not bound by the latter in any way, shape, or form."

"Did the Grand Admiral know this when he accepted your unit's presence here?"

"I must assume so."

"We'll see about that. I intend to raise your disregard for the chain of command with him."

"As is your right, General. In the meantime, I expect the full cooperation of everyone in Fleet Security who might have information concerning the late Captain Montoni."

"You expect a lot for an officer of your comparatively low rank, Assistant Commissioner. Terak, out."

I gave Arno a wry smile. "If I wasn't in her bad books before, I most assuredly am now."

Arno gave me a half-shrug, eyes twinkling with amusement. "It's your curse, Chief. You make more enemies than friends wherever you go."

"Thanks for that, I think."

"Speaking of friends, did you update Admiral Talyn on the Montoni case?"

"No. And I really should."

But when I tried to call her, I only got a message — supper at her place at eighteen-thirty. And so, at eighteen-twenty-nine and a half, I walked up to her front door from the street. It opened at my approach, and her voice called out, "I'm in the kitchen."

I joined her, and the first thing she did was shove a glass of gin and tonic into my hand before picking up her glass.

"I think you need this after the last three days," she said. "Your health."

"And yours."

We both took healthy sips. Then she nodded at the kitchen table. "Let's sit right here. The weather's about to go bad on us, anyway. So, tell me about Montoni. I understand she died in the brig last night."

I gave Hera the whole story, beginning with our weekend getaway to Horizonte.

"We have our home away from home close to there."

"I remember you mentioning it."

"That's quite the chain of events. Montoni must have been out of her mind to take you on."

I made a face. "As you know, she seems to have left a trail of vanished friends during her career — two that we're aware of, and the Almighty knows how many more. Montoni was merely planning on making me the latest one. Although how she figured she'd get away with it still puzzles me. But now I'll never find out."

"And you figure she didn't die of natural causes?"

"No." I sighed. "Yet that's something else I'll likely never determine for sure. Any trace of fast-dissolving poison was gone by the time they autopsied her. The main reason I'm determined to press on with the investigation is Fleet Security's obstinacy in trying to shut me down."

"Which makes you believe someone in Security is involved."

"Yes. And that, in turn, leads me to wonder whether there's another traitor in Security, one who worked covertly with Montoni. Did the Black Sword people operate in clandestine cells?"

"Most of them did, and I'm sure we missed a few sleeper cells back then."

"I guess I'll need to broaden my investigation and dig into Security so I can figure out who might have the means and opportunity to induce Montoni's death, be it voluntarily, meaning suicide, or involuntarily, meaning murder."

"Any idea how you'll tackle that?"

I gave her a tight smile. "Hopefully, the analysis of the brig logs will provide something to show they've been tampered with. Otherwise, I'll be stuck. Mind you, there's still the fact that Terak knew Montoni. I'll have to see who else in Security had a personal relationship with her."

Hera gave me a speculative look. "You don't think Terak is involved?"

I thought about it for a few seconds before grimacing. "At this point, I figure she could be as guilty as the next senior officer. She certainly hasn't been particularly helpful, although she referred a whole lot of cases to us last week."

"Perhaps Terak is trying to swamp you so you don't have the resources to look for traitors."

I let out a bark of laughter. "Now that's verging on paranoia."

Hera smirked. "Even paranoids have enemies."

"And so do I, Terak among them."

Later that evening, as I sat on my balcony with a glass of Glen Arcturus, I thought back to our conversation and realized that General Tania Terak had been figuring large in my subconscious as being somehow involved in Montoni's death. I didn't know how or why, but my instincts rarely led me astray. Arno would probably say it was because I had a touch of a Sister of the Void's eldritch abilities. I simply figured my subconscious had a way of putting together disparate clues and eventually presenting me with plausible theories.

***

"They've definitely tampered with the logs, sir." Destine, Arno hard on her heels, entered my office the next day with a triumphant air. "An expert job that would have fooled just about anyone but a member of ACU 12 wielding the PCB's document analysis program."

"Sit." I pointed at the chairs in front of my desk. "And tell me all about it."

Both obeyed, and Destine said, "There's a distinct cut in the sequence at oh-one-fifteen and another at oh-one-thirty-three, indicating eighteen minutes' worth of record was replaced with nothing."

"More than enough time for someone to visit Montoni and give her a suicide pill."

"Wouldn't it be simpler to just stop the log recording?" Arno asked.

I shook my head. "Can't. Any attempt to stop it will trigger all sorts of alarms, just like our detention logs."

Arno slapped his forehead theatrically. "Right. How silly of me."

"Okay. There are two people involved — Sergeant Otreya and Lieutenant Colonel Horik. Otreya because she obviously let in whoever visited Montoni."

"If Montoni died from anything other than natural causes," Arno said. "Let's keep in mind we're still dealing with very circumstantial evidence, most of which is no evidence at all."

Destine half grimaced. "The fact someone tampered with the log minutes before Montoni's death pretty much establishes that something wasn't right in the brig that night."

"Granted." Arno raised both hands in surrender. "And do you think Anton Horik fiddled with the log?"

"It's his brig, and he doesn't strike me as a fool. He either did it himself or knows who did."

"Question is, at whose behest? I don't think he acted on his own. So, Chief, when do we interrogate both of them?"

"Tomorrow morning. Otreya when she comes off shift at oh-eight-hundred and Horik right after."

— Twenty-Five —

A sullen, scowling Sergeant First Class Otreya showed up in our offices at eight-fifteen the following morning, having been summoned by Arno an hour earlier. When she didn't want to come at first, he'd threatened her with arrest and confinement to her own brig on charges of perverting the course of justice. That had done the trick. Of course, it would take more than refusing to show up for an interview to make such charges stick, but she didn't appear to realize that.

But it was clear she wasn't happy and wouldn't be an easy witness.

Arno placed her in one of our interrogation rooms and left her to stew while we watched remotely from my office. Otreya didn't take being locked into a windowless space and ignored terribly well. She paced, sat, drummed her fingers on the tabletop, looked for video pickups, and paced again. After fifteen minutes, we — Arno, Destine, and I — entered the room, interrupting another pacing session.

Otreya immediately dumped herself in one of the chairs, staring at me as if to say, 'finally.'

"Thank you for coming, Sergeant," I said, sitting across from her. Arno sat beside me while Destine took one of the remaining chairs and settled just beyond Otreya's field of vision.

"Chief Inspector Galdi didn't leave me much choice," she paused for a fraction of a second, just long enough to make her point, "sir."

"Someone entered the brig and the late Captain Montoni's cell between oh-one-fifteen and oh-one-thirty-three the morning of her death. Who was it?"

"No one entered the brig between midnight and oh-six hundred that night." Her eyes shifted to one side as she spoke.

"Are you sure about that?"

She stared at me and replied in a tone verging on hostile, "Yes. Quite sure."

"Then why was the log changed between oh-one-fifteen and oh-one-thirty-three?"

"I beg your pardon, sir, but the log can't be changed. It's impossible."

"And yet someone did, presumably to hide a visitor who didn't wish to be recorded. There's no other rational reason to tamper with something that difficult to modify and in such an expert manner. It further stands to reason said visitor was for Captain Montoni, considering she died minutes later, we presume of a self-ingested, fast dissipating poison."

"Sir?" She glanced at me in astonishment. "I understood she passed of natural causes."

"Many poisons vanish within an hour or two after ingestion, and the autopsy wasn't conducted until over six hours after death. Now, who visited her at the time I mentioned?"

"No one."

I slapped my hand on the tabletop, making a loud crack that caused Otreya to jump.

"Stop lying, Sergeant. Someone visited Captain Montoni in the wee hours of the night. Who was it?"

Otreya leaned forward, eyes on me. "As I keep repeating, no one."

"And you were at the front desk during the time in question?"

She glanced away again, and that's when I knew the next words out of her mouth would be a lie.

"Yes, I was."

"No, you weren't."

Otreya gave me a defiant glare. "Suit yourself. But I still didn't see anyone enter the brig, nor do I know how the log was tampered with."

And strangely enough, I believed her, which meant she didn't see who entered the brig shortly after oh-one-fifteen.

"Who sent you on break not long after oh-one hundred?"

She bit her lip and looked at the tabletop.

"Come on, Sergeant. You and I know you weren't at the front desk when Captain Montoni's visitor showed up. That can only mean someone else, someone higher in rank than you, temporarily took your place. Who was it?"

"I'm sorry, sir, but I cannot answer that question." She sounded like a woman who knew she was caught in a falsehood but couldn't admit it because doing so wouldn't just open her to retribution but would bring her life crashing down around her ears.

"Cannot because you have no idea who took your place or because telling me means whoever it was will make you pay?"

Otreya crossed her arms, eyes fixed on the tabletop, and didn't reply.

"We can protect you."

Still nothing. Time to try a different approach.

"Does Colonel Horik show up a lot in the wee hours?"

Her eyes came up and briefly met mine before dropping again. "Sometimes. He runs a tight ship and likes to conduct unannounced inspections."

"Did he come on the night Captain Montoni died?"

This time, she looked away to one side, eyes narrowed as if debating whether to answer.

"No comment," she finally said, glancing at me for a second or two.

Those two words told me all I needed to know.

"Thank you, Sergeant. You're free to go."

She stood and wordlessly left the room.

"So," I looked at Arno and Destine in turn, "Horik was there that night. He sent Otreya on a break and doctored the logs afterward. At least that's what I get from Otreya's non-answers."

Arno scratched his beard. "It's what I get as well, Chief. She was clearly unwilling to answer your questions and yet uncomfortable not doing so, perhaps because she knows what happened that night or thinks she knows and isn't happy about it."

"Let's take a deeper look at Sergeant First Class Otreya. And at Lieutenant Colonel Horik."

"Will you interview him this morning?"

I shook my head.

"No. Probably not for a day or two. I'm presuming Otreya will report back and I would rather let Horik wonder why we're not calling him in for a chat right away." A thought occurred to me. "And let's examine every death in custody for the last five years. Horik said they had two or three per year, which, now that I think about it, seems a tad excessive for a supposedly well-run brig."

✳✳✳

"None of the deaths in custody appear suspicious at first glance, Chief." Arno dropped into a chair across from my desk that Friday morning. "Fourteen over five years, not including Montoni. Five suicides, nine deaths from natural causes — all of them ruled as cardiac arrest, meaning the doctors don't have a clue why they died."

"Do the deaths from natural causes have anything in common?"

"Destine is looking at that right now, but they were older — two lieutenant commanders, one major, three chief petty officers, and three senior sergeants. They were arrested on various charges, one of the lieutenant commanders for extortion, the other for embezzlement. The major was arrested for assault causing bodily harm, as were two of the chief petty officers. The third was awaiting trial for murder. Of the three sergeants, one was arrested for sexual assault, one for blackmail, and the last for attempted murder."

"And the suicides?"

"A leading spacer, arrested for sexual assault, a buck sergeant for assault causing bodily harm, a petty officer for murder, and two Navy lieutenants, one for embezzlement, the other for attempted murder."

"Seems like quite the variety of crimes."

Arno made a face. "It does. Which helps us not one whit."

"But they happened on Horik's watch. Let's look at the record of the previous brig commander."

"Already done. He had one death per year, five during his entire tenure."

My eyebrows shot up. "So the deaths in custody under Horik literally tripled, and nobody found it strange?"

A sly smile appeared on Arno's lips as he tapped the side of his nose with an extended index finger. "I thought you might find that interesting. Perhaps no one found it strange because Fleet Security, to use Colonel Butler's description, is a closed shop."

"Meaning?"

"Something might be going on, but outsiders will never know what that is."

"And we're the ultimate outsiders." I grimaced. "Okay. Keep plugging at it. In the meantime, I'll summon Anton Horik for thirteen hundred hours this afternoon. It's time we had a chat."

— Twenty-Six —

I'd decided to tackle Horik in my office rather than use one of the interview rooms, and at thirteen hundred, he appeared in my open doorway. Arno was already seated at the small conference table on one side of the room while Destine occupied a chair across from it.

"Colonel, come in." I stood, walked over to the conference table, and sat beside Arno. Then I indicated the empty chair across from us. "Please take a seat."

"Assistant Commissioner, Chief Inspector." Horik nodded once as he obeyed, ignoring Destine, his face an inscrutable mask. "What can I do for you? I am rather busy, so if we can jump right in?"

"Certainly. Let me see." I studied Horik's expression. "Do you often visit the brig at odd hours, such as in the middle of the night?"

"Yes." Judging by the look in his eyes, the question had come as a surprise, meaning Sergeant Otreya hadn't told him we'd asked it of her. "I think the best way of ensuring a continuously operating unit like the brig functions smoothly is to show up at least once per shift every so often."

"And did you visit the brig the night of Captain Montoni's death?"

Horik hesitated for a fraction of a second, just enough for me to notice, confirming my earlier suspicion Otreya had remained silent.

"Yes."

"Approximately what time was that?"

"Shortly after oh-one hundred. I did my inspection tour and left at around oh-one-thirty."

"Sergeant Otreya was the duty sergeant that night, correct?"

He nodded, a guarded expression creeping into his eyes as if he were wondering where I was going with my line of inquiry. "Yes."

"And you sent her off on a break while you stood at the desk sergeant's post." I did not voice it as a question.

Realization set in as his guarded expression turned to one of alarm.

"Is that what she told you?"

"Did you send her on a break, Colonel? Yes or no?"

He glared at me, jaw muscles working, then said, "Yes."

"And who showed up at the brig while Sergeant Otreya was on a break, and you were alone at the front desk?"

"No one." The answer came quickly while he held my eyes, daring me to gainsay him, and I knew he was lying.

"A section of the log between oh-one-fifteen and oh-one-thirty-three that night was tampered with. We have irrefutable evidence of that fact."

"I have no idea what you're talking about, Assistant Commissioner. The brig logs are impossible to change without leaving traces, and there are no such traces."

Gotcha.

"So, you're saying you checked the log at those times and found nothing to show they were changed? Why ever did you do so?" He looked flustered for the first time since I started the interview. "Do you routinely check the logs for tampering when you come in during silent hours? That must take an inordinate amount of time."

His jaw muscles worked again as he looked for a plausible answer, and one came. "I checked the logs for the night of Captain Montoni's death to make sure no one tried to tamper with them. Are you saying I missed something?"

"Why were you concerned someone might have modified the log that night?"

"I check the log for inconsistencies every time a detainee dies in custody." The answer came too quickly and was too smooth for my liking.

"I see. And you have a lot of those. Deaths in custody, I mean. Three times more than your predecessor. He had one a year, while you average three. Can you explain that?"

My change of tack had visibly flummoxed Horik because he simply stared at me for several heartbeats. But he quickly recovered.

"I wasn't aware of my predecessor's record regarding custodial deaths, Assistant Commissioner. Yet considering we see hundreds of detainees pass through each year, an increase of two isn't statistically significant."

"It is for the deceased, Colonel."

He inclined his head. "True. However, they weren't the finest examples of Fleet personnel. Some were downright nasty examples of debased humanity and no loss."

Something in his tone, if not his words, was faintly disturbing.

"Weren't they awaiting trial? You know, innocent until proven guilty?"

Horik's eyes lit up with a meanness I'd not seen before. "All were denied bail because the evidence against them was overwhelming. Notwithstanding the fact they hadn't yet had their day in court, there was no doubt about guilt. As I said, they were no loss to our species. Now, was that everything you wished to discuss?"

"Who showed up in the brig at oh-one-fifteen the night Captain Montoni died?"

"I don't know what you're talking about."

"Oh, come now, Colonel. You took over the front desk from Sergeant Otreya to let someone in, someone who visited Captain Montoni and offered her a suicide pill. You then erased that visit from the log. Four minutes later, Montoni was dead from so-called natural causes, which were anything but. Now who was it?"

A smirk appeared on Horik's face. "I'm definitely sure I don't know what you're talking about, Assistant Commissioner. Now if you'll excuse me — unless I'm under arrest — I'd like to carry on with the rest of my day."

He made as if to stand, but I relied on that tried-and-true tactic, the slap on the tabletop with the palm of my hand, the one that sounded like a sonic crack.

"Sit, Colonel. You'll leave when I let you."

Horik fell back in his chair, startled by my quiet vehemence. "I beg your pardon. You can't keep me here unless you caution me."

"Is that what you want? To be cautioned? Now why is that I wonder?"

He raised both hands, palms facing outward. "I'm only going by the rules of the game, Assistant Commissioner."

"Is that what this is to you? A game? A woman who was healthier than most humans in this star system died in your cells the other night. And yet you dismiss it as natural causes, no need to inquire further. I'll tell you what this is, and it isn't a game — I'm looking at you for accessory to murder, at the very least." I speared him with my eyes and asked, in a tone as cold as the depths of space, "Who visited Montoni at oh-one-fifteen?"

He leaned forward, visibly angry. "Nobody. And I'm not an accessory to murder or any other crime. I'm a senior Fleet Security officer, thoroughly vetted and therefore beyond suspicion."

"No one is beyond suspicion."

A sardonic smile appeared on his lips. "Except the officers of ACU 12. But here's a question for you — *quis custodiet ipsos custodes*? Who will guard the guards themselves?"

"Bravo. You know your Juvenal. However, we're talking about you and what you did the night Montoni died."

"I did nothing out of the ordinary." Horik crossed his arms as he sat back.

"And yet someone tampered with the log."

He shrugged. "So you say, but I've seen no proof."

"I can assure you the evidence is incontrovertible and will be accepted by any court. Either you did it, or someone in your unit did. This means you have a problem, and I need to know what was cut out of the log."

His eyes slid to one side. "I have no idea. But I can tell you considering Montoni's death as other than from natural causes is insane. I've seen plenty of that sort, and hers fits. Now, are you done accusing me of everything under the sun?"

I smiled at him. "I'm just beginning, Colonel. And I still want an answer on the changes to the log. It's your brig and ultimately your responsibility."

He grunted. "Perhaps. If the log was modified."

"It was, and it's your responsibility. I suggest you figure out who did it and tell me as soon as possible. That's all, Colonel. You're free to go."

Horik stared at me for a few moments, taken aback by his sudden dismissal, then stood and walked out of my office without saying another word. At my gesture, Destine got up and closed the door before joining us at the conference table so we could discuss the interview in private.

"Thoughts?"

"He was lying. That's almost a certainty," Arno said. "But he recovered quite well when you first talked about the tampered log."

I grimaced. "Yes. I thought I had him there, but his subsequent explanation was just plausible enough. The question is, what next?"

"Wait for him to get back to you on the log?" Arno suggested. "When people start to lie, they head ever deeper into a rabbit hole until they tangle themselves up. Since we're not under time pressure to solve this one, let Horik figure out a story that'll give him more problems than solutions."

"Okay. It's not like we have anything better to do, what with Fleet Security having closed ranks against us."

— Twenty-Seven —

The following day, since it promised to be beautiful sunshine from morning to evening, I decided to hike one of the popular paths in the hills north of the Nestor Valley. It would allow me to recharge amid nature, all by myself.

Evidently, half the population of Sanctum had the same idea because I was never out of sight of other people during the entire day, but things were still pleasant, and everyone wore a smile. It was after sixteen hundred when I returned to the parking lot and my car — I'd splurged on a used model sold by a Navy commander being posted away from Caledonia — but I didn't want to go home yet.

Instead, I headed to downtown Sanctum and the pedestrian district at its heart, so I could window shop, browse market stalls, and find a restaurant for supper.

After parking my car in the Hope Street parkade at the fringes of the pedestrian district, I ambled along crowded avenues, feeling at peace with myself and the galaxy, the Horiks of the universe be damned. My stomach suddenly grumbled, and instead of window shopping, I looked for a likely restaurant. The choice was almost overwhelming, but I eventually settled for a little joint called Heck's Kitchen that offered the sort of meat platters I sometimes craved.

I took a small table by the window, looking out on one of the main pedestrian streets, ordered, and sat back, watching people walk by while sipping on a surprisingly decent house red wine. A vaguely familiar individual, a man in his late forties or early fifties with short dark hair and a square face, wearing hiking clothes, stopped in front of the restaurant. I racked my brains trying to find where I'd seen him before, and then it struck me — we'd shared the same trail throughout the day, him mostly one curve behind me. Strange that of the hundreds of thousands of people who called Sanctum home, we'd stumble across each other again, so to speak. But coincidences happen. The man moved beyond my field of vision, and I let my eyes roam over the passing crowd.

The kebab platter I'd ordered showed up soon afterward, and I dug in, enjoying every bite of the filet mignon, chicken, and lamb over a generous layer of rice dotted with bits of caramelized onion and raisins. I had a cup of coffee afterward with dessert, a slice of creamy, chocolaty cake. By then, night had fallen, and light globes, floating everywhere, lit up the streets.

I paid, finished my coffee and climbed to my feet, stretching. I left the restaurant and stood outside its door for a few moments, looking around, then crossed the street to window shop a clothing store on my way back to the parkade. As I admired a business suit, I caught the reflection of the same man as before in the window. He was standing about two or three meters behind me, consulting a small tablet in his hand, and the immortal words of a twentieth-century writer came unbidden. Once is happenstance, twice is coincidence, and three times is enemy action — and this was the third time I'd seen him in the space of a few hours.

I drifted down the street, stopping in front of a jewelry store, and he moved along with me. Oh, he tried to stay inconspicuous in the crowd, but once I'd spotted him, I couldn't help but see his reflection in every store window. The man was definitely shadowing me, and I could only assume it was for nefarious purposes. I carried my sidearm in a hip holster beneath the loose shirt I wore untucked and suddenly felt its reassuring weight, although I was able to keep from touching it.

A tavern stood next to the jewelry store, and, on a whim, I entered. It was a casual sort of place, with many small, round tables and a copper-topped bar that ran the length of the room. Three-quarters full, the buzz of conversations fought with the ambient music but not at an offensive level. Otherwise, I would have turned around since I'm less tolerant of noise than I used to be. One of the many signs of aging gracefully.

I took a stool at the end of the bar and sat on it sideways to keep the door and windows within my range of sight. I ordered a single malt whiskey with a splash of water. It appeared quickly, and I took an appreciative sip, eyes on the entrance, but saw no sign of my tail. Either he was staying outside and waiting, or he'd left.

But when I exited the tavern half an hour later, I spotted him sitting on a bench on the other side of the street, eyes on his tablet once again. I stopped in front of another clothing store half a block away, and sure enough, I spotted his reflection in the window. The Hope Street parkade was fast approaching, and if he was going to do something, it would be there, where the afternoon crowd had already left and the evening crowd hadn't started arriving.

I turned off the street into an alley leading to the underground parkade's entrance. There were fewer people here, and unfortunately, there were no convenient reflecting windows to gauge his progress. I reached the entrance built into the ground floor of a three-story building, and the doors opened silently at my approach. Risking a glance over my shoulder, I realized he was much closer than I expected, a mere four paces behind me, but I kept the same stride.

Once in the lobby, my eyes went to the stairs beside the bank of elevators, and I knew I had to make a split-second decision. I chose the stairs. My car was on the third level below the surface, so it wouldn't be much of an inconvenience.

As I went down the first flight, I kept listening to footsteps following me, and when I didn't hear anything, I stopped on the first-floor landing. Nothing.

Perhaps I was just being extra paranoid and the man was an innocuous citizen of Sanctum whose path happened to cross mine several times. Then he took one of the lifts to whichever floor he'd parked his car. Or to the third floor, where I'd parked mine. Surely, he'd know where I put it if he was after me.

And so I quickly went down to the fourth level and let myself out into the elevator lobby. One of the lifts was on the third level. The rest were on the ground floor. I returned to the parking area, found the roadway used by vehicles, and quietly made my way to the third floor. Everything was well lit, the concrete painted white with pillars at regular intervals. The level was almost full of cars, with mine tucked away in a corner.

I saw the man lurking between two cars near the door leading to the stairs, weapon in hand, waiting. For me. There could be no doubt. I drew my sidearm and made my way to my car, slipping between vehicles and keeping to the shadows. By now, he must have known something was wrong since I hadn't appeared, and as I was about to cross an open area, he turned to look in the direction of my car. And he spotted me.

His weapon came up — it was a needler — and I ran. I heard a soft whizzing behind me, needles passing through the space I'd occupied a fraction of a second earlier. I ducked behind another car and drew my gun, an honest blaster, not an assassin's weapon like a needler. Just then, I saw the lift open, and three people stepped out. My would-be killer's gun vanished before he could fire another salvo, and I stood and ran to my car.

I climbed aboard, locked the doors, flicked the power plant on, and peeled out of my spot, tearing past the man who stared at me with expressionless eyes. Within moments, I was up on the second level, then the first, then I emerged onto the street and turned left toward the southern part of town and Joint Base Sanctum.

— Twenty-Eight —

By the time I reached the ring road, my heartbeat had returned to normal, though I could feel my skin slick with stress perspiration. Why was an assassin after me? Was it for past sins, or did it have anything to do with my current cases? I tapped my car's communicator and had it open a link with Hera's home.

"What's up, Caelin?"

"Some joker with a needler tried to put me down in a parkade on the fringes of the downtown pedestrian zone."

I explained how the man had been following me all day.

"Right," she said when I finished describing the man. "You're coming straight here to spend the night. Chances that your assassin can access the base are slim, but why take the risk? My residence is about as secure as it gets around Sanctum. It's a perk of the job."

"Okay. I'll be there in about fifteen minutes."

"Don't stop at your apartment for a toothbrush and spare underwear. I have everything you need right here."

"I wasn't intending to."

"Good. I'll see you in fifteen."

After threading my way through the main gate security barriers, I turned right toward the residential sector, and as I came to Hera's house, the garage door opened, showing a vacant space beside her car. I pulled in, and the door closed again. Then, as I got out of my vehicle, an inner door opened, and Hera appeared.

"I've alerted some people who'll try to track your would-be assassin, not that there's much of a chance, but the parkade will have security video, so at least we'll get a good look at his face."

"If that's his real face. From what I saw, it was probably a good disguise."

"True." She led me into the living room. "A wee dram of the good stuff?"

"Oh, yes. And then a shower, if you don't mind."

"Not at all." Hera went to the bar, pulled out two tumblers and a bottle of Glen Arcturus, poured a splash in each, then handed me one. "Slainte."

"Slainte." I took a healthy sip and let the amber liquid burn a path down my throat. "That hit the spot."

"Follow me, and I'll show you to the guest quarters. Fortunately, you and I have almost the same build, meaning my clothes will fit you. Don't worry, I have new, still-in-the-package stuff I keep just in case of an emergency like this."

And so she did. I found underwear, a t-shirt, and shorts waiting for me on the bed and a spacious shower enclosure in the ensuite bathroom. Ten minutes later, with damp hair hanging on either side of my face and wearing borrowed clothing, I rejoined Hera in her living room and poured myself another Glen Arcturus.

"Who do you think is after me?" I asked, taking a chair across the low coffee table from where she sat, legs tucked under her, on the sofa.

She shrugged. "You've made a lot of enemies over the years, and you're still making more. But I'm going to concentrate on our friends from the Sécurité Spéciale. They have reasons to want you gone if they're behind the late Captains Wils and Montoni and the other you're investigating — Young. We're aware they have a large contingent on Caledonia, not all of whom are known to us. That being said, I would suggest you confine yourself to the base until further notice to not tempt fate."

"No problems there. If I hadn't recognized the man from seeing him several times on the hiking trail, I'd probably be dead by now."

"A good thing you have a cop's sharp memory for faces."

I smiled at her. "Isn't it? Did you hear from Zack recently?"

She nodded. "Yes. He's settled in on Mykonos by now and has made contact with his family. It was strange, to say the least."

"Why?"

"Family history. Zack joined the Marine Corps the day he turned eighteen — against the express wishes of his father and grandfather. Call it an act of rebellion. He doesn't talk much about those days but figures if he hadn't enlisted, he'd have been utterly miserable as the heir apparent to part of the family fortune."

"And you two wouldn't have met."

A smile. "Indeed, and the Corps — the Fleet — would have been poorer for not having him in its ranks. I'm curious how his inevitable reunion with his family went."

"Why inevitable?"

"They're big shots on Mykonos, well known to move in the rarefied upper circles of government and politics, and Zack is swimming in those waters. You see, he's an old high school chum of the

Mykonosian President, Eugenius Van Kirten. It was just a matter of time before Zack came face-to-face with his family for the first time in over three decades. How I wish I could have been there when it happened. I'll just have to wait until Zack comes home and interrogate him about the not-so-tearful reunion."

"Do you think this constitutional convention on Mykonos will do any good?"

Hera made a face. "Personally, I doubt it. The differences between the OutWorlds and the Home Worlds have become too great. Even if Earth accepts proposals to strengthen the sovereign star systems principle, it'll only paper over them for a generation at best, and Earth has already said it didn't consider the convention legitimate."

"What's your guess on the likely outcome?"

"Either the status quo or the OutWorlds seceding from the Commonwealth because the status quo can no longer be tolerated. The chances of constitutional amendments being accepted wholesale strikes me as next to nil."

I took a sip of my Glen Arcturus. "And what happens to the Fleet if the OutWorlds secede?"

"Caledonia is an OutWorld." Her smile returned. "As is Wyvern."

"Isn't that a thought?"

A sudden yawn overcame me, and I finished my drink. "I think I'm off to bed. It's been a long day."

"Sleep well."

I stood. "Thanks."

The next morning, I woke up at daybreak only to find Hera already up and preparing breakfast. She thrust a mug of coffee in my hand before either of us spoke, and I wandered out onto the terrace, sipping the bitter liquid.

Once I drank that first cup and felt human again, I returned inside just in time to find a copious plate of eggs, bacon, sausage, beans, potatoes, toast, and fruit waiting for me.

"It's what Zack calls the Marine Meal Deal," Hera said, sitting across the kitchen table from me. "Not my favorite, but you looked like you could use a heavy protein load this morning."

I gave her a quick smile. "Thank you." Then, feeling surprisingly hungry, I attacked my plate with gusto, polishing off every bit.

"Tell me," I said, sitting back with my second cup of coffee, "did General Terak call you about senior officers I might investigate at your behest?"

"No. She wouldn't in any case. Terak and I aren't on friendly terms, and she tries hard to avoid me and my division."

I recounted my latest conversation with the general, and Hera gave me a half-shrug. "You did the right thing, not that it'll stop her from being a pain."

"Is there any reason Terak tries to stay away from you?"

"She's vaguely aware of what we do in Special Operations and disapproves mightily because we're an affront to her sense of propriety. However, she's learned that I, too, have a direct line to the Grand Admiral and that he not only relies on me for many things but respects my opinions and advice." A smile appeared. "Larsson let me know he told her so when she complained. That said, Terak is good at her job and was personally picked by Larsson as the Armed Forces Provost Marshal, so we're not talking about a holdover from the previous regime."

"Just like you."

She raised a hand, held it palm down, and waggled it from side to side.

"I wasn't picked by him but by the Chief of Naval Intelligence to take over the Special Operations Division. Although I suspect Kruczek ran my appointment by Larsson. But back to Terak. As I said, she's good at her job, yet she has problems with things she can't control, but figures should be in her ambit, such as ACU 12, or thinks shouldn't exist, such as my organization. The best thing you can do is keep her at arm's length, no matter what. I'm sure Larsson will back you, if necessary since he understands your role in the Fleet's ecosystem, something Terak doesn't. Mind you, many senior officers, if not most, don't understand either, so it's not solely Terak's failing." She smiled again. "Although it would be easier if you wore a commissioner's star, the mentality of people here at HQ being what it is."

"The story of my life, being under-ranked compared to the people I investigate and arrest. But it has its advantages, most of all the shock value at being hauled in by a lowly PCB officer."

"No doubt. But for the purposes of Fleet HQ?" Hera cocked an eyebrow at me.

"Perhaps, but I am what I am."

"Maybe I should have a talk with ACC Sorjonen and see what can be done."

I groaned. "Please don't. I'm still fairly junior as an assistant commissioner."

"Seniority has nothing to do with the needs of the Service. Besides, didn't you spend more time than necessary as a chief superintendent?"

Her tone was so reasonable, and her expression so innocent, I scowled. "Don't do it, Hera. Just don't."

She raised both hands in a gesture of surrender. "Fine. But I think you'd carry more weight as the conscience of the Fleet wearing a star."

"Conscience of the Fleet?" I guffawed. Deputy Chief Constable Hammet, the head of the Professional Compliance Bureau, was known as the Conscience of the Constabulary. I could hardly compare myself to him, especially since the Fleet was bigger than the Constabulary by more than an order of magnitude. "I don't think so, Hera. I'm merely the head of Anti-Corruption Unit 12, whose mandate is the military, and the heads of the ACUs are assistant commissioners, nothing more."

She scoffed. "I'm not so sure of that. You and your people are the Last of the Incorruptibles. You are who the Fleet turns to when it suspects corruption in its ranks, and you will extirpate the guilty no matter what while incontrovertibly clearing the innocent. And you stand apart from the Fleet, watching over it. If that's not the very definition of being the Fleet's conscience, I don't know what is."

"Don't let General Terak hear you say that, Hera. She might have a fit of apoplexy."

Hera made a dismissive gesture. "It doesn't matter if she hears it. In fact, maybe she should, just so she's clear on where you stand."

"Please don't. If I'm to be the conscience of the Fleet, let me be a subtle, understated one."

"Says the assistant commissioner who almost fell victim to an assassin's needler last night. You're already high profile for at least one or more people. Might as well embrace it and become a visible force to be reckoned with. The military doesn't do subtle and understated."

— Twenty-Nine —

Hera's people gave me the all-clear to return to my apartment later that Sunday, and I spent the day quietly sitting on my balcony, reading and watching the rain, which had settled in for the duration. The events of the previous evening began seeming distant and strange as if they'd happened to someone else, a sure sign I was assimilating them and putting them aside. Would they try again? Perhaps not, since their first attack failed, yet I intended to stay on Joint Base Sanctum for the foreseeable future.

Monday morning, bright and early, I headed for the office and a fresh week of sleuthing and administering. But I first briefed my wingers and team leads on Saturday evening's attempt on my life.

"Admiral Talyn, with whom I stayed that night, thinks it might be the Sécurité Spéciale, although I have my doubts. It didn't seem polished enough to be them. Now that I think back on it, there was something a bit too amateurish about the entire business."

Arno nodded slowly. "You may be right based on what you just told us and what we've seen of the Sécurité Spéciale. Which then begs the question of who."

"I can only surmise that it's related to one of our cases since we arrived here, and the only ones aware they were under investigation so far were Jacques, Wils, and Montoni, and they're all dead. Well, Jacques and Montoni are dead. Wils is presumed so. Which leaves Young, who, as far as I know, isn't aware he's being investigated."

I glanced at Frederick Vasiliev, who shook his head. "There's no way Young would realize we're looking into his life and times, sir."

"There's also Anton Horik, Chief. In fact, the more I think about it, the more I like him for the attempt. There's something uncanny about the man. Maybe he's a sociopath beneath that Marine Corps veneer. He wouldn't be the first."

"But from being interviewed by ACU 12 to attempted murder? It seems a bit hard to believe."

"In that case, maybe past sins are catching up with you."

"Could be. In any case, that was it. Needless to say, not a word about this incident to anyone, not even your teams. Thank you." As they left my office, my communicator chimed. Hera. I touched it to accept the link. "Good morning. What's up?"

"Good morning to you, too," she replied in a cheerful voice. "I just finished speaking with the Sécurité Spéciale's Caledonia station chief." When she saw my astonished look, she chuckled. "Yes, we occasionally talk, even though they're the opposition. It keeps the body count low, and yes, the station chief is known to us, although we don't socialize. Anyway, he said the Sécurité Spéciale isn't interested in you and not responsible for Saturday's attempt on your life. Take that with as many grains of salt as you want. More importantly, I made it crystal clear that you're on the same protected list as Zack and me, meaning if they try anything against you, we will massively retaliate, up to targeting the Sécurité Spéciale's director general on Earth. They take that very seriously."

It took me a few seconds to process what she said. "Thank you, I guess."

"No thanks necessary. You're my friend. I probably should have put you on the protected list before this. But it doesn't mean you should go out into town on a Saturday night just yet. If it wasn't the Sécurité Spéciale, then there's an unknown gunning for you."

"We were speculating that Lieutenant Colonel Horik, the brig commander, might be after me since I put him on notice that he was part of my investigation into Captain Montoni's death." I gave Hera a rundown of Horik's interview the previous Friday.

By the time I was done, a faint frown creased her forehead. "Hmm, I must have my people look at him to see if he's the sort who might become violent. That wasn't him who made the attempt, right?"

"No. Unless he was disguised."

"And I should know how good disguises can be. Okay, let me have a crack at Horik while you stay away from him for a few days."

"I was going to let him stew for a while anyway, to see if he comes up with a fresh lie about how the brig log was tampered with the night of Montoni's death, something to let me pull on a thread that will unravel his story."

"Good. Oh, I almost forgot. I have the surveillance video from the parkade. Your people should get a copy momentarily."

"Excellent, thanks."

"My pleasure. Talyn, out."

Protected list with the Sécurité Spéciale? Just when I thought Hera's world couldn't be more bizarre, she went and proved me wrong. Still, it was nice of her to put me on it.

Arno poked his head back into my office. "Chief, we've just received a copy of the parkade's surveillance video for Saturday evening, though from an unknown source."

"One of Admiral Talyn's operatives, no doubt. Pipe it over to me."

"Already done."

I gestured at Arno to come in and sit while I called it up on my primary display. After going through several minutes of nothing, I finally appeared on the screen, entering the parkade at ground level, the man who shot at me a few paces behind. I stopped the video and enlarged his image.

"Does he look like anyone we know?"

Arno scratched his beard. "Not really. Young is shorter and fatter, so that leaves him out. Horik under a good disguise? Possibly. Our man has the same general build and facial structure."

I let the video run again, and the view soon changed to the level I'd parked on. We watched the man pull a gun from beneath his jacket and take aim. I froze the playback again.

"Notice anything, Arno?"

"He's left-handed. Can you focus on that hand?"

"Sure." I pulled the hand in until it filled the display.

"See on his pinkie? There's an indent at its base as if he's removed a ring he usually wears. Now, who do we know is left-handed and wears a pinkie ring?" Arno gave me a cocked eyebrow.

I thought back to the people we've met since arriving on Caledonia.

"Horik."

Arno nodded, his beard bobbing. "Just so. It could be a coincidence that your would-be killer shares two distinct characteristics with Anton Horik, but I doubt it. Only ten to twelve percent of humans are left-handed, and based on my admittedly anecdotal evidence, the number of men who wear pinkie rings is much less than that. Plus, the man who shot at you is of the right size and shape to be Horik. And Horik is almost certainly a sociopath. There is nothing behind his eyes, no soul. However, if he is, he controls it admirably."

"What do I do with this knowledge, or at least this suspicion?"

Arno shrugged. "Not a clue, Chief. I suppose you could go up to him and ask where he was last Saturday, around nineteen hundred. But he'll almost certainly have an alibi, maybe even an ironclad one."

"Admiral Talyn asked me to stay away from Horik for a few days while her people check him out, so that's not an immediate possibility."

"Well, I suppose you'll have to make do with administrative work for now." He climbed to his feet and ambled out of my office.

Leaving me to face the tasks of the commanding officer, Anti-Corruption Unit 12, because I had nothing else. I did, however, tell Hera about our suspicions concerning the man who shot at me.

***

Three days later, I received a call from Hera.

"He's quite the lad, our Lieutenant Colonel Anton Horik," she said after we exchanged the usual pleasantries. "It appears he's a protégé of General Terak, for one thing. She got him promoted to lieutenant colonel and command of the Fleet's number one brig here in Sanctum. Before that, he was the commanding officer of a Fleet prison colony on Parth, one of five on the planet, and reputed to have been the most brutal during his term. Over two dozen prisoners, lifers mostly, died during his tenure, more than twice as many as under his predecessor and three times as many as under his successor."

"Let me guess — all of natural causes and suicides."

"Yes."

"And no one thought his death rate was worth investigating?"

"General Terak likely shut down any questions. She was the officer in charge of brigs and military prisons before becoming Provost Marshal of the Armed Forces."

"Convenient. And I'll bet his record of losing detainees in the Sanctum brig is being equally suppressed by Terak."

"Without a doubt."

"So why is Terak loyal to Horik, and I assume vice versa?"

"I don't know, but they first served together when Terak was a military police company commander as a major, and Horik was her first sergeant over twenty years ago on Cascadia. Something might have happened back then to cement their relationship because when Terak was promoted to lieutenant colonel and assigned to command the brig in Sanctum, Horik was promoted to sergeant major and came with her. From there, she's either taken him with her or arranged for a plum assignment. She also likely pushed for his commissioning as a captain when she was a full colonel on the brigadier general's promotion list, even though Horik wasn't considered that suitable."

I smirked. "And now he's a lieutenant colonel who may or may not be going around trying to assassinate Constabulary assistant commissioners. What a career progression!"

"Yes. Let's discuss that for a moment. Everything my agents have picked up about the man shows he's cold, methodical, and dangerous. Perhaps even very dangerous because he isn't particularly bright. If you're right about him being the shooter, and you probably are, that means he'll try again because, to his eyes, you represent a peril not only to himself but to his patron, General Terak."

"Surely Horik knows my death won't change anything regarding the investigation into Montoni's death and his involvement. In fact, it'll make things worse because my second in command will scrutinize him even more than I have so far."

"Anton Horik could be the sort to get tunnel vision and focus on one element to the detriment of all others. And you're the element of immediate threat he sees. Meaning you remain in danger."

"Don't worry. I won't leave the base. It'll be strictly the office, the gym, and home for the foreseeable future. But now that I know more about him, may I interview Horik again?"

Hera let out a snort. "If I said no, you'd do it anyway, so have fun."

"Thanks."

"Talyn, out."

So Lieutenant Colonel Anton Horik was General Terak's creature. Interesting. After interviewing him last Friday, I was surprised I didn't hear from the general. Surely she knew about that by now. Maybe she was merely keeping clear so she could strike more decisively later if I got too close to Horik, like after the next interview.

— Thirty —

"Colonel Horik, thank you for coming." I entered the interview room with Arno on my heels early that afternoon. Destine would watch from her desk.

He gave me an appraising stare as we sat across from him. "It's not like I have much choice when summoned by the head of ACU 12."

"Indeed, not." I locked eyes with him and was struck once more by how there was nothing behind them, no soul. "Colonel, did you figure out who tampered with the log and what was removed?"

"No."

"Meaning you tried and failed or didn't try?"

He briefly glanced over my right shoulder. "I noted no evidence of tampering and left it at that."

"Not the answer I was hoping for, Colonel. But let's move on to something else." I saw a flash of interest in his eyes and perhaps a bit of worry. "Where were you between seventeen-hundred hours and twenty hundred hours last Saturday?"

His stony expression didn't change. "At home."

"Can anyone verify that?"

"Yes."

"Who?"

"I'd rather not say."

"You're unattached and live alone, which means you had a visitor."

"Congratulations, Assistant Commissioner. You got me there. Yes, I had a visitor. Now what's this about?"

"On Saturday evening, someone tried to kill me with a needler in the Hope Street parkade."

Horik immediately scoffed. "And you're accusing me?"

"Could I examine your left hand?"

He raised it.

"Please remove your pinkie ring."

Horik complied.

"Now imagine you have a weapon in your hand, and it's pointing to your right."

I touched the controls embedded in the tabletop, and the image of the hand holding the needler appeared on the interview room's primary display.

Arno and I compared Horik's hand to the image, then glanced at each other. We had a match.

"What is this?" Horik asked, alarmed by the view on the display.

"That, Colonel, is the hand of the man who shot at me in the Hope Street parkade just before twenty-hundred hours last Saturday, taken from the security video." I zoomed the image out so we could see all of him. "I'd say that even though he doesn't look like you, his left hand is a match. Can you explain it?"

Horik shrugged with irritation. "How the hell should I? That's clearly not me, and a visual match on a hand is hardly proof of anything."

"Yet the man is of the same height and build as you and has the same underlying facial structure. He may not look like you, but a good disguise, the sort used by undercover operatives, will do that."

"As I told you, I was at home with a guest."

"And I'll need your visitor's identity so I can ask him or her to corroborate your alibi."

"Oh, this is ludicrous." A scowl appeared on his square features. "Why would I, a lieutenant colonel in Fleet Security, commanding officer of the most important brig in the Service, attempt to murder a Constabulary assistant commissioner?"

"That's what I'd like to know. Now, who was your guest?"

Horik glanced away again. "Colonel Saul Butler. He dropped by for supper and a drink."

"And Colonel Butler will confirm this?"

"Yes."

"Why were you reluctant to name him?"

"Because you were getting up my nose, Assistant Commissioner and I become uncooperative when someone does that."

"Do you now? That's not a good idea when you're dealing with me. I get annoyed at deliberate obstruction and charge people with perverting the course of justice. Now please hold up your hand again in the same way you did just now."

When he complied, after staring at me with overt hostility for a few seconds, Arno raised his tablet and took a picture.

"You can put your ring back on."

"This isn't evidence of anything." Did he sound a lot less self-assured than a moment ago, or was it wishful thinking on my part?

"On the contrary, Colonel." I glanced at Arno, and we stood. "You're free to go. For now."

Then, we left the interview room without another word.

"I think you rattled him, Chief," Arno said once we were in my office. "Will you call Butler?"

"Oh, right away, before Horik has the chance to line up a story with him."

But Colonel Butler was in a meeting with General Terak and, therefore, not immediately available. When he called back forty-five minutes later, he was unctuously apologetic.

"So sorry I couldn't get back right away. And what can I do for you, Assistant Commissioner?"

"Do you mind telling me where you were last Saturday, between seventeen-hundred and twenty hundred?"

"Of course not. I was at Anton Horik's place for drinks and supper. I arrived around seventeen-thirty and left shortly before twenty-one hundred." He gave me a winning smile. "Was that all you wanted?"

"Do you and Anton sup together often?"

"Once every few months, I suppose. Anton and I go way back to when he was a sergeant major, and I a junior captain freshly commissioned from command sergeant."

"When you worked at the Sanctum brig?"

"No, the 102nd MP Battalion here in Sanctum, back when General Terak was the CO and Anton, the battalion sergeant major, after their tours at the brig. I was her adjutant and worked closely with Anton. We've been friends ever since. In fact, Anton was commissioned the same day I became a major. May I ask what this is about?"

"Colonel Horik gave you as an alibi for Saturday evening."

"Oh dear. And why does he need an alibi?" Something in Butler's eyes told me he knew damn well the reason.

"I'll have to pass on telling you that, Colonel. This is a matter pertaining to my investigation into Captain Montoni's death."

"And did you get what you needed from me?"

"I did, thank you. Enjoy the rest of your day."

His image faded as I sat back and contemplated my office's far wall. We'd have to do this the hard way. I summoned Arno and Destine and told them about my conversation with Butler.

"What I'd like you to do is canvass Horik's neighbors about last Saturday and determine if anyone noticed Horik or Butler. Find out about any security systems in the area as well and figure out whether they'd have a visual record of Horik's home."

Both nodded, and Arno said, "Will do, Chief. We'll leave right after we change into civvies."

"Good idea — you'll be less noticeable."

"That was the plan."

***

Arno and Destine returned late in the afternoon and came to see me directly as I was wrapping up for the day.

"We got little from the neighbors. It's a nice, leafy suburban area with plenty of space between houses but no nosy old people who spend their days spying on everyone. Horik's been living there for several years, yet he keeps to himself and isn't well known beyond the fact he's a senior Marine Corps officer. However, we got a copy of the surveillance sensor record from the house across the street. It should give us something." Arno pulled a data wafer from his suit pocket. "Do you mind if we watch it here and now?"

"No. Give it to me." I placed the wafer on my desktop reader and called up its sole file, scrolling through to seventeen-hundred and letting it play at an accelerated rate. We saw the neighbor's front yard and the front of Horik's house across the street, with the occasional car zooming by. When the time counter hit eighteen hundred without showing Colonel Butler pulling up, I stopped the playback.

"I guess Butler has been telling me lies."

"Let's run it from twenty-hundred onward," Arno suggested.

I cued up the recording, and we watched Horik's house, darkened save for a porch light until twenty-one hundred when a car pulled up and drove into the garage.

"That's Horik's vehicle," Arno said. "Meaning he was out and not hosting Colonel Butler. We'll dial it back to earlier in the day and see if we can catch him leaving, Chief. You might as well hit the gym."

"Thanks." I returned the data wafer to him and stood, stretching. "It's a wonder Horik didn't think about the surveillance suite of the house across the street."

Destine made a face. "He probably didn't figure he'd become a suspect so easily, sir. Or, like Admiral Talyn said, he was suffering from tunnel vision at the time, focused only on eliminating you."

"And an amateurish attempt it was, Chief."

"I doubt Horik has killed anyone other than inmates under his care, Arno. He's no professional assassin, and the admiral did say he wasn't all that bright."

"A true meathead, eh?" Arno grinned at me.

"You like that slur on Fleet Security, don't you?"

"Hey," he raised both hands in a gesture of surrender, "I didn't come up with it. The term goes back to the twentieth century, which makes it hoary if not honorable — I checked. And if the term fits…"

As I entered the gym, I felt myself under observation but couldn't find by who, and so I exercised with less vigor and more alertness, to no avail, unfortunately.

Since it started raining while I was exercising, I took the subterranean shuttle back to the senior officers' block, and at that time of day — it being past eighteen hundred — there were few others aboard. Still, when I hopped off and headed for the lower-level entrance, my senses were at heightened vigilance until I reached my sixth-floor apartment and let myself in. A sudden rush of relaxation overcame me as the door clicked shut, proving that I'd been more keyed up than I had figured.

If the noose was slowly tightening around Anton Horik's neck, why did it feel as if another noose was searching for mine?

— Thirty-One —

"Horik left home at oh-seven-hundred Saturday morning and didn't return until twenty-one-hundred Saturday evening," Arno announced when I poked my head into his office early the next day. "Or at least his car did. We couldn't see exactly who was inside, but I doubt he'd have sent it off by itself for fourteen hours. Besides, there was no activity at his home during that time."

"Well, that corresponds to my movements. He probably picked me up as I left the base and followed me to the hiking trail, but didn't find any spot where he and I were alone."

"Have you checked your car for a tracking device?"

"No. But I'll do so when I get home."

"Will you interview Horik and Butler again today?"

I nodded. "Yes, this morning, if I can get a hold of them."

Horik was unavailable when I called his office, but Butler was, so I invited him over to mine for ten-thirty without giving a hint about why I was interviewing him.

At ten-thirty on the dot, he appeared in my open doorway, smiling. "Good morning, Assistant Commissioner."

"Good morning, Colonel. Please come in and sit." I gestured at one of the chairs across from my desk. Arno was occupying the other while Destine watched remotely from her desk.

When he'd done so, I studied him silently for several heartbeats, our eyes meeting, his questioning, mine revealing nothing.

"You told me you were at Anton Horik's place Saturday from seventeen-thirty to twenty-one hundred."

He inclined his head. "Yes."

"What if I said we have evidence you weren't there, that Anton wasn't even at home?"

"And what evidence would that be?" He was as suave as always, but there was a definite glint of alarm in his steady gaze.

"We have surveillance video from a neighbor whose sensor pickups happen to cover the front of Anton Horik's house. It shows Horik's car leaving at oh-seven hundred and returning at twenty-one hundred. What it doesn't show is you arriving. Can you explain that?"

"Does your surveillance video cover the right day?"

"It's date-time stamped, so yes."

Butler glanced away, jaw muscles working.

"I could charge you with perverting the course of justice for lying to me during the conduct of an investigation, Colonel, so if you had a good reason, now's the time to speak up."

I could almost see the gears in Butler's brain moving as he parsed his choices.

"All right, so I lied. Anton asked me to cover for him," he said, still looking at a spot somewhere beyond my left shoulder. "I wasn't with him on Saturday."

"Why did he ask you to cover for him?"

Now that he'd chosen his course, Butler's eyes met mine again. "He didn't say, and I didn't ask."

"Do you provide your friends with alibis often?"

He shrugged. "Occasionally. You know how it is when someone has a forbidden romance or engages in activities that aren't considered salubrious by their close friends and relatives."

"And you, a senior Fleet Security officer, thought it would be a good idea to lie to me?"

A rueful smile tugged at Butler's lips. "I obviously underestimated your resourcefulness, Assistant Commissioner. However, no harm done."

"Oh, but there is harm done, Colonel, certainly to your credibility as a witness, for one thing."

"Will you charge me?"

I thought about it for a few seconds, then shook my head. It wouldn't do much good. Butler might receive a slap on the wrist, nothing more.

"Since you confessed, no." I held his gaze in silence for several seconds. "Care to speculate why Anton Horik asked you to give him an alibi?"

Another shrug. "Not particularly. I did it out of friendship, and I now see that might not have been the best idea."

Now why did I get the impression that Butler was aware of Horik's attempt to kill me? Or at least that we were looking at him for it. Perhaps it was time I let him know about our suspicions.

"Then let me tell you why. We think your friend Anton tried to assassinate me at approximately twenty-hundred hours last Saturday in the Hope Street parkade after shadowing me all day, looking for an opportunity."

Butler's eyes widened at the revelation, but there was something phony in his reaction and I was convinced he'd been aware all along.

"Really? Oh, my. That is serious. Are you sure it was him?"

"Whoever it was wore a disguise, a good one, but he had certain indicators that linked him to Horik."

"Why? Why would Anton try to terminate you?"

"I can only think of one reason, Colonel, and that's because he's somehow involved in Captain Montoni's death. A death which I continue to investigate as suspicious, notwithstanding Horik's assertions it stemmed from natural causes. And I have reason to believe he or someone he knows is involved."

Butler shook his head. "I'm sorry, Assistant Commissioner, but I have a hard time visualizing Anton as a merciless killer. And because you're continuing your investigation into Montoni? Please. That doesn't sound plausible."

"Yet here we are, Colonel, with mounting evidence against your friend." I paused. "Unless you know of things I don't, such as what happened at the brig the night Montoni died. You see, we have evidence the log was tampered with. Eighteen minutes were excised and replaced. An expert job, one which most investigators would have missed, but not us."

"I have no idea what happened in the brig, but tampering with the logs is a serious matter that can result in a court martial for those responsible. You see, we rely on the logs to ensure detainees are properly recorded and treated."

"I'm aware of that, which is the main reason why I'm still investigating Montoni's death. It can't be a coincidence someone changed the log minutes before she died. Thank you, Colonel. You may go.”

Butler seemed taken aback by the abruptness of his dismissal but climbed to his feet and left without another word.

“Impressions?”

“He was lying,” Destine said via the intercom. “He knew why Horik asked him to provide an alibi.”

Arno nodded. “Agreed.”

“Question is, does he know Horik did it or merely that we suspect him of doing so?”

“If the latter, then maybe we’ve sown doubt in his mind about his friend’s sanity, which could prove useful, Chief.”

“And if the former, then he’s an accessory to attempted murder.”

“What do you want to bet he’s talking with Horik right now — or will be when he gets back to his office?”

“No bet, Arno. In fact, I’m counting on it.”

He cocked a questioning eyebrow at me. “You want Butler to stampede Horik into doing something stupid?”

“Or at least get him worried enough that he makes mistakes. It’s the only way we get ahead on this one. We have plenty of circumstantial evidence but nothing concrete enough to justify an arrest.”

Yet Horik remained unreachable that day, and by the next morning, he’d gone off on leave for a week, destination unknown. When Arno and Destine checked his residence, no one was home. The helpful neighbor who'd provided the surveillance sensor recording said Horik had left around twenty-two hundred hours in his car the previous evening.

And so, I did the next best thing — I issued a 'be on the lookout' or BOLO for Lieutenant Colonel Anton Horik with the Caledonian Police Service, the star system's civilian cops. I deliberately didn't issue one with Fleet Security because I didn't know who to trust at this point, though I figured my notice would make its way back to them in due course. It did.

"Why did you put out a BOLO on Anton Horik?" A visibly irritated Colonel Butler asked me a few days later.

"I see your friends in the Caledonian Police finally got back to you. I put a BOLO on Horik because I need to speak with him, and he's made himself mysteriously incommunicado just after you and I spoke about his possible involvement in an attempt on my life and the death of Captain Montoni. You wouldn't happen to know where your friend vanished to, now would you?"

"No, I wouldn't. But I think your actions are going beyond the bounds of good policing, Assistant Commissioner. Putting out a notice on an innocent senior Fleet Security officer is a bit much."

"Innocent, Colonel? I'd be careful characterizing Horik in such a manner, considering the evidence we're accumulating," I replied in a tone as dry as the Great Caledonian Erg. "His taking leave at the last minute, a few hours after you and I last spoke, isn't just suspicious. It's more evidence that something isn't right in Fleet Security. I think I'll be further enlarging my investigation to encompass you and your actions."

"Oh, be very cautious, Morrow. You don't know who you're dealing with."

"As a matter of fact, I'm beginning to understand. Good day, Colonel."

I cut the link before he could reply and settled back in my chair, wondering what I'd unleashed. Hopefully, it would be something that brought me closer to the truth, but I feared I might find myself facing renewed peril. Butler had sounded like a man getting close to the end of his patience, which, in turn, made me wonder about his involvement beyond giving Horik a fake alibi.

And since Butler was Terak's executive assistant, I also had to wonder about the general herself. I'd immersed myself back in my work when my communicator chimed again and speak of the devil.

"Good day, General. What can ACU 12 do for you?"

"Saul Butler told me about the BOLO you issued for Anton." She came across as aggrieved, though her eyes smoldered with repressed anger. "He's done nothing criminal, so you're going to rescind it.

Now. Before Fleet Security's reputation suffers through your thoughtless actions."

"No."

"What do you mean, no?"

"I'm not sure how I can make myself any clearer, General. I do not take orders from you or anyone else in this star system. We've accumulated a lot of circumstantial evidence pointing toward Anton Horik having engaged in criminal activities. I need to speak with him now, not in a week or whenever he returns from his impromptu leave."

"Yes, Saul told me about those alleged crimes. I cannot believe Anton would do anything of the sort, and I've known him for a long time. Now rescind the BOLO, or I will make an official complaint to Assistant Chief Constable Sorjonen."

"Be my guest, General, but ACC Sorjonen won't countermand me."

She glared at me and my air of self-confidence. "You're sure of that?"

"He's not in the habit of second-guessing his officers in the field. Now was that everything? Because I have a file I need to get back to."

"This isn't the last of it. Terak, out."

I'd barely touched the file when my communicator chimed. This time, it was the Caledonian Police Service. They'd found Anton Horik.

— Thirty-Two —

"Where is this place?" Arno asked after I told him and Destine we were heading north to see Horik, who was apparently occupying a lakeside cabin.

"Near a lumber town by the name Frejus."

Arno called up a map and grunted. "A thousand kilometers, and no superhighway leading up to it. I think we should sign out an aircar."

"Good idea. I'd like to get to him before Butler does." When Arno gave me a questioning gaze, I said, "Butler has friends in the Caledonian Police who informed him about my BOLO. They're sure to tell him I've been informed of Horik's location."

"I'll get us an aircar from the base motor pool." Destine left my office for hers.

An hour later, having quickly packed overnight bags just in case, we climbed aboard an unmarked military aircar and, with Destine at the controls, drove out through the main gate before lifting off since there was no flying allowed on the base. Destine pointed us north, and we gained altitude under the direct guidance of the civilian centralized traffic control system. Then we left Sanctum and the sub-tropics behind as we headed toward more temperate climes.

"What do you think we'll find, Chief?"

I shrugged. "Not a clue. Horik relaxing by the lake? Doing some fishing? Does this planet have comestible fish?"

"I'm not sure."

"You mean you haven't studied the matter?" I gave Arno a mock surprised look, complete with raised eyebrows.

"No. Sorry, Chief. Some things are a little too far out for me, and comestible Caledonian fish are even further out than that."

"I'm stunned, Arno."

He looked away from me and muttered something that suspiciously sounded like, "We're aware."

But I knew it was in good fun, so I winked when he glanced in my direction again with a sheepish air.

The rest of the two-and-a-half-hour trip mainly passed in silence, Destine keeping her eyes on the autopilot, Arno snoozing in his corner, and me fretting about what I'd do when I came face-to-face with Anton Horik now that his alibi had been thoroughly destroyed.

The rays of Caledonia's sun were lengthening along with the shadows of the Northern Alps when we finally flew over Frejus, a town of some thirty thousand inhabitants in the alpine foothills whose key industries were lumber and mining on a grand scale. Lake Harfang, along whose shores Horik's cottage lay, was in the first valley to the north of Frejus, a forty-five-minute ride by ground car but a five-minute run for us.

Destine slowed our aircar to one-tenth of its maximum speed as she threaded the way through the pass at low altitude, emerging over a long, narrow body of water with houses dotting its banks. The one purportedly occupied by Horik was two-thirds of the way down, and we flew over the lake a few dozen meters above the surface and a hundred meters from shore. The cottages we saw between stands of native trees appeared rustic from the outside, many seemingly built of logs but with modern, polarized windows. Most had decks overlooking the lake. However, since the day was blustery, we saw no one outside.

"There it is." Arno pointed out the window at an L-shaped, single-story structure sitting almost on the shoreline. "And it looks like he has company."

"An aircar just like ours parked beside Horik's vehicle," Destine said. "How much do you want to bet that's Colonel Butler?"

"No bets. He must have arrived within the last hour or so if his civilian police buddies informed him at the same time as they told us."

Destine landed us beside the other aircar, and after checking our weapons, we climbed out and headed for the front door, which opened at our approach. Anton Horik appeared in the opening, face like stone, dead eyes staring at us. He wore civilian clothes — a loose checked shirt over khaki slacks and moccasins.

"Go away, Assistant Commissioner. I have nothing to say to you."

"And I have a lot of questions for you. So no, I'm not going away. Now we can do this on your front porch or indoors. I don't care which." I approached the door until I stood almost nose to nose with Horik, close enough to prevent him from slamming it in my face. "Is Colonel Butler with you, perchance?"

"He is," Butler's voice called out from behind Horik. "And glad to see you've not wasted any time getting here. How about you let them in, Anton?"

Horik glanced over his shoulder. "Fuck 'em, Saul. I have nothing to say."

But then he stepped back, clearing the way. Saul Butler stood in what appeared to be the main living area, wearing his silver-trimmed black uniform and an air of concern as he watched us enter the cottage. Once Destine and Arno had followed me into the room, Horik closed the door behind them.

"Say your piece, then get the hell out of here."

I turned to Horik. "How about we sit?"

"No."

"Okay. Did Colonel Butler tell you we discovered you have no alibi for last Saturday, that we have evidence you left your home at oh-seven hundred and came back at twenty-one hundred?"

"Yeah. That still doesn't prove I shot at you."

"Where were you between those hours?"

I saw Horik and Butler exchange a brief glance.

"I was out of town, hiking on the Skyline Trail until about seventeen-hundred, then I came back into Sanctum and enjoyed a leisurely supper at the Gaetano Pub." He stared at me defiantly.

As stories went, this one wasn't too bad. The Skyline Trail's parking lot also served the Wolf Trail, which I'd taken, meaning if we found evidence of his private car being there on Saturday, he'd already given us an explanation.

"This pub, where is it?"

"On the western outskirts of town. And before you ask, I paid with cred chips, not my card. Sorry."

"So, if I ask the pub's staff, they'll recognize you?"

"I doubt it. The place was jammed, and it was my first and only time there."

He was lying. I could see it in his eyes.

"And yet, we've matched your left hand to the gunman's in the surveillance video from the parkade."

Horik shrugged. "A hand isn't sufficient to indict me. Look, Morrow, all you have is circumstantial. If you ever uncover any factual evidence, we can talk. Until then, get the hell out of my house."

"You own this place?"

"Yes. Not that it's any of your business."

I saw Destine, standing behind Horik, casually shove her hand in her trouser pocket out of the corner of my eye and withdraw it moments later, and I knew she'd pulled out a tiny listening device. She glanced at me, then over my shoulder, indicating I should distract Butler. I turned toward him.

"Colonel, why did you come here?"

"Because I knew you'd be on an aircar to find Anton the moment you heard a result from your BOLO, and I only thought it fair to warn him so he wouldn't be taken unawares. I owed him that."

"You took a two-hour trip just to warn Anton? I find it hard to believe."

"He didn't have his communicator on, and I didn't know where he was until the police found him. Besides, Anton's a friend, and we tend to be rather serious about covering each other's backs in Fleet Security."

"Up to and including false alibis," I replied dryly. "It makes me wonder what else Fleet Security is covering up."

"Come now, Assistant Commissioner. There's no call to be nasty." Butter wouldn't have melted in his mouth, yet his eyes remained hard as flint. "We're all on the same side, that of law and order in the Fleet."

"Indeed. Thank you for your time, Colonel Horik, and yours, Colonel Butler." I nodded toward the door as I looked at my wingers. "Let's go."

We trooped out to our aircar and climbed aboard.

"Am I right in thinking you left them with a bug, Destine?"

"Yes, sir. A short-range model, however." She pulled her tablet from a tunic pocket and touched its controls, and Butler's voice filled the passenger compartment.

"You panicked, Anton. Twice. The first time when you took a pot-shot at her in the parkade and the second time when you fled here. Make it three times, and you're out."

"I'm out? What is that supposed to mean?"

"Look, Anton, we can't afford a weak link. You need to get a grip on yourself. Morrow thinks she knows what happened, yet she doesn't have incontrovertible evidence and won't find any. By all means, stay here until the end of your leave, but then come back to

Sanctum and your job. Morrow will eventually tire of pursuing you and move on to something else."

"Then how about you find her something else, Saul? Right now. To get her off my back. Or maybe make sure she has an accident. A fatal one."

"It might still happen if — and that's a big if — she gets too close. But I doubt she will. As for Montoni, that case is closed. They'll never prove she ingested rapidly dissolving poison."

There was silence, then Butler said, *"They're still parked outside. I wonder…"*

"Waiting for you to leave so they can go at me again?"

"No. But they might have dropped a listening device. That tall warrant officer did reach into her pocket."

"Aw, fuck. That would mean they have all they need to arrest me."

"No. They'd need a warrant to record our conversation, and I doubt they had the time to obtain one before they left Sanctum. Anything they may have heard is inadmissible."

"But they still know about me in the parkade, and from there it's not much of a stretch to infer I tried to kill her because of Montoni's death and the gap in the brig log. Damn it, why did Montoni have to get caught by Morrow? It's all her fault."

"And she paid for it with her life. Aha. Here we go."

Moments later, the link with the bug broke, and Destine said, "Butler must have found the device and neutralized it."

"Alright. Let's get out of here before they burst through the door waving blasters."

Destine flicked on the power plant, fed the thrusters, and we leaped straight into the air before turning south and speeding away.

"A shame the recording we just made isn't admissible in court, Chief. That would have wrapped up the case nicely."

"Not quite. We still don't know why they killed Montoni or induced her into committing suicide, nor do we know in what organization or cabal Horik is a weak link. Let's assume Montoni, Butler, and Horik are part of a cell of some kind and that Montoni was a traitor. It means Butler and Horik are also traitors. But for who do they work?"

"Sécurité Spéciale would be my guess."

"It is the most plausible," Destine said. "Are they remnants of Black Sword, I wonder? Or some new attempt at subverting the Fleet?"

I gave her a shrug. "If Montoni was recruited four or five years ago, I lean more toward a new attempt."

"Speaking of attempts, Chief, I'd take Butler's comment concerning you suffering a fatal accident seriously."

"You mean us suffering one, Arno. At this point, you and Destine are just as vulnerable as I am since you heard them speak via the bug."

A grim expression appeared on Arno's face. "True."

— Thirty-Three —

It was dark when we returned to Joint Base Sanctum and parked the aircar in the motor pool lot. We went our separate ways, each to our blocks, and I felt extreme fatigue once the door to my apartment shut behind me. A quick autochef supper, and then I sat on the balcony with a glass of Glen Arcturus, wondering what to do with the revelations we'd overheard. It was the worst sort of situation. The enemy knew we were aware, but we couldn't do anything with it because of admissibility. That we'd become targets was almost a foregone conclusion.

The following day, I'd barely settled behind my desk when my communicator chimed — Colonel Butler.

"Good morning, Assistant Commissioner."

"Colonel, What can I do for you?"

"We need to talk about what you heard yesterday, face-to-face."

I let out a bark of laughter. "Do you think I'll be putting myself at your mercy? You want to talk, well, let's talk. I assume our link is secure at your end because it certainly is at mine."

"Look, let's meet in the quadrangle in ten minutes. Nothing will happen to you there."

The quadrangle was the perfectly sculpted miniature park fronting Fleet HQ's main building. It had stone paths cutting through grassy areas lined with bushes and trees and a statue of Grand Admiral Kathryn Kowalski at its center.

"Isn't it a bit too public for your purposes?"

"You carry a jammer? Well, so do I. We can both activate ours and enjoy perfect privacy out in the open. What I have to discuss with you, I'd rather not commit to a link, no matter how secure."

"Plus, with jammers going, there's no way for me to record anything you say."

A cold smile appeared. "Just so. Please humor me, Assistant Commissioner. In ten minutes by the Grand Admiral's statue."

His image vanished, leaving me to decide whether I'd accept his invitation. My instinct said go, so I crossed the hall to Arno's office.

"I'm meeting with Colonel Butler in the quadrangle in ten minutes, and I'd like you to come with me and watch from a distance."

"What?" He stared at me as if I'd grown a second head. "How did this happen?"

"He just called me, saying we needed to talk about yesterday."

"And you'll blithely go? Are you mad?"

"The quadrangle is hardly the place for an assassination, and I'll be careful to stay out of reach in case he plans on slipping me a slow-acting dermal poison."

"You're determined to do this, aren't you?" Arno shook his head. But he stood and put on his beret, then checked his sidearm, which he carried in a pancake hip holster under his tunic.

I returned to my office for my beret and checked my sidearm as well, then we headed out to the quadrangle. When the statue came into sight, I left Arno and closed the remaining distance alone. As I got nearer, Colonel Butler appeared, coming from the other direction. He glanced at Arno, then back at me.

"You brought your faithful chief inspector, I see. Well, no matter. So long as he's out of hearing range and both our jammers are working, it's fine." He pulled a small flat rectangle from his tunic pocket and showed it to me. "Mine is on, as you can see."

I fished out mine, switched it on, and showed it to him. "Now, what did you want to discuss, Colonel?"

"Shall we sit?" He gestured at a bench facing the bronze, life-sized replica of the Fleet's most influential leader.

Since it was long enough to allow more than arm's length separation, I said, "Sure."

He sat at one end, I at the other, both of us facing each other. "Okay. I'm listening."

"Did you ever hear of Smert Shpionam?"

"No. What language is that?"

"Russian. It means Death to Spies."

"And?"

"After the Black Sword business, a few of us in Fleet Security formed a loose grouping of like-minded people dedicated to eradicating spies working for the enemy since Naval Intelligence would never catch all of them. We call ourselves Smert Shpionam, known by its abbreviation SMERSH. Historically, it referred to an organization working for a long-gone Earth nation. Its role was to find and eliminate any subversives infiltrating that country's military."

"How apt a name." My mind was racing at Butler's assertion he and presumably Horik was doing the same sort of work I was. "But why should I believe you?"

"Because I'm telling you the truth. We eliminate the bad guys, those who infiltrate the Fleet on behalf of the Sécurité Spéciale, the zaibatsu intelligence organizations, organized crime, and the like."

"So you're responsible for Montoni's death."

He nodded. "I visited her that night — it was my presence that was erased from the log — pretended I was from her secret employer and handed her a suicide pill to atone for getting caught."

"What if she hadn't taken it?"

"Then I would have had to return and use a more direct method. But people in her situation, who know it's hopeless, will often take the easy way out."

"You seemed to have some experience in the matter."

"She wasn't my first termination."

"Let me guess, the excess deaths in the brig under Anton Horik, they were also your handiwork?"

"Some. Others were Anton's. He has a minor character flaw that's nonetheless proved useful. You see, Anton enjoys killing people."

"You couldn't tell me what happened to Captain Gunter Wils and Brigadier General Aldous Greer, could you?"

A faint smile appeared. "Mine, I'm afraid. And Greer's spouse, Raylee Redvers. Wils and Redvers' bodies will never be found since they no longer exist. And please don't ask."

"Why leave Greer's body for us to discover?"

"So you could close his case and blame Redvers."

"And Wils?"

"I sent his yacht into the storm under remote control. Wils himself didn't suffer, and he didn't leave land."

"Why tell me this? We may be on the same general track, but I work within the law. You're nothing but a murderous vigilante, one who I'll put out of business. You can count on that."

"Please, Assistant Commissioner. You have nothing. This conversation never took place since our jammers ensure no recording is made, and even your chief inspector can't read our lips, let alone hear us." His smile returned. "As to why I'm telling you this? It's quite simple. I want you to understand that we're not traitors to the Fleet. Quite the contrary. You may be the Fleet's conscience, but we — Smert Shpionam, SMERSH — are the Fleet's guardians. And every organization needs its guardians, people who will go beyond the law for the common good."

The way he spoke, his gentle tone, his relaxed smile, and his words told me one thing for sure. This was a man who'd lost touch with reality long ago.

"Yet you and I are both charged with enforcing the law, Colonel. Not going beyond it. The fact you're killing people or forcing them to commit suicide makes you a murderous thug, even though your victims are criminals themselves."

His gaze hardened. "You can call me many things, but you will never call me a traitor."

"Perhaps. Is General Terak aware of your extracurricular activities?"

"No. Leave her out of this." The speed with which he answered made me doubt his veracity. Interesting.

"Again, why are you telling me all that?"

"So you can stop pursuing Montoni's death and bedeviling poor Anton. You have no evidence. You'll never get any evidence, and there are more of us than there are of you. I'd rather you keep going after the corrupt bastards and leave us to take care of traitors."

"You know I can't do that, Colonel. We of the Professional Compliance Bureau are the Last of the Incorruptibles, the ones who will uncover the truth and see that the guilty are punished no matter the personal cost to us."

A faint smile appeared though it didn't reach his eyes.

"You have the truth, and we are not guilty, or at least no more than Naval Intelligence was when they did a wholesale purge during the Black Sword business." Butler stood. "It would pain me to terminate you and your colleagues, but I will if necessary. Good day, Assistant Commissioner."

Then, he walked away, giving Arno a nod in passing.

When he'd vanished from view, I rose and joined Arno.

"What did he have to say, Chief?"

"Let's wait until we're in my office."

"Right."

Once there, I gave Arno an almost verbatim rundown of our conversation, leaving him to stare at me in amazement.

"Smert Shpionam? Is he for real?"

"Oh, I think reality left Butler long ago. Him, Horik, and the rest of the cabal. But that makes them even more dangerous than we thought."

"What are we going to do about it?"

"The first thing I'll do is call Admiral Talyn and bring her up to speed. She may have ideas. You might as well stick around."

I opened a link with Hera's office, and wonder of wonders, she was available, so I told her about my meeting with Butler.

"Do you realize what's funny about this? When we first stumbled across Black Sword, they were eliminating our fellow Naval Intelligence operatives by the dozens, and Zack called them Smert Shpionam. That the title would be used by people hunting enemy agents nowadays is a bit ironic."

"Indeed. But I'm at a loss about what to do with Butler's revelations. He admitted to murdering Wils, Greer, and Redvers, as well as giving Montoni a suicide pill, and has the Almighty only knows how many other deaths on his conscience. That's if he has one. Yet he claims the same level of guilt as you and your people during the Black Sword purge, meaning none at all."

Hera made a face. "The Black Sword business wasn't our finest hour. We ended up with blood on our hands, but it was necessary so we could cut out the rot before it became too pervasive and threatened the Fleet's independence. Nowadays? Not so much. We know we have traitors in our midst, but they're manageable, especially now with your unit on Caledonia. Unfortunately, I have no advice for you about how to deal with this Smert Shpionam. Butler is right. With nothing more than the circumstantial evidence you have at this point, you're dead in the water. But let me think about it."

"All right, Hera. And thanks."

"For you, anything. Talyn, out."

I gave Arno a wry look. "If Hera has no ideas, maybe we are truly stuck."

Then a thought struck me. It must have shown on my face because Arno frowned.

"Oh, no," he said. "Whatever you're about to come up with, forget it."

"At least let me explore the notion."

I explained, and he grudgingly admitted that it might just work, although he didn't like it one bit.

— Thirty-Four —

We bided our time until Horik returned from his vacation, doing nothing that would attract Butler's attention, although Frederick Vasiliev was getting close to arresting Colonel Young, who would surely fall victim to Smert Shpionam once we did so. And that wasn't going to happen on my shift.

I occupied my days carrying out the sort of administrative work commanding officers hate, but it had to be done. My evenings and weekend were spent at home, imitating a hermit, although I had supper with Hera at her place occasionally. I'd explained my plan to her, and she'd agreed it might work, although she considered it just as risky as Arno did.

Butler must have thought me convinced it would be best if I no longer pursued him and his friends because whenever we met, be it in the hallways or the officer's mess, he was unctuously polite with me, all smiles and expressions of friendship. He even took to calling me Caelin, demanding I address him as Saul rather than colonel since both of us wore the same rank insignia. I did so to further allay his suspicions.

But the moment Anton Horik was back in town, all that changed.

Arno, Destine, and I headed for the brig and his office on his first morning back, where we found him and his adjutant discussing matters that had cropped up during his absence.

"Out, please, Captain," I said, pointing at the adjutant and then the office door.

He looked at Horik, uncertain what to do. Horik himself seemed momentarily taken aback by our appearance and my harsh tone and had no immediate answer.

"I said out."

Destine reached for his arm, but the man finally complied. When he was gone, Destine closed the door.

"Lieutenant Colonel Anton Horik, I am Assistant Commissioner Caelin Morrow of the Constabulary's Anti-Corruption Unit 12. With me are Chief Inspector Arno Galdi and Warrant Officer Destine Bonta. I am arresting you on suspicion of falsifying documents, aiding and abetting murder, attempted murder, and perverting the course of justice. You do not have to say anything. But it may harm your defense if you do not mention when questioned something which you later rely on in court. Anything you do say may be given in evidence." I paused. "Do you understand?"

He stared at me with his soulless eyes, then nodded once. "I do. What I don't understand is how you have enough evidence to prove anything against me. Besides, Saul Butler spoke with you, didn't he? Explained what we were doing?"

"He did. Now, you're coming with us, either voluntarily in which case we won't manacle you, or involuntarily, in which case we will."

Horik didn't move a muscle. "Where are you taking me?"

"To our interview room."

"And then?"

I gave him a cold smile.

"You'll be held in the Sanctum Police detention cells until your bail hearing." When he cocked his head as if to say, you can't do that, I added, "There's no way we're leaving you in your own brig, Colonel Horik. For one thing, it would be inappropriate. For another, it might save your life."

"Save my life? What the hell are you talking about?"

"You might find yourself with an oh-one-thirty visitor offering you an honorable way out. A visitor whose powers of persuasion you might find hard to resist. At least in the civilian police cells, I can be assured you won't get any visitors, period."

Horik scoffed. "If anyone faces termination, it's you, Morrow. Arresting me is going too far. Much too far. My friends will make sure you pay."

"By friends, you mean the murderous little cabal that goes under the ridiculous name Smert Shpionam? Good luck to them."

"Since you've arrested me, I get to make one call. When will that be?"

"Once we're in our offices."

"So you can listen in."

"Of course. Now get up."

He stared at me for several heartbeats before complying. Then, he put on his beret. "Lead the way, Assistant Commissioner. I expect I'll be back behind my desk before the day is out."

Arno opened the office door and stepped aside to let us go first. When a curious adjutant looked up from his desk, Horik smiled.

"I need to help Assistant Commissioner Morrow with a few things. I should be back later today or tomorrow morning."

"Yes, sir."

None of us spoke during the drive back to our offices, and I let Horik have his one call before we interrogated him. Not surprisingly, it was to Saul Butler who told him to hang tight and not answer any questions. He'd show up with a lawyer within the hour. Butler sounded angry, although his face remained expressionless.

I then showed Horik to the interview room and left him alone to stew until his lawyer arrived since there was no point in attempting to question him. Forty-five minutes later, I had Butler in my office while Lieutenant Commander Amon Galindez of the Judge Advocate General's Defense Services was conferring with Horik.

"What's the matter with you, Morrow?" Butler asked as he shut the door behind him. I noted that it no longer was Caelin and supposed our false friendship was over before it had begun. "Arresting Anton when you have no evidence worth a damn."

"But I do, Saul. I have his hand, with a ninety-nine percent match, holding the needler. That's enough to arrest and keep him behind bars until his trial."

"Bullshit!" The word echoed across the room like the crack of a whip. "You need more, and you know it."

"I'll start with that and work my way through to the rest. Your little Smert Shpionam is going out of business, and you'll spend the rest of your life in a penal colony on Parth."

"I should have known you being so quiet for the last week hid evil intent."

"You're one to speak about evil, Saul, seeing as how you have what? A dozen deaths or more on your conscience?"

"All of them guilty of betraying the Fleet in one way or another."

"That still doesn't give you the right to commit murder." I stood. "You can watch my interrogation from the observation gallery next to the interview room."

"You won't get anything from Anton. He's a good man who doesn't speak out of turn."

"We shall see." I met Arno outside the interview room after dropping Butler off in the gallery where Destine already waited. "Ready?"

"Yup."

We entered the room, interrupting Galindez, who gave me a frown of annoyance, and sat across from Horik and him.

"Commander. Glad to see you again. Hopefully, your current client won't follow the previous one into the Infinite Void because of death by natural causes."

I gave Horik a significant look as I spoke that last sentence, but he seemed unmoved, his face carved from stone, his eyes expressionless and without a soul behind them. As an opener, I repeated the charges for which I'd arrested Horik and asked him if he had something to say concerning any of them or a statement to make.

"No comment."

"Were you acting on your own when you tried to assassinate me, or were you under orders?"

He crossed his arms and sat back in his chair. "No comment."

"I'll assume you were under orders when you tampered with the brig logs the night Captain Victoria Montoni died. Who gave those orders? Colonel Saul Butler?"

Did I see a brief flash in his eyes?

"Did he enter Captain Montoni's cell and convince her to take a suicide pill?"

"No comment."

And so it went for almost half an hour. I'd ask a question, and he'd give me the same answer — no comment. I had to give him props for consistency, but I knew this would be the interview's outcome anyway. Fortunately, I wasn't interrogating him in the hopes of getting answers.

"Alright. We're done here. Commander Galindez, I assume you'll be putting in for bail?"

"Indeed." He nodded. "And considering the scant evidence you apparently have, I'm sure it will be granted."

"In the meantime, I'm remanding Colonel Horik into the custody of the civilian police since he cannot be held in his own brig."

"Understood." Galindez turned to Horik. "It won't be for long. I have enough time to put in a bail application this morning, and, with any luck, the judge will grant it before the end of the day."

"Thanks."

"Do you need more private time with your client?"

"No, Assistant Commissioner." Galindez stood and tucked his tablet into a tunic pocket. Then, he gave Horik a nod and left the room.

"Okay, Colonel. Here's how we're going to do this. We secured brig coveralls in your size, and you'll exchange your uniform for them here, in this room. Chief Inspector Galdi will observe the switch and secure the bag with your belongings. It will be returned to you if you make bail. Then, Chief Inspector Galdi and Warrant Officer Bonta will take you to the central police station's detention cells to be held incommunicado except for your lawyer and members of ACU 12. Do you understand?"

His icy stare got even chillier. "Yes."

I rose and left the interview room, making way for Destine, who carried the navy-blue brig coveralls and shoes. Instead of returning to my office, I entered the observation gallery.

"You were right. Anton isn't a man who speaks out of turn. In fact, he says very little, as you may have noticed."

Butler didn't reply. Instead, he kept his eyes on the display showing Horik disrobing down to his underwear.

"It must be humiliating to go from commanding officer of the brig to detainee."

Butler glanced at me. "Anton will deal with it. However, I'm not so sure you'll be able to deal with the consequences of your actions today."

"And what's that supposed to mean?"

"Taking on Smert Shpionam could prove fatal for you."

"If I didn't know better, I'd consider that a threat."

A cruel smile appeared. "Oh, but it is."

"Surely you don't mean that."

"I never say things I don't mean, Morrow." He gave the display one last glance, then left the observation gallery. When I exited it moments later, he'd vanished.

The bait had been cast upon troubled waters. Now all that remained was for me to hook the fish and stay alive while I did so.

— Thirty-Five —

Lieutenant Commander Galindez was good. He got Horik bailed by sixteen hundred that day, and we returned the bag with his uniform and personal effects after he spent less than six hours in the Sanctum Police detention center.

The next morning, Horik was back at his job as commanding officer of the largest brig in the Fleet. And he was mad as hell. Fit to be tied, in the quaint expression Arno used after fetching him and driving him home.

I just hoped it would be enough to provoke him and Saul Butler into taking action against me, the sort I'd survive, but they wouldn't. Yet, as Arno had said, only half joking when I proposed my idea, I had better ensure my affairs were in order.

I met with the military prosecutor, and although he was a bit hesitant to take on the case based solely on identifying Horik's left hand, he eventually agreed, provided I keep digging for more evidence — a confession being preferred. And he wouldn't push to have it heard earlier rather than later.

Then, I called in Colonel Butler and Lieutenant Colonel Horik for formal interviews.

Butler's annoyance was plainly visible when Arno and I entered the room.

"Is this really necessary, Assistant Commissioner?"

"It is." We sat across from him. "You're not under caution, but we're recording the interview anyway. Now, did you visit Captain Victoria Montoni shortly before her death?"

"No comment."

"Did you give her a suicide pill and strongly suggest she take it since her usefulness to her employer was at an end?"

"No comment."

"Did you order Lieutenant Colonel Anton Horik to tamper with the brig log so that any record of you visiting Montoni was removed?"

"No comment."

"Are you a member of a group that calls itself Smert Shpionam?"

"No comment."

"And is that group responsible for the deaths of Brigadier General Aldous Greer, Raylee Redvers, Captain Gunter Wils, and the following?" I rattled off the names of those who'd died in the brig over the last five years.

"No comment." He was growing more exasperated with each question.

"Other than you and Anton Horik, who else is part of Smert Shpionam?"

"No comment."

"Or are you two the only members?"

Butler's eyes narrowed as he leaned forward, arms crossed. "No." A pause. "Comment."

I was finally getting to him and allowed myself a faint smile. "Is General Terak involved with Smert Shpionam?"

Butler exhaled loudly, nostrils flaring. "I told you to keep her out of this, Morrow."

"Oh, so there is a Smert Shpionam — a 'Death to Spies' — but the general isn't involved."

"Don't twist my words."

"How am I doing that?"

Butler looked away, clearly frustrated.

"What was the poison you gave Victoria Montoni?"

"No comment."

"Did you spend the entire eighteen minutes of the tampered log with her, and if so, what did you discuss?" Before he could answer, I said, "No comment, right?"

He glared at my mocking tone. "I don't appreciate your flippancy, Assistant Commissioner."

"Who decides that a putative traitor to the Fleet gets murdered? You? The general? Someone else?"

This time he remained silent, lips compressed into thin lines as if he was blocking words trying to escape his mouth.

"Colonel Butler is being non-responsive to the question."

"No comment."

At that moment, Destine entered the interview room. "Lieutenant Colonel Horik has arrived, sir."

"All right. That's it for now, Colonel Butler. Thank you. You're free to go, but I reserve the right to recall you at any time for further questions." I turned to Destine. "Warrant Officer Bonta, please escort Colonel Butler out of our offices and then show in Colonel Horik."

"Sir."

Butler left without a word, and thirty seconds later, a truculent Anton Horik entered the interview room, accompanied by Lieutenant Commander Galindez.

"Congratulations on getting your client bailed so quickly, Commander."

He gave me a half-shrug. "It's what I do, Assistant Commissioner, and I'm pretty good at it."

I turned my attention to Horik as he and Galindez sat.

"Did the brief stint behind bars cause you to reconsider whether you'll cooperate?"

"No comment."

"I guess not. You're still under caution, Colonel. Do I need to refresh your memory and repeat it?"

He shook his head once, hostile eyes meeting mine.

"Who besides you and Saul Butler have been killing so-called traitors?"

"No comment."

"Is Smert Shpionam merely you, Butler, and General Terak?"

"Leave the general out of this."

"Funny, but Saul Butler said the same thing when I mentioned her. I wonder why that is? So, it's just you and Butler, is it?"

He crossed his arms. "No comment."

"You know, I'll bet this whole Smert Shpionam nonsense was dreamed up as an excuse for two sociopaths who enjoy killing. You and Butler, you're nothing but a pair of vile murderers who wrapped themselves in a cloak of self-righteousness."

A flash of anger appeared in his eyes, but he didn't speak.

"Are you a murderous sociopath, Anton?"

Lieutenant Commander Galindez raised a hand. "Please, Assistant Commissioner."

I speared him with my gaze. "Please, what?"

"That sort of question goes beyond the bounds."

"Not in my interrogation room." I turned my attention back to Horik, who was growing visibly angrier by the second. "Are you a murderous sociopath?"

"No comment," he said between clenched teeth. His fingers were turning white from their death grip on his elbows, and he was shaking with suppressed rage. Not a lot, but enough to notice.

"I think you are, Anton. I think you enjoy killing or watching people die, just like your friend Saul Butler."

He looked away. "So what if I do? Prove it. But you can't because you have no damn evidence. About anything."

"We have your hand holding the gun that fired at me. That's enough for an appearance in front of a judge." I glanced at Arno and gave him a slight nod. We both stood simultaneously. "Thank you, Colonel, Commander. That was it for today. I reserve the right to recall you for further questioning at any time."

Then we left the interview room.

"I don't know about Butler," Arno said once we were behind closed doors in my office, "but Horik seems on the verge of cracking and doing something unforgivable."

"I sure hope so."

"Let's hope it won't end up with you on the ground bleeding out, Chief."

I gave Arno a wry grin. "I don't intend to finish my life that way, but unless you come up with a better idea, it's the best I've got to nail the bastards."

Arno held up a hand in a gesture of semi-surrender. "I know. And I admire you for putting your life on the line in a good cause. But I still don't like it, and neither does Destine. I couldn't begin to say what your team leads would think if only they knew what you were up to, except they wouldn't like it either."

"Good thing I'm the boss, then. None of you can stop me."

"No, but we will watch over you even more closely as of now."

"That's what I'm counting on, Arno."

I wished I was as sanguine as I gave out to be, but worry gnawed on my insides nonetheless at what I'd unleashed. Butler and Horik were dangerous, unpredictable, violent men who'd think nothing of making me vanish. Something about my thoughts must have shown because Arno frowned.

"Chief, Destine and I will have your back," he said softly. "And you'll come out of this with a commissioner's star."

I scoffed. "Let's see this through one step at a time. First, we take down Butler, Horik, and anyone else in their cabal."

I called Hera later and told her I thought I might have reached the trigger point with Horik at the very least, and she said she'd have a pair of her agents watching over me whenever I left the office. Plus, I'd stay with her from now until it was over since her house was one of the most secure residences on the base.

When I called it a day and headed for my apartment to pack a bag with my clothes and toiletries, I looked for her operatives but saw no one who might be them until I reached the senior officers' block, and they revealed themselves via the code word Hera had given me. One of them, a middle-aged woman, wore a Navy uniform with lieutenant commander's stripes at the collar; the other, an equally middle-aged man, wore Marine Corps black with a chief warrant officer's bars. Both displayed no more than the usual fruit salad on their left breasts and had eminently forgettable faces.

They entered my apartment ahead of me, cleared it, and waited outside while I gathered my things. Then, they took me to Hera's place aboard a car they'd pre-positioned in the block's garage. Hera was at home when I arrived and settled me in her guest suite before handing me a gin and tonic. We walked out onto the covered patio and took facing chairs at the table.

"Have you decided how you'll draw them out yet?"

"No. It has to be in an environment I can control but which will simultaneously make them confident they can get at me without too many problems. A tall order if there ever was one. I thought about going for a hike on Saturday, weather permitting, perhaps one of the lesser used trails west of Sanctum, in the foothills."

"It's an idea." She took a sip of her drink, eyes watching me over the glass rim. "And a trail has the merit of being sparsely populated, which gives you a certain amount of control. But you will be wearing a subcutaneous tracking device as well as a tiny communicator."

I gave her an amused smile. "Will I?"

She nodded once. "In fact, why don't we implant the subcutaneous tracker tonight? I happen to have one on hand. Oh, and by the way, my people placed surveillance on your apartment. If anyone tries to enter it, we'll know."

"Do you think they'd try anything in an apartment block full of senior Fleet officers?"

"You'd know better than me, but it's best if we don't discount the possibility. Who knows, if we catch one or both of them entering your apartment, you may have enough to end their careers, if not their lives as free humans."

"I'd rather hold out and put an end to their freedom for good." I took a big gulp of my drink. "You do not know how much their continued existence as officers of the Fleet offends me."

Hera gave me a crooked smile. "I think I do now."

— Thirty-Six —

When I woke the following day, Hera was already up and bustling in the kitchen. She shoved a mug of coffee in my hands and announced, "Your apartment had a visitor during the night, proving that I was right to have you come here."

"Who?"

"You tell me."

She gestured at the kitchen's primary display, which lit up with an image of my apartment door taken shortly after oh-two hundred, according to the timestamp. A man approached it and fiddled with the locking mechanism.

"Looks like my would-be assassin from the parkade."

"Indeed. Keep watching."

The door gave within moments, and he entered.

"He used an electronic lock override, and he's wearing gloves this time."

The view changed to inside my apartment, where the man stood stock still after closing the door behind him, listening in the darkness. He quietly moved toward my open bedroom door, stared at my empty bed for a few seconds, and then turned toward my bathroom. But finding it devoid of any personal items, he moved on to the kitchen, where he opened the refrigerator and appeared to put something in the bottles of juice and milk.

"We had them tested," Hera said, "and both were poisoned with a substance that causes almost immediate cardiac arrest."

I gave her a surprised glance. "They're really upping the ante, aren't they?"

"Keep watching."

I did so and noticed the man put something in various food containers. "Also poison?"

"Yes."

"He's certainly covering all of my larder save for the autochef packs."

"Do you think it's Horik wearing a disguise?"

I nodded. "Yes. It's virtually the same man as in the parkade, and watching him just now, he moves like Anton Horik."

We watched him leave my apartment, and then the display turned dark.

"It didn't take them, or at least Horik, long to come after you, Caelin. They definitely want you dead, and I'm beginning to wonder whether your plan is such a good idea."

"I can't live in fear forever, nor can I hide behind you for the rest of my life."

She raised both hands, palms facing outward. "All right. We'll do it your way, but my agents will shadow you."

"As will Arno and Destine."

"My people have removed all the items touched by the intruder from your apartment, but I still wouldn't return until this is over."

"No problems. Tomorrow is Saturday and, hopefully, the end of this entire business. Or at least the beginning of the end. Can I get a copy of the recording from my place? I suddenly have the urge to confront Horik with it."

"Why?"

I gave her a predatory smile. "To make sure he takes the bait tomorrow. Oh, and could your people check my car to see if they planted a tracking device. If they did, leave it, but let me know where it is."

"No problems." Hera tapped her communicator, lying on the kitchen counter. "You have a copy of the video in your queue."

***

"Was that you, Colonel Horik?" I asked after showing him the recording. "We know it's the same man as the one who shot at me in the parkade, and he moves just like you do."

"No comment."

I could read irritation in Horik's expression, stolid as it was, perhaps at having been caught by surveillance sensors rather than because he was back in my interview room.

"The man poisoned most of my foodstuff with a substance that will cause cardiac arrest in short order, and poison seems to be yours and Saul Butler's favorite means to dispose of someone."

"No comment."

"I don't understand how you can accuse my client," Lieutenant Commander Galindez said. "That man doesn't look like him, and he's wearing gloves, which means you can't repeat the trick of the matching hand."

"Let's see — an unknown got on base, found my apartment, and used an electronic lock override to get in. Please spare me, Commander. The only one with motive, means, and opportunity is your client. I shudder to think what he would have done to me had I been asleep in my bed." I turned my attention back to Horik. "No doubt you were surprised I wasn't there. I spent the night at a friend's place, as I sometimes do."

"No comment."

But I could tell by the flash of anger in his eyes that my absence had annoyed him, that he'd expected me to be there, a sleeping victim unknowingly waiting for death.

"Aren't you curious about my friend's identity? About where I was last night?"

Horik looked away, jaw muscles working.

"No comment."

"Aren't you curious why I had surveillance sensors watching over my apartment, one in a secure block on the most secure installation in the star system?"

"No comment."

"I'll tell you why, Anton. Because I expected something like what we saw on the video recording to happen. That's why the surveillance and why I wasn't there. Nice try, but you'll have to get up earlier in the morning to put one over me. Oh-two hundred just isn't cutting it."

He gave me a glance filled with pure malice. "No comment. And since that'll be my answer to any question, there's no point in continuing this charade."

I gave Horik a sweet smile designed to infuriate him. "Maybe I enjoy hearing you say it. What was the poison you put in my food and drink?"

"No comment."

I turned to Arno. "Do you have any questions for Anton?"

"Yes, I do. Tell me, Colonel, do you really think you'll get away with it? That we won't nail your ass to a cross when we're done? Yours and Butler's."

Horik stared contemptuously at him. "I don't talk to the likes of you, Chief Inspector."

"And what likes would that be?"

"Inferiors in rank." He turned his eyes away again.

"Look at me," Arno snapped. "Look at me, Anton."

Against his will, Horik glanced at Arno, who winked at him. "It's got nothing to do with rank, my friend, and everything to do with character. And you don't have any."

I stood, immediately followed by Arno. "That's all I had for now. Enjoy your weekend, Anton. It may be the last one you spend as a free man."

We left Horik and his lawyer to stare at our receding backs in silence, and once in my office, I said, "Hopefully, that'll get him and Butler to try something tomorrow since they planted a tracking device on my car last night as well."

"Did they now? Well, then, I suppose it's on." Arno sighed. "The things we do to collar our perps."

I grinned at him. "We do the incredible before lunch. The impossible will take us a little longer. I wish I had a good reason to recall Butler as well, but it'll have to do."

That evening was spent quietly with Hera, discussing the constitutional convention on Mykonos coming to a head with a brazen mercenary attack on the convention's site, mercifully repelled by Zack's Marines and the local police. Still, a half dozen delegates had died. Zack suspected the mercs were Hashashin, members of a shadowy cult that sold its services to the highest bidder. Apparently, dying on a mission was a sacrament to them, a promise of heaven.

I slipped into my bed at twenty-two hundred but had a restless night that left me more tired than when I turned out the lights. I recalled dreams plaguing me but not their substance, and I didn't get much uninterrupted sleep.

The next morning, I was up at oh-six-hundred and made coffee for both of us, Hera joining me on the patio to greet the day shortly after six-thirty.

"Still determined to go through with it?"

I nodded. "Yes. I got Horik riled up enough yesterday that he's bound to do something stupid."

"Alright. My agents will leave shortly and position themselves at the trailhead to wait for you. What are Arno and Destine doing?"

"They'll be following me at a discreet distance in a rental car Arno picked up last night."

"You know the rental's make, model, and color?"

"Yes. Arno sent me an image. It's a nondescript, mid-sized Caledon Car Company product, dark green."

"Good. Let's have breakfast, and then I'll drive you to your block's underground garage."

An hour later, I pulled out of the base and headed for the ring road, conscious of Arno and Destine several cars behind me. I didn't spot any other vehicle, suspicious or otherwise, taking the same lanes and exit as I did, and I began to wonder whether we'd left too early for Horik and Butler. Or whether they'd be after me at all.

Forty-five minutes later, I pulled into the trailhead parking lot, where the two operatives were waiting. They were the only human beings in sight, and the woman gave me a nod when I climbed out of my car. Then they headed out on the trail to stay ahead of me. I set out myself once Arno and Destine arrived and parked in a shady corner of the lot, their car's polarized windows making it impossible to see them within. They would stay there all day and send me a warning when and if Horik or Butler or anyone suspicious looking, for that matter, showed up.

But no one did.

I was back in my car by fifteen hundred, tired yet happy with a day spent wandering up and downhill through the woods. We drove away from the lot in a small but loose convoy — the agents in the lead, me, and then Arno and Destine. I was disappointed that nothing had happened, but relieved as well, a contradiction I tried hard to ignore.

Still, I kept alert as we made our way through the back roads until we reached the main road leading into Sanctum, yet I saw no sign of anyone paying attention to me. Once on the highway, I debated letting the centralized traffic control system take me the rest of the distance, but decided to drive myself instead. Which worked fine for the first five minutes.

Then, the car sped up on its own and changed lanes. I checked to make sure it hadn't accidentally switched over to the CTC system and found myself locked out of the controls, no matter what I tried. Someone had taken over my car, and I could do nothing about it.

I pulled out my communicator to call Arno and let him know, only to discover I was being jammed. In effect, I was a mute prisoner of my car, which seemed to be trying to shake Arno and Destine off my tail.

— Thirty-Seven —

The car suddenly veered onto an offramp and screamed up the incline toward a cross street in the industrial outskirts of Sanctum, turning right at the top and speeding along a mostly empty road. At the first intersection, it turned left into a narrow lane between grimy warehouses, then right into another, even narrower one. I looked behind me, but there was no sign of Arno and Destine, let alone the two agents.

As the car slowed, I tried to open the driver's side door, but it was locked, and I couldn't override the locking mechanism, so I pulled out my sidearm and held it loosely in my hand, which was resting on my right thigh. Adrenaline pumped through my veins, and I could hear my accelerating heartbeat in my ears as my body was experiencing the rush of the fight-or-flight reflex.

The car turned left through an open freight door and entered an empty warehouse. Tall windows and skylights let in plenty of daylight, revealing a grimy concrete floor, steel pillars supporting the roof at regular intervals, and four people-sized doors at the far end of a space that must have been fifty meters a side easily. The freight door rumbled shut behind me as my car came to a halt in the center of the open space, and one of the people-sized doors opened. Four humans wearing black tactical clothing, harnesses, and helmets with full face masks emerged. All carried slung carbines and pistols in holsters at the hip. They cautiously approached my car, stopped a few meters from the driver's side door, and raised their carbines.

Without warning, my car door began to open. I just had time to reach for my left shirt cuff to activate the miniature communicator embedded in it before the door opened fully, revealing me and my sidearm.

"Toss your gun out," one of them said in a rough voice that sounded as if his words were being fed through a speech modifier. "And then your communicator."

I complied since there was no way I could take all four down before one of them killed me. My weapon, followed by my communicator, skittered on the floor, ignored by the four men who kept their blank visors on me.

"Get out and put your hands on your head."

I undid my restraints, swiveled in my seat until my legs dangled through the opening, and stood.

"Hands up and turn toward the car." The man gestured with the barrel of his carbine, and I obeyed. He walked up to me and expertly manacled my hands behind my back, exactly like a police or security officer would do, taking mere seconds.

He then produced a sleep mask and slipped it over my eyes, effectively blinding me, before grabbing my right arm and dragging me away, presumably toward the door they'd come through. I was proved right a few minutes later when he released my arm and placed his hand on my shoulder to help me navigate through the opening.

I fervently hoped that they'd shut down whatever jamming device they'd been using so that Arno, Destine, and the agents could home in on both the communicator and the subcutaneous tracking device implanted in the web of skin between my left thumb and forefinger.

We eventually exited into the open air — I could suddenly feel the sun on my skin, and the scents surrounding me had changed.

"You're about to climb aboard a vehicle." He pulled me to a stop. "Take one step forward and up."

I did so tentatively until I found my footing first with my right foot, then both feet.

"Two steps forward."

Once I'd complied, he pushed me sideways and down onto a bench seat. Not having to duck meant I was aboard something large, a bus or a truck. Moments later, I heard the other men climb aboard and the doors shut, then I felt forward motion as the driver engaged.

"You're taking me to see Colonel Butler and Lieutenant Colonel Horik, I presume?"

"Shut up."

"Oh, come on. You can at least tell me where I'm going."

"I said shut up." A hand grabbed me by the throat. "If I have to repeat myself one more time, it won't go well for you."

Somehow, I believed he meant it and bit my tongue.

We drove for perhaps half an hour before slowing and coming to a stop. My internal clock was disturbed by my circumstances and wasn't as reliable as usual.

"Get up and turn to your left. Take two steps and dismount."

After doing so and stumbling, I found myself standing on a hard surface. One of the men took me by the arm again and dragged me along. Since I couldn't feel sunshine or fresh air, I surmised we'd stopped inside another building. The hand on my arm released me to grab my shoulder, and I was guided through several turns until we stopped and the face mask was removed.

I found myself in a well-lit, concrete-walled, and floored room, three meters by three meters, with absolutely nothing in it, no windows, and a single door. One of the men removed my manacles and backed out before slamming the metal door shut.

I was tempted to try my miniature communicator but figured the room would be under surveillance. Instead, I examined every square centimeter of it before settling on the floor across from the door and composing myself to wait.

After little more than an hour, according to my internal clock, the door opened again, and Anton Horik stepped in. He wore the same black, unmarked tactical clothing as the men who'd captured me, minus the helmet, and I wondered whether he'd been among them all along.

Horik stood still for a moment, hands on his hips, as he contemplated me with an air of satisfaction.

"Not so high and mighty now, are you, Morrow?"

I climbed to my feet. "What do you want with me?"

"I want to see you die, but first, we got to bring in your wingers, that fat, old chief inspector, and the warrant officer who looks like she might be a bit of fun."

"How did you get me?"

A cruel smile appeared. "We reprogrammed your car to accept commands from a third-party source when we put the tracking device on it. Then it was just a matter of keeping an eye on you, which we did with a loitering drone. It also caught your wingers waiting at the trailhead. When you were in the right place, we took control of your car and brought you to the empty warehouse. From there, we brought you here to a place your chief inspector and his warrant officer will never find."

"Impressive."

He smirked. "Fleet Security can do pretty much anything and get away with it."

"And the goons who took me, do they normally wear a Marine Corps uniform too?"

"Sure. They're all SMERSH, so you see, it is more than just Saul Butler and me. We're not quite legion, but there is a fair amount of us."

"Why this elaborate charade when you simply want me dead?"

"After my failed attempt in your apartment, I knew you'd deduced that we were going to kill you and had taken precautions. It's nice to have friends in high places, such as Admiral Talyn, by the way." Another smirk. "So, we decided to bring you and your wingers in and make the three of you vanish. Your chief inspector and his sidekick will surely have tracked your communicator to the warehouse by now, where several of my people are waiting for them."

I felt my heart give a jolt of joy. They were relying on my regular communicator when Arno and the agents would be looking for the subcutaneous tracking device and the miniature communicator embedded in my shirt cuff.

"You realize my disappearance won't stop the investigation into your affairs or those of Saul Butler."

"Maybe, but it will buy us time, and that's all we need."

"Time for what?"

"To expand SMERSH until no one and nothing can harm us while we keep the Fleet safe from traitors."

If I hadn't thought so before, this pretty much established that he was delusional, just like Butler. How he got enough people to go along with him so that he could run my kidnap operation and keep it secret boggled the mind. Mass psychosis, maybe?

"I seriously doubt that will ever happen, Anton. The Fleet has far too many honorable men and women in its ranks to allow your SMERSH a foothold, let alone become untouchable."

A look of disgust crossed his face. "What the hell does a civilian cop know about honor? The fact that your unit even exists is dishonorable beyond belief."

"And yet the Fleet needs us. You're proof of that."

Horik took a step toward me, fingers flexing. "I think it's time I taught you a lesson, Morrow. After all, you need not be intact when we finally execute you."

The fury in his eyes, coupled with his muscular bulk, lit a spark of fear within me. He was a sociopath and, therefore, unpredictable, and I had my back against a cold concrete wall.

"Let's not harm her right now, Anton," a familiar voice said from the corridor. "In case we have issues bringing her people in. Besides, she's just trying to get under your skin, as she's been doing all along."

Colonel Saul Butler appeared in the doorway to my cell, smiling. He wore a dark civilian suit, the tunic open to display a gun in a holster at his waist.

"Good afternoon, Caelin. I trust you survived your abduction with nothing more than a fright."

— Thirty-Eight —

"Getting your hands dirty, Saul?"

Butler made a face and shrugged. "Anton is reliable, but since you're more dangerous than anyone we've dealt with over the years by an order of magnitude or two, I figured I'd best come along. And a good thing I did. Anton was about to do things to you that would have been unpleasant. He rarely gets the chance since he has to be on his best behavior in the brig, and we don't deal with traitors outside of it all that frequently."

"Gee, thanks. So, what's the plan once you've caught Arno and Destine?"

"A quick shot in the back of the head, then we'll load your bodies aboard an aircar and drop them into a deep chasm in the mountains approximately three hundred kilometers northwest of Sanctum. It's a little place we use to make people vanish."

"Perhaps before," Horik rumbled, "I'll have some fun with the tall warrant officer. You can take Morrow if you want."

"We won't do that, Anton. Our Constabulary friends are honorable enemies, not worthless traitors."

Horik scoffed. "Honorable? I doubt that."

"Nevertheless, we will not misuse them before they die." Though Butler's tone was soft, it held the power of command.

"Aye, aye, sir." Horik gave him an ironic salute.

"Why don't you check with our people at the warehouse? Caelin's friends should have shown up by now."

Horik fished a communicator from his pocket and held it to his lips. "Hotel Two Two, this is Sierra Niner."

"Hotel Two Two," a voice replied moments later.

"Did the follow-on targets arrive?"

"Negative. No sign of them."

"Sierra Niner, out." Horik glanced at Butler, frowning. "Something's wrong, Saul."

Butler gave me a hard look. "Could it be? Search her for a hidden communicator, a transponder, something like that, Anton."

Horik approached me until we were almost touching, his eyes boring into mine, and then he expertly ran his fingertips over me from top to bottom. He made me turn around to face the wall and did the same again.

"If she has something, it's well hidden."

"Did you bring a battlefield sensor?"

Horik grunted. "No."

"Did any of your men?"

"I'll check."

Horik left me facing the wall, and Butler said, "You can turn around again, Caelin."

I did and leaned back, my gaze on Butler.

"You're really going to kill Arno, Destine, and me?"

He gave me a sad smile. "Yes, I really am. And I'm sorry. If only you had let well enough alone, we wouldn't be here."

"You know I couldn't."

"Yes." He nodded. "Because you're the Last of the Incorruptibles. What makes this worse is that I truly like you. We have a lot in common, you and me. We're both driven to do the best we can. We both have the welfare of the Fleet foremost in our minds, and we're very good at what we do. A real shame it has to end this way."

Horik's return, brandishing a handheld sensor, excused me from replying. "Now let's see if you have anything so well hidden, I couldn't find it."

He ran the sensor over me and uncovered both the miniature communicator in my shirt cuff and the subcutaneous tracking device in my hand.

Horik shook his head. "You've been extremely naughty, Assistant Commissioner. What shall we do with her little secrets, Saul?"

"Leave them be. They'll attract her people here, and that's almost as good as the initial plan, except we should be ready to receive more than Galdi and Bonta. I'm sure Admiral Talyn has set a few agents to watch her. Recall the men you left at the warehouse." Butler gave me an amused look. "You're always full of surprises, aren't you? Ah, well. This place is almost impregnable to a small force. And now, we must leave you to prepare."

With that, both vanished, and the door to my cell slammed shut, leaving me to fret about my friends coming into a situation they couldn't handle against a determined team of rogue Fleet Security personnel.

The place wasn't well soundproofed because after a while, I heard indistinct shouting and the faint buzz of plasma weapons fire, and I stood, tensing up. Without warning, my cell door opened, and Arno stumbled through, propelled by one of the men in black tactical clothing and helmet. He was wounded in the right arm, his face contorted with pain. I took a step forward to help him when another of the men dragged Destine in and dumped her on the floor before leaving us and slamming the door behind him.

I immediately dropped to my knees at her side and examined her. She had several shot holes in the chest, and although she was still breathing, it was labored. Her eyes fluttered open.

"Sir," she said in a thready voice, "I'm so sorry we messed up."

Then, her eyeballs rolled up in their sockets, and her chest fell for the last time. I touched her carotid artery but got no pulse, and I knew she was dead.

I looked up at Arno, who was puffing hard, fighting the pain, his face pale, and realized my vision had blurred from tears. Shaking my head, I reached down and closed Destine's eyes before laboriously climbing to my feet, feeling rage building, filling me and turning my blurry vision red.

Hatred such as I'd never felt before seized me, and I wanted nothing more than to wrap my hands around Horik's and Butler's throats and slowly squeeze the life out of them.

But Arno needed my help, and after a few deep breaths, my vision cleared as my heart rate dropped.

"How are you?"

"Better off than poor Destine," he answered between clenched teeth. "Bastards."

"Let me look at your arm."

"No need. It's inoperative. They blew a hole through my biceps."

I examined the wound, then removed my jacket and my t-shirt and tore the latter into strips. First, I made an improvised tourniquet above the shot hole, then I bandaged it. Then, I put my jacket back on.

"What happened?"

Arno, bleeding stemmed for the moment, leaned against a wall and slumped down until he was sitting. "We walked right into an ambush."

He winced as he settled his arm in his lap. "Let me see. When your car suddenly took off on the highway and swerved, we tried to contact you, but to no avail. Your communicator and tracking device literally disappeared from the surface of Caledonia."

"They were jamming me."

"Figures. We missed the offramp you took and circled back at the next one, but it was hopeless to try and follow you by then. Not long afterward, your regular communicator, the miniature one embedded in your cuff, and the subcutaneous tracking device came back online, except the first stayed put while the other two were in motion. I alerted the Admiral's agents, and we homed in on the tracking device, assuming that whoever took control of your car forced you out of it and left your regular communicator for us to find and perhaps capture us."

"That's pretty much it."

Arno shook his head. "You really need to stop letting yourself be abducted, Chief. It's turning into a bad habit."

"But it always gets results. Where are we, by the way?"

"In an industrial park on Sanctum's north side. This building is in the middle of a row of adjoining businesses."

"So why did you come in knowing there were likely more of them than there were of you instead of calling for the cavalry and sitting tight until it arrived?"

"The agents did call for backup, but we figured the bad guys might kill you at any moment." He grimaced. "In any case, our friendly operatives were supposed to go in through the back door and us through the front, and since we only picked up six life signs, we thought the four of us would be enough if we struck hard and fast. And at first, Destine and I got inside with no problems, though the agents faced a locked door that wouldn't give up its secrets. Then, they ambushed us. We winged two of them badly, mind you."

"They wanted you and Destine to join me in death, Arno. That's why you were allowed in, and the agents weren't."

He glanced at Destine's rapidly cooling body. "In that case, one down, two to go. What do we do now, Chief?"

"We sell our lives as dearly as possible. You stay where you are to attract the attention of whoever's going to open the door, and I'll stand beside it, ready to jump him."

He grunted. "Not much of a plan."

"Sorry, it's the best I can do."

"I know. What a mess."

I moved over to stand beside the door.

"Enemies who are much more sophisticated and more ruthless than we imagined outmaneuvered us. Horik and Butler might be out of touch with reality when it comes to their long-term plans, but they have a good grip on the bottom line, and that bottom line is to protect their Smert Shpionam at all costs."

"How many are there?"

"I saw at least four besides Horik and Butler, and I suspect there are a few more, those who were waiting for you in the warehouse where they left my car and communicator for you to find. Say ten in total for this operation."

Arno made a face. "So, there are more than merely our two colonels involved. I wonder how many others they have in Fleet Security."

"Judging by the sophistication of my abduction, probably more than we might think."

We suddenly heard more shouts and shots fired and exchanged glances.

"The agents?"

The door to our cell opened, and I braced myself to jump the first individual who entered, but it was the female agent, wearing gray body armor and a helmet with the visor raised.

"Assistant Commissioner, am I ever glad to see you." She glanced at Arno, then at Destine's body, and grimaced. "I'm sorry about Warrant Officer Bonta. We need to haul ourselves out of here. My partner is holding them off."

As if to punctuate her words, more shots went off somewhere to my left.

I helped Arno stand, and we both looked at Destine. The agent, correctly interpreting our thoughts, said, "We can pick her up later."

She led us along the corridor to our right, across a large, empty space, and then through an open door toward their car, waiting around the corner. The male agent burst out of the door moments later and joined us just as we were climbing aboard.

"Go, go, go," he said, dropping into the front passenger seat. "I shot one of them, but at least three remain."

We peeled out of the rear parking lot as a nondescript ground car pulled up and disgorged four men in black tactical clothes.

"The ones who were waiting for you and Destine at the warehouse, no doubt," I said, glancing through the rear window. "We evacuated just in time."

"Where to, Assistant Commissioner?" The female agent asked.

"First, the base hospital so Chief Inspector Galdi can be seen to, then Admiral Talyn's residence."

"Aye, aye, sir."

As we hit the ring road to make our way across Sanctum, my mind returned to Destine's body, lying in SMERSH's lair, and I wondered whether we'd see it again. When I voiced that thought, the male agent chuckled.

"They're about to get a visit from a troop of the 1st Special Forces Regiment. They won't have time to make Warrant Officer Bonta's body vanish. In fact, let me call them, and they'll pick her up. Where would you like it brought?"

"The base hospital's morgue."

"And any prisoners they take?"

"Do they have a brig in Fort Arnhem?"

"No, but they have detention cells that are never used except for training."

"Then that's where the survivors should go."

"You got it, sir." He spoke quietly into his helmet microphone before he turned to me and said, "Done and done. They're within sixty seconds of splashing down."

After a few minutes, the agent tilted his head to one side, the unmistakable and unconscious gesture of someone receiving a message.

"The troop picked up ten prisoners, three of them injured, and they secured Warrant Officer Bonta's remains."

The relief I felt almost made me light-headed. "That means they got all the rogue Fleet Security people involved in my abduction, Horik and Butler included. They're done, and SMERSH will go out of business."

— Thirty-Nine —

"Your operatives saved the day, Hera," I said when I walked into her house, Arno with his upper arm immobilized in a regen sleeve hard on my heels.

"I know. They reported while Arno was being treated at the hospital. Consider it part of the service the Special Operations Division offers its closest allies. I'm very sorry about Destine Bonta, though. She deserved better."

"Yes, she did. Loyal to a fault, our Destine." I felt tears well up but managed to hold them back.

"Let's get you some food and a drink." Hera turned toward her kitchen, motioning us to follow.

"The drink first, I think. What'll it be? A healthy slug of Glen Arcturus?"

"Yes, please." I glanced at Arno, who nodded emphatically.

"Shipping the prisoners off to Fort Arnhem was an excellent idea, by the way. They'll give the 1st SFR's interrogators some good practice."

"Field interrogations on Fleet personnel? Isn't that a bit beyond what's allowed?"

Hera poured two glasses and gave us each one.

"You haven't arrested them, and they were caught fighting Constabulary officers as well as Naval Intelligence operatives, which makes them hostiles subject to intelligence's rules. But I would encourage you to sit in on the interrogations, especially those of Horik and Butler. Once that's done, we'll have to figure out what's next, although the Sanctum brig will need a thorough cleaning from top to bottom before you can think of housing them there."

"I'll make arrangements with the civilian police to lodge them."

"Or we can simply make the whole lot vanish."

The matter-of-fact way Hera spoke, coupled with her emotionless eyes, reminded me of Horik and it sent a faint shiver up my spine. But then I reminded myself that Hera was not only more intelligent than him but on the side of angels rather than a barely controlled psychotic.

"I'd rather we let justice take its course."

"There is natural justice in my proposal, but I understand."

The bugger of it was that I could see her point of view as well, but I had to uphold the law as it was written. Otherwise, I was no better than those who I arrested.

"Do you mind putting Arno and me up for the night?"

"No, not at all. I'd have insisted on it." The autochef chimed, and Hera smiled. "Now sit and eat. We'll take care of the logistics after supper."

And take care of them she did. Her agents visited Arno's apartment and retrieved his toiletries and a set of clothes. I had already moved in with Hera, so I needed nothing. We spent the rest of the evening on her covered patio, discussing the day's events and where we would go from here.

The next day, Sunday, Arno and I visited the base hospital's morgue and made Destine's funeral arrangements. Since she had no close family and was Pathfinder qualified, I decided she'd be buried in the Fort Arnhem cemetery with due military protocol, but only after we broke the Smert Shpionam conspiracy.

Then, Arno and I headed for our empty offices and recorded our statements on the previous day's events — in great detail in case it came to a full court martial for all involved. That evening, we returned to Hera's place, it being our temporary home until the conspiracy was neutralized, but she was such a good hostess we felt pretty comfortable.

Monday morning saw us board an aircar for Fort Arnhem, one under the control of a lance corporal of the 1st Special Forces Regiment. We were both back in uniform for the occasion, although Arno still had his arm in a sling. It was a comparatively short run between Sanctum and the fort, thanks to the lance corporal flying us up the Nestor Valley at maximum speed. Once near the front gate, he landed, and we passed through the security arch on the ground.

I'd last visited Fort Arnhem a while back when Zack Decker and Hera Talyn were married in the chapel. The reception following the ceremony was still talked about to this day. It had been the biggest blowout in the fort's history, and yet the Pegasus Club, Fort Arnhem's all-ranks mess, remained standing.

On a Monday morning, there was little visible activity. I knew that Ghost Squadron was on Mykonos, along with the regimental Aviation Squadron and both Marine Light Infantry battalions stationed here, meaning approximately half of the base's occupants were gone. If the Pathfinder School was running any serials, they were indoors at the moment.

The lance corporal drove us to a two-story building separate from and behind the regimental headquarters. Unlike most in Fort Arnhem, it had no sign announcing its function or occupants.

"The detention barracks, sir," he announced as we stopped by the front doors.

They opened, and a man in Marine black wearing a captain's three diamonds on the collar emerged. He was of average height but muscular, in his thirties, and dark-complexioned with intelligent brown eyes. As I alit, he raised his hand in a crisp salute.

"Good morning, Commissioner. I'm Captain Evan Ferron, one of the regiment's NILOs."

I returned the compliment. "Good morning, Captain. I assume you're overseeing the interrogations?"

"Yes, and I'm about to interrogate Colonel Butler myself. I was just waiting for you to begin. We started on the troopers yesterday. They're Fleet Security senior noncoms, by the way. The injured ones are in the fort's infirmary enjoying the comforts of a secure ward."

We followed Ferron into the silent building and along a bare, clean, brightly lit corridor.

"Anything interesting come from those noncoms?"

"Plenty, sir. None of them are conditioned, so they sang like little birdies. For instance, there are many more of these Smert Shpionam or SMERSH clowns out there. I have a list of names, ranks, and assignments. They also thoroughly implicated

Horik and Butler in your abduction and the death of Warrant Officer Bonta. You'll be able to use the interrogation records in court, by the way. We stuck to the rules of engagement."

"Excellent."

He ushered us into an observation gallery with an interview room on either side. Both were occupied, one with Butler, the other with Horik. Both wore black overalls and sat at metal tables. Their hands were manacled, the cuffs fastened to a staple in the middle of the table. After tamping down a surge of rage toward them for Destine's death, I studied their demeanor and saw men facing defeat, demoralized and alone.

"They've been confined in solitary since their arrival, with no one speaking to them, the lights in their cells on all the time, and their meals delivered at random intervals. It's interesting to see how quickly they appeared to have collapsed. Most opposition agents we bring in can last a long time before they give up."

"That's because they're not trained agents but Fleet Security officers with delusions of adequacy," Arno said in a gruff tone. "In other words, meatheads."

Ferron gave Arno an amused look. "I see you know the ancient pejorative for military police, Chief Inspector."

"Arno is a fount of exotic knowledge, Captain."

"Then we must compare notes. I love digging up bits of old history."

"So what's the plan?" I asked to bring the conversation back on track.

"I thought we'd do Horik first since based on your assessment, he's not as smart as Butler and, therefore, likely easier to break. Do you know if either of them is conditioned?"

"No."

"Well, we have ways of finding out before their systems shut down. Shall we begin?"

I nodded. "Yes."

Arno stayed behind in the observation gallery as Ferron and I entered the interrogation room. Surprise showed on Horik's face as he saw me accompanied by a Marine Corps captain wearing the 1st SFR's winged dagger badge on his beret. We sat across from him.

"Lieutenant Colonel Anton Horik." Ferron glanced at the tablet in his hand, then up at Horik again. "I'm Evan Ferron, one of the 1st Special Forces Regiment's Naval Intelligence Liaison Officers. Commissioner Caelin Morrow, you already know. Are you aware of the reasons you're here?"

"No comment."

"That no-comment line won't work, Anton. We have you dead to rights in leading Commissioner Morrow's abduction and the murder of Warrant Officer Bonta. You can either answer our questions, or I'll inject you with drugs that will loosen your tongue and turn you into a drooling imbecile. In some cases, they can cause death."

"I've been conditioned."

"And I seriously doubt that. Fleet Security personnel aren't routinely conditioned, especially brig chasers. You're simply not important enough."

I saw Horik bristle at Ferron's dismissive tone and his use of the term brig chaser, which was a colloquial term for troopers assigned to escort detainees to and from the brig.

"Now, what will it be? Will you answer the questions or risk dying from interrogation drugs?"

"I'm a dead man, anyway." But I heard the uncertainty in his voice as his bloodshot eyes went from Ferron to me and back again.

"You understand that there's no coming back from this, Anton," I said. "No one will swoop in to save you, not even General Terak. Your noncoms already implicated you and Butler in my abduction and Destine Bonta's death, and their testimony is enough to have you spend at least twenty years in a prison colony on Parth. You might as well tell us everything and take your punishment like a Marine rather than allow the interrogation drugs to make you a shadow of the man you are."

Horik looked away, jaw muscles working.

"Ask," he finally said.

"You understand that you're still under caution?"

"Yes."

"How many people did you kill in the last five years?"

"Twenty-four." He went on to name them without prompting, several of them being on the list of those who died in the Sanctum brig. "All of them traitors to the Fleet who deserved their fate."

"Why not denounce them and let the military justice system take its course?"

He stared at me with defiance. "Because they would have gotten away with their treason. You must understand — this is a matter of life or death for the Fleet. If treason prospers, we're done for."

"How about Captain Victoria Montoni?"

"Saul slipped her a suicide pill while I modified the brig logs to erase his being there."

"And the attempt on my life in the parkade?"

"Yeah, that was me. I also entered your apartment and poisoned your food since you weren't there for me to kill."

"Let's talk about Smert Shpionam, SMERSH, as you call it. Who is your superior in the organization?"

"Saul Butler."

"And his superior?"

"I don't know. We're compartmentalized. Maybe Saul is the top boss."

"How many people work for you?"

"Two dozen."

"Are there any others reporting to Butler?"

"No idea. As I said, we're compartmentalized. But I think there may be more like me."

Extirpating SMERSH was shaping up to be a significant effort. I wondered whether I could borrow some of Hera's operatives to help.

"And General Terak? Is she involved?"

"Not that I'm aware."

I glanced at Captain Ferron. "That's all I have for now."

"Very well. I can continue with the prisoner at a later date." He stood, and I followed suit. Then we left a pensive Horik to contemplate his bleak future and joined Arno in the observation gallery.

"Anything to add?" I asked him.

"No. We got what we wanted from him and within the rules, so his interview is admissible in court."

"That's if it goes there," Ferron said. "I suspect we'll be offering Horik and Butler a chance to take their own lives."

"And the senior noncoms who followed them?"

A faint smile danced on Ferron's lips. "They might well be offered a transfer to the Marine Light Infantry and sent to take its basic training course on Parth under new identities rather than face a court martial."

"Who is so eager to make them disappear, Captain?"

"Admiral Talyn, sir. I gather she wants Smert Shpionam quietly dismantled and buried so deep no one will ever suspect it existed. Unless you object, of course, in which case you'll need to take it up with the admiral."

"For the good of the Fleet."

He inclined his head. "Yes, sir. Exposing it for all to see would be detrimental."

And the Almighty help me. I could just about agree with that. Considering Butler and Horik's crimes were such that a court martial would likely impose the death penalty, or if not, exile on Parth's Desolation Island, allowing them to commit suicide was an acceptable alternative. Besides, it gave us time to winkle out the rest of SMERSH if there were more than just Butler, Horik, and their two dozen.

"Shall we tackle Saul Butler?"

— Forty —

"Anton Horik has told us everything," I said once we sat across from Butler.

"Has he now? What did you do? Inject him with interrogation drugs?"

"No. I simply gave him a chance to make a clean breast of things after making it quite clear he was utterly screwed."

Butler grimaced. "I suppose it was inevitable. Anton's strange sense of honor would demand he talks under those conditions."

"Will you do the same?"

"Why? If Anton spoke, then there's nothing left for me to say. I'm just as screwed as he is and will face the same penalties."

"Not quite, Saul. You were Anton's superior in SMERSH. Tell us about your superior and your other subordinates."

Butler chuckled. "I have no superior because I run the organization — founded it, in fact. As for other subordinates, I'm sorry to disabuse you, but Anton was the only one."

"You mean to tell me Smert Shpionam was two officers and twenty-four senior noncoms, nothing more?"

"Yes."

Something told me he was lying. Captain Ferron obviously thought the same because he said, "Come now, Saul. You and I know that's not the truth."

"It is, and that's 'colonel' to you, *Captain*."

"Are you conditioned against interrogation?"

"No."

"Then you won't object if I use interrogation drugs on you."

Butler's face hardened. "Of course, I object. I'm a senior serving officer of the Commonwealth Marine Corps. You can't do that to me."

"At the moment, you're a hostile who's been taken prisoner. I can inject you if I wish. And since you've decided not to answer, I will do so."

I was surprised Ferron would go to the drug stage so quickly. But I figured he'd decided Butler wouldn't answer no matter what, seeing as he was already implicated beyond any doubt and faced an extremely grim outlook.

Ferron stood and pulled a hyperdermic syringe from his tunic pocket, then walked around the table until he stood behind Butler and placed the syringe tip against his neck. It gave a slight hiss, and after pocketing the now empty device, he sat beside me again.

Butler's face quickly became slack as the drug took effect, and a tiny bit of drool appeared at the corner of his lips.

"All right, Colonel, do you have a superior in the organization called Smert Shpionam?"

Butler nodded. "Yes." The word came out slightly slurred.

"And who is that?"

He shook his head as he became visibly and intensely agitated. "Can't tell anyone."

"Do you have any subordinates other than Anton Horik?"

"Yes."

"Who are they?"

Butler's breathing became increasingly labored, and his skin slowly turned blue.

"Aw, shit." Ferron jumped to his feet and went around the table again, placing his fingers on Butler's neck. "He's having an adverse reaction to the drug. Are you conditioned, Colonel? Did you lie to me?"

An imbecilic smile appeared. "Yes. Goodbye. Say farewell to the general for me."

Then his eyes rolled up, and he slumped forward, dead.

"We won't have to give him a suicide pill," Ferron said, straightening his back. "Damn, damn, damn. I should have tested him. The admiral won't be happy with me."

"Butler committed suicide, Captain. That's clear. Except he did it by lying about his conditioning. We wouldn't have gotten anything out of him either way."

"True. But at least we know he has a superior and more subordinates. Now we just need to find them."

I thought back to Butler's last words — *say farewell to the general for me*. Clearly, he meant Terak. Could she be the actual head of Smert Shpionam? When I voiced my thought, Ferron frowned.

"It's possible, I suppose. Terak has the clout to quash any investigation into her own people."

"Until I came along."

"Yes. Until ACU 12 showed up and was embedded into Fleet HQ, but not of it. Proving she's involved will be difficult, though. With Butler dead, we might have lost the sole thread leading back to her."

"Which was the entire point of his committing suicide by conditioning, since he had nothing left to lose anyway." I let out a heartfelt sigh. "Whoever his superior is, he or she certainly inspired loyalty. I suppose I'd better get back to Sanctum and let General Terak know Butler is dead, and Horik is…"

"Dead as well, Commissioner. You can tell her they and their people died during your rescue by the 1st SFR after they turned rogue and abducted you because of your not letting the Montoni matter go. Or you can tell her anything else you want."

Ferron's tone showed he would brook no discussion, and for the first time, I wondered who he really was. Probably not a mere Marine Corps intelligence captain, but I wasn't about to ask.

"Very well. If she's the head of SMERSH, then she'll receive a warning. If she isn't, she'll face a mystery that will never be solved."

"Indeed, Commissioner."

"By the way, in the Constabulary, we don't abbreviate titles like in the Fleet. It's assistant commissioner."

"Oh. My apologies. How about you and Chief Inspector Galdi return to Sanctum while I clean up around here? You can find your way back to the front door, right?"

"Yes, we can. Thank you, Captain. It's been a most enlightening experience."

Arno and I didn't discuss the morning's events during our trip back, each of us lost in our thoughts. I knew he was excruciatingly uncomfortable with

Naval Intelligence's solution to deal with the guilty parties, and I was as well, but to a much lesser degree than I would have been even a few years ago. Perhaps it was true that the higher one got in rank, the more flexible one became, and that was why Arno didn't want any further promotion. He tried to cling to his more rigid views of our business until the bitter end, something I could no longer afford.

Hera called when we were ten minutes out, telling me she'd been fully briefed by Captain Ferron and asking that I come to her office before seeing Terak. As a result, I had the car drop us off at the Naval Intelligence entrance rather than the one that led to our offices.

I found her office door open, and she waved me in, pointing at a chair across from her desk while Arno waited in the antechamber.

"A reasonably satisfactory outcome, I'd say. A shame Butler died ahead of schedule, but at least he left you with two other threads to pull on."

"And I'm about to yank on the first of them, Terak, though I doubt I'll get anything." I made a face. "She's too canny to let anything slip. Especially to a mere assistant commissioner."

"Well, that's one reason I wanted to see you beforehand. A message came through from Wyvern earlier this morning. You're promoted to acting while so employed, Commissioner. Congratulations."

I gave her a sharp look. "You promised you wouldn't approach Sorjonen with the idea."

"And I lied. Congratulations. I understand the acting becomes permanent after twelve months?"

"It does."

Hera reached into a desk drawer and retrieved a small silver object. "Flag officer stars are the same across the Services, the Constabulary included. Would it be too much if I offered you my old commodore's star?"

"No! I'd be honored."

"Then how about my executive assistant drag in the camera drone, and we take a picture of me pinning the star on your collar? If Chief Inspector Galdi is nearby, perhaps he can join us."

***

When I called General Terak's office to request a meeting with her, I was told she'd see me immediately, and surprising me even more, I was ushered into her office the moment I appeared. Of course, she noticed the star on my collar right away.

"Did you just get a promotion, Morrow?" She asked, her face pinched as if she was smelling something horrible.

"Yes, General. Thank you for receiving me so promptly." I took a chair across from her unbidden. "I have the sad duty to report the deaths of Colonel Saul Butler and Lieutenant Colonel Anton Horik."

"What?" She sat up. "How?"

"It appears that they turned rogue two days ago and came up against a SOCOM unit which, quite naturally, didn't mess around. I investigated their deaths and concluded they were caused by factors within their control. The cases are closed."

Terak seemed stunned and unable to speak for a moment. "Hold on, now. Under what authority did you investigate?"

"Under my authority as the commissioner in command of Anti-Corruption Unit 12. All details of the incident are classified."

"No. You do not have the right to simply mark the deaths of two honorable officers with the word classified."

"They were not honorable, and if they hadn't died, I would have them under arrest in the Sanctum Police cells with no chance of bail, facing charges of murder and attempted murder. One of my officers died because of them on Saturday, and she was a dear friend as well as a colleague."

I watched her appalled expression, wondering whether it was because she'd lost an arm of Smert Shpionam or simply because two officers she'd known for decades were revealed as criminals.

"You'll also be losing several senior noncoms who will be reassigned to the Marine Light Infantry on Parth."

When she didn't immediately reply, I stood. "That's what I came to say, General. Their bodies are being held in the Fort Arnhem morgue if you'd like to take care of the disposal."

I turned on my heels and left her office. This wasn't over, not by a long shot, but I could do nothing in the short and perhaps even medium term except dig deeper. But I knew I might never find Butler's superior or the rest of his subordinates if they had any sense and kept quiet for the foreseeable future.

— Forty-One —

We buried Destine in the Fort Arnhem cemetery that Thursday. She was escorted to her final resting place by a company from C Squadron, 1st Special Forces Regiment, in a ceremony so solemn yet touching that I bawled openly as her casket was lowered into the ground after the firing party, six troopers under a sergeant, shot three times. A flight of shuttles then passed overhead, one breaking away from the others and escorting her spirit up into the Infinite Void. Even Arno shed silent tears. I was presented with the folded flag that had been draped over her casket and bought a small transparent case to display it on the wall outside my office — the first member of ACU 12 to die in the line of duty.

***

On a Wednesday, two weeks later, all flag officers at Fleet HQ were summoned by the Grand Admiral to appear in the main auditorium at fifteen hundred hours, no exceptions allowed. I received an invitation rather than a summons, not being in Larsson's chain of command, but a flag officer, nonetheless. With the rumors running rampant about the outcome of the constitutional convention on Mykonos — it had sent its proposals to Earth a week earlier — I figured something momentous might have happened.

When I called Hera, she merely smiled and told me to wait until Larsson spoke to us.

And so, at fourteen-fifty-five, I filed into the auditorium with the other flag officers and found it was assigned seating by Service and by seniority. Since I was the most senior and sole Constabulary flag officer in the star system, my seat was at the front, with the Service chiefs, who all wore four stars. But they were as polite to me as I was to them.

When the clock struck fifteen hundred, Grand Admiral Larsson bounded onto the stage as we were called to attention.

"At ease," he said, his augmented voice reaching every part of the vast space. He let his eyes roam over the assembled flag officers in silence for a few heartbeats.

"You've all been following the news of the constitutional convention on Mykonos and know it sent recommendations for changes to Earth. Those recommendations were rejected without debate or discussion, leaving no hope for reform, let alone reconciliation." He paused for effect. "As a result, earlier today, the convention unanimously voted for the secession of the OutWorlds from the Commonwealth and the formation of a new Federation of Sovereign Star Systems."

He fell silent to let his audience react and did they ever. First came a buzz of voices, then isolated cheers, which grew as more and more people understood what Larsson's announcement meant.

After a bit, he raised both arms, demanding quiet. When it returned, he said, "Since the Fleet is primarily based on the OutWorlds, and Caledonia is an OutWorld, we will become the Federation Armed Forces."

Larsson noticed me in the front row.

"The Constabulary as well will belong to the Federation since it is mostly based in the OutWorlds. For now, we remain a unified force until the details of the Fleet's split between the Federation and the Commonwealth are promulgated and put into effect. But in essence, those who wish to remain in the Commonwealth will be allowed to move there and continue serving the Commonwealth Armed Forces. Those in what is now the new, much smaller Commonwealth sphere and who wish to serve the Federation will be repatriated.

"This is the most momentous event in our history since the Second Migration War and a logical consequence of it, the split Grand Admiral Kowalski foresaw and tried to stave off until we were ready. Well, whether or not we're ready, it's happened, and we need to face the future of a divided humanity, one which, in due course, will unite again when the time comes, but under a different sort of constitutional system. Instructions will filter down over the coming days and weeks. As I said, we remain a unified force for now, and since humanity's borders will stay the same, except under Federation control, nothing will change where it counts, along the frontiers."

Another pause to let his words sink in.

"I will not be taking any questions at this time but feel free to send them up your chain of command. However, much will shortly become evident as the process to separate the Fleet between the Commonwealth and the Federation unfolds. And for those of you staying with us, your duties will remain the same. That was all I had for now. Thank you."

A disembodied voice called us to attention as Grand Admiral Larsson left the stage. Once we were released, the sound of countless conversations became deafening, and I made my way out as fast as I could. Hera intercepted me by the auditorium's main door.

"So, what do you think?" She asked as we walked out into the afternoon sunshine.

I gave her a crooked smile. "That life for ACU 12 will go on as before, looking for perils so dire the Fleet needs the Last of the Incorruptibles."

About the Author

Eric Thomson is the pen name of a retired Canadian soldier with thirty-one years of service, both in the Regular Army and the Army Reserve. He spent his Regular Army career in the Infantry and his Reserve service in the Armoured Corps.

Eric has been a voracious reader of science fiction, military fiction, and history all his life. Several years ago, he put fingers to keyboard and started writing his own military sci-fi, with a definite space opera slant, using many of his own experiences as a soldier for inspiration.

When he's not writing fiction, Eric indulges in his other passions: photography, hiking, and scuba diving, all of which he shares with his wife.

Join Eric Thomson at
http://www.thomsonfiction.ca/
Where you'll find news about upcoming books and more information about the universe in which his heroes fight for humanity's survival.

Read his blog at https://blog.thomsonfiction.ca

If you enjoyed this book, please consider leaving a review with your favorite online retailer to help others discover it.

Also by Eric Thomson

Siobhan Dunmoore

No Honor in Death (Siobhan Dunmoore Book 1)
The Path of Duty (Siobhan Dunmoore Book 2)
Like Stars in Heaven (Siobhan Dunmoore Book 3)
Victory's Bright Dawn (Siobhan Dunmoore Book 4)
Without Mercy (Siobhan Dunmoore Book 5)
When the Guns Roar (Siobhan Dunmoore Book 6)
A Dark and Dirty War (Siobhan Dunmoore Book 7)
On Stormy Seas (Siobhan Dunmoore Book 8)

Decker's War

Death Comes But Once (Decker's War Book 1)
Cold Comfort (Decker's War Book 2)
Fatal Blade (Decker's War Book 3)
Howling Stars (Decker's War Book 4)
Black Sword (Decker's War Book 5)
No Remorse (Decker's War Book 6)
Hard Strike (Decker's War Book 7)

Constabulary Casefiles

The Warrior's Knife
A Colonial Murder
The Dirty and the Dead
A Peril So Dire

Ashes of Empire

Imperial Sunset (Ashes of Empire #1)
Imperial Twilight (Ashes of Empire #2)
Imperial Night (Ashes of Empire #3)
Imperial Echoes (Ashes of Empire #4)
Imperial Ghosts (Ashes of Empire #5)

Ghost Squadron

We Dare (Ghost Squadron No.1)
Deadly Intent (Ghost Squadron No.2)
Die Like the Rest (Ghost Squadron No.3)
Fear No Darkness (Ghost Squadron No.4)

9 781989 314968